Penguin Folklore Library

SCANDINAVIAN FOLKTALES

Advisory Editor: Neil Philip

Dr Jacqueline Simpson was born in Worthing in 1930 and obtained a first-class degree in English at Bedford College, University of London, followed by an MA in Medieval Icelandic at King's College, London. Throughout her career of research and writing, her main interests have been folk beliefs and oral narratives, both Scandinavian and British, and early Scandinavian history. In 1981 she received a D.Litt. from London University for her work in these fields.

Her books include *Icelandic Folktales and Legends* (1972), *The Folklore of Sussex* (1973), *The Viking World* (1980), *British Dragons* (1980) and *European Mythology* (1987). She is a member of the Viking Society for Northern Research and of the Folklore Society, and since 1979 has been Honorary Editor of *Folklore*.

SCANDINAVIAN
FOLKTALES

Translated and edited by

JACQUELINE SIMPSON

PENGUIN BOOKS

PENGUIN BOOKS
Published by the Penguin Group
27 Wrights Lane, London W8 5TZ, England
Viking Penguin Inc., 40 West 23rd Street, New York, New York 10010, USA
Penguin Books Australia Ltd, Ringwood, Victoria, Australia
Penguin Books Canada Ltd, 2801 John Street, Markham, Ontario, Canada L3R 1B4
Penguin Books (NZ) Ltd, 182–190 Wairau Road, Auckland 10, New Zealand

First published 1988

Made and printed in Great Britain by
Richard Clay Ltd, Bungay, Suffolk
Filmset in Monophoto Bembo

CONTENTS

Acknowledgements

The author and publishers are grateful to the following from whom permission was sought to translate legends:

Rosenkilde og Baggers Forlag, Copenhagen, for legends from Laurits Bødker, *Danske Folkesagn* (copyright Laurits Bødker, 1958).

H. Aschehoug & Co., Oslo, for legends from Reidar Th. Christiansen, *Norske Sagn*, (copyright Reidar Th. Christiansen, 1938).

H. Aschehoug & Co., Oslo, for legends from Edvard Grimstad, *Etter Gamalt: Folkeminne frå Gudbrandsdal*, (copyright Edvard Grimstad, 1948).

Norstedts Förlag, Stockholm, for legends from Bengt af Klintberg, *Svenska Folksägner*, (copyright © Bengt af Klintberg, 1972).

The translations of Icelandic tales on pp. 42, 51, 74, 93, 95, 110, 112, 139, 150 and 171 appeared previously in Jacqueline Simpson, *Icelandic Folktales and Legends*, B. T. Batsford and University of California Press, 1972; those on pp. 129, 130, 136 and 139 in Jacqueline Simpson, *The Master Magicians of Iceland*, Mistletoe Books, The Folklore Society, 1975. We are grateful for permission to reprint them here.

Every effort has been made to trace copyright holders, but in some cases this has proved impossible. The author and publishers apologize for these unwilling cases of copyright transgression and would like to hear from any copyright holders not acknowledged.

GENERAL INTRODUCTION

To English speakers, the term 'folktale' is commonly taken as synonymous with 'fairy-tale' – that is, an exciting and fanciful oral fiction, full of supernatural marvels, and set in a never-never land of once-upon-a-time, which is told by adults to children as pure entertainment. Such fairy-tales form the substance of the classic collections made by Charles Perrault in France and by the Grimm brothers in Germany, and subsequently by other collectors all over Europe, including Scandinavia. Modern English-speaking scholars have given such stories the technical name of Wonder Tales; in French, they are termed *contes*, and in German *Märchen*.

The present book, however, is not about Wonder Tales. It is devoted to an equally important and widespread but comparatively neglected type of oral narrative, called a *Sage* in German, a *sägne* in Swedish, and a 'legend' in English. Its first defining feature is that it is based on beliefs and assumptions which are generally accepted in the social group to which the teller and the hearers belong, and are relevant to their everyday concerns: ghosts of murdered men cannot rest, for example; cattle diseases are caused by witchcraft; gypsy curses come true; God sends dramatic catastrophes to punish sinners. Normally, therefore, a legend is told by someone who believes it really happened, and in the expectation that the hearers will accept its truth and draw the desired moral. Tellers may reinforce their credibility by explaining how they first heard the tale from wise, trustworthy elders, or asserting that it happened to a relative or acquaintance of their own. If, as often is the case, the legend includes a reference to some material feature – a stain on a church wall, say, or a landscape peculiarity – the existence of this is held to prove the truth of the tale. Naturally, since the parameters of socially acceptable belief shift with time, it does happen that tales once told as true lose their plausibility and are only told in a tone of humorous half-belief, to impress or entertain. Even so, they can still be distinguished from Wonder Tales by their localized setting and by a more sober style, which implies a claim to veracity. The vast majority of legends, however, do reflect the sincere and serious beliefs of a community; those chosen for this book represent ideas current among considerable sections of the population of pre-industrial Scandinavia. Many can be proved to have medieval roots; a few may preserve pre-Christian ideas in modified forms; all are important as evidence of their countries' cultural history up to the early years of the present century.

The second defining feature of a legend is that it is a proper story and not just a bare statement of belief, nor even a spontaneous, unshaped anecdote about some personal experience of the teller which has reinforced one of his beliefs. The legend has a plot, however brief, which has been fixed through tradition into a stable, recognizable pattern. Passing orally from one teller to another over several generations – or, in some cases, several centuries – its basic structure has been shaped for maximum memorability and dramatic effect, forming a strong framework to sustain whatever variations of detail individual narrators bring to it.

Legends can be classified into subgroups according to subject-matter, distribution, or function. As regards subject-matter, almost all the stories I have chosen here are 'mythical' – they concern supernatural beings and uncanny events, even though they are told as facts. The other major subject-category is the 'historical', covering real personages and public events. Unfortunately, the majority of these stories hold little appeal for foreign readers since they assume one is familiar with the historical background in which they are set. Only a handful of historical tales, which can be enjoyed without special knowledge of Scandinavian history, have been included here.

Distribution forms the criterion for another important distinction – that between the 'local' legend and the 'migratory' legend. Local legends comprise stories linked exclusively to one spot – for instance, those designed to explain a place-name or some peculiarity of a building or of the landscape. The migratory legends are those existing in several versions widely separated in time or space; they consist of a stable core of plot which remains recognizable even though it has been adapted to each new setting by incorporating appropriate allusions to local places, persons or customs. It must be stressed, however, that this distinction is made by scholars only, never by story-tellers themselves. To story-tellers, all legend narratives seem specific to their own community. They would be amazed, and probably offended, to be told that an identical tale is known elsewhere.

Only experience can guide a scholar in classifying a legend as 'local' or 'migratory'. The Danish story 'Ram's Mound' (p. 62) looks convincingly 'local', both because of its specific link with a landmark and because the anecdote it tells, though highly dramatic, is within the bounds of physical possibility. One could easily take it to be an orally transmitted memory of something that did once occur at Rolfsted. But this cannot be; it must be migratory, for exactly the same story is known at no fewer than twenty-five sites in England, generally told with reference to some local boulder nicknamed 'Hangman's Stone'. Research might well uncover further instances in Germany, France, or elsewhere, each rendering it increasingly doubtful whether this striking story-pattern originated from real life, or whether it has always and everywhere been simply a warning story rather than a true record. In any case, it obviously is not 'local' in the exclusive sense, however firmly the people of Rolfsted claim it for their own.

One of the great fascinations of legend-study is to watch the constant recurrence of themes, motifs and whole plots in the stories of one country after another, and to spot the presence of characteristic regional variants ('eco-types', to use a term borrowed by folklorists from biologists). To facilitate cross-referencing, scholars have assigned code numbers to the most widespread stories. The code-system best suited to Scandinavia is that devised by the Norwegian folklorist Reidar Th. Christiansen in *The Migratory Legends*; where applicable, I have cited his number in the reference note at the end of each tale. References to the numbering of Antti Aarne and Stith Thompson's *The Types of the Folktale*, are also sometimes relevant. British readers who would like to explore our own comparable traditions will find plenty of material in Part B of Katharine M. Briggs's *A Dictionary of British Folk Tales in the English Language* (1970); in the same author's briefer work, *A Sampler of British Folk Tales* (1977); and in Jennifer Westwood's *Albion: A Guide to Legendary Britain* (1985). Many similar German stories had been published by the brothers Jacob and Wilhelm Grimm in 1816, but were overshadowed by their far more famous and popular collection of fairy tales; they have been recently translated and annotated by Donald Ward in *The German Legends of the Brothers Grimm* (1981). Ward's excellent commentaries and bibliographies make this essential reading for any student of European oral narrative and belief.

The third way of classifying legends is by their functions, though with the proviso that the same story can easily be made to serve two or more functions at once, and that different narrators may use the same story for different purposes. Swedish scholars, led by C. W. von

Sydow, have devoted much attention to this classification. One important category they call *vitnessägner*, 'testimony legends' or 'witness legends'. These are intended to support the truth of some belief by telling a story which reinforces that belief. Thus, 'Lapp Wizards' (pp. 154–5) 'proves' that shape-changing can happen, and that Lapps have evil magical powers. Most stories involving encounters with witches, ghosts or fairies fulfil this function. One particularly revealing example is 'The Troll in the Chimney' (p. 185), where the narrator unwittingly demonstrates how readily a group of people can interpret a natural but alarming event in terms of their pre-existing beliefs. The thunderstorm described there was real enough, and the 'something big and black' which rolled out of the chimney must have been a mass of soot dislodged when the lightning struck it. However, guided by Old Jonte, who 'could see things that other people couldn't see', the startled haymakers convinced themselves it was a troll, rolling along as trolls were said to do, and pursued by God's thunderbolts. And it was in that form that the tale was handed on through two more generations.

Akin to 'witness legends' are those aiming to teach their hearers what to do, or not do, when encountering the supernatural. Such didactic legends in turn shade into tales of warning, describing what happens to those who break the moral code or who offend supernatural beings (which often amounts to the same thing). These three categories mentioned above are educative; they pass on the community's beliefs and ethics to new generations.

A few legends can be classed as wish-fulfilments, in particular those about luck-bringing protective spirits (as in Part Six) and buried treasures. Admittedly, in most stories the treasure-seekers lose their booty, but such traditions do at least offer hope that there is wealth to be had without working, if one is lucky enough to find it. The traditions about magically skilled huntsmen, coachmen, rat-catchers and so on in Parts Five and Seven also involve an element of wish-fulfilment, besides bolstering the prestige of these crafts in the eyes of outsiders.

Then there is the ætiological function – one of the commonest, since very many legends serve to explain the origins either of material objects, or of place-names, or of customs and taboos. This function is easily combined with others. In this way 'The Sunken Castle' (p. 75) and 'Ram's Mound' (p. 62) are moral warnings which simultaneously explain the origin of a lake and of a place-name respectively. The purpose uppermost in a narrator's mind would vary from one teller to another, and from one occasion to another. In a more abstract sense, too, stories can 'explain' misfortunes and disagreeable experiences in daily life. Disease in humans or cattle, the birth of deformed or mentally handicapped children, the panic of losing one's way in forests, the uneasiness created by unfamiliar surroundings at dusk – innumerable unpleasantnesses, great or small, can be interpreted as the work of fairies, witches, ghosts, or the Devil. Any explanation, however sinister, was apparently psychologically more acceptable than to admit that misfortune strikes at random and that one can do nothing about it. A supernatural 'explanation' is often accompanied, in traditional lore, by information on ways to counteract the force involved: hauntings can be stopped by exorcisms, milk-stealing 'carriers' (see. pp. 150–3) can be destroyed in prescribed ways. The explanatory and the didactic functions of the tales are thus often combined.

Some scholars add one more function: entertainment. This rarely occurs in isolation, though there are a few light-hearted stories which seem to have no point but to amuse or excite their hearers, for example, 'New Clothes' (p. 177) and 'The Solunna Hag' (p. 214). It can be argued, however, that even the grimmest tale of warning or the most sincere testimony to belief has to be told effectively if it is to impress its hearers. The conscious purpose may simply be to tell them something the narrator considers true and important, but the more he or she employs artistic skills – concision, suspense, drama and so forth – the more impact the tale will have. To this extent, every telling has an element of 'entertainment' in it. There were also occasions when story-telling became more self-consciously a 'performance'. This could happen among guests at weddings and wakes, among families after the day's work was over, among people engaged on some monotonous indoor task. 'Hunters' Tales' (p. 225) is a good instance of one of these informal story-telling sessions: a group of friends passing time, at dusk, by swapping anecdotes relevant to their present occupation, in a mutually informative and mildly competitive way. Nevertheless, the vast majority of tellings were quite casual and unplanned; a topic would crop up in conversation and lead someone to tell a story bearing upon it. That is one reason why legends are, typically, very short; unlike Wonder Tales, they must not be on too large a scale, or they would disrupt social communication instead of contributing to it. The main exceptions to this rule come from Iceland, where detailed, leisurely narration was appreciated, especially in the evening story-telling sessions.

Anybody could tell legends; they were not restricted to specialists, as long Wonder Tales often were in rural communities. Even so, it would be useful to know more about the personalities, opinions and lives of the informants from whom collectors gathered these stories – until recently, folklorists were regrettably uninterested in tellers, as opposed to tales. Archives often record no more than the name and age of an informant. Nevertheless, as the Swedish scholar Bengt of Klintberg points out, certain patterns emerge even from these meagre records. Gender roles determine certain choices of subject-matter; stories about changeling babies and those involving cattle and dairy work were almost all collected from women, while those about hunting and encounters with forest spirits were from men. Some tellers told many tales about magic and the second sight; others seemed deliberately to avoid these, preferring anecdotes with a religious tone. But many questions must remain unanswered so long as collectors merely note down the story itself, stripped of its context of comment and discussion.

The amount of material in the folklore archives of Scandinavian universities and museums is truly immense. Writing in 1964, Reidar Th. Christiansen stated that there were then 'some 4,000 to 4,500 recorded versions' of Norwegian folktales in print or in manuscript archives; in 1972, Klintberg said there were over 100,000 in the four main Swedish archives. These figures of course include many instances where the same story has been recorded from many different informants. Even so, English visitors cannot but be astounded at the richness of these vast treasuries of traditional lore.

The stories I have selected for translation do not come directly from these archives but from printed sources of different periods. The nineteenth century is represented by four major collections: Andreas Faye's *Norske Folke-Sagn*, J. M. Thiele's *Danmarks Folkesagn*, Jón Árnason's *Íslenzkar þjóðsögur og Aefintýri*, and P. C. Asbjörnsen and J. I. Moe's *Norske Folkeeventyr*. These great pioneers did not set out to record stories word-for-word but to publish a 'best' version of each, tactfully combined from several informants. Occasionally, in order to sketch the background to a particular group of tales, they would summarize common beliefs in their own words, as Jón Árnason does for 'The Carrier' (p. 150), and Andreas Faye for 'Nisses' (p. 171). Besides their own fieldwork they made use of a network of correspondents among the educated classes – usually clergymen or teachers – who collected and sent in stories from their own localities. It must be admitted that this process of mediation has left the tales somewhat improbably smooth and impersonal; one misses the voices of the primary narrators. However, editorial intervention did not destroy the crisp vigour of the style; Scandinavian folklorists in the nineteenth century all seem to have been blessedly free from the verbosity and heavy-handed, patronizing jocularity so often displayed by Victorian English gentry when handling folk material. However, George Webbe Dasent's translation of Norwegian tales are free from this fault, and I have included one of his stories here (p. 187).

So much has been published in the twentieth century, both as books and in specialist journals, that my choice of tales was inevitably arbitrary. The works I have taken as my sources each represent a different approach to the task of folktale collecting. Reidar Th. Christiansen's *Norske Sagn* contains stories sent in by Norwegian readers of a popular newspaper, the *Allers Family Journal*, in response to an appeal for traditional local tales. Some contributors include illuminating comments on how, when and from whom they had first heard the stories – see, for instance, 'A Tale about St Olav' (p. 19), 'The Solunna Hag' (p. 214) and 'Hunters' Tales' (p. 225). Edvard Grimstad's *Etter Gamalt: Folkeminne frå Gud-brandsdal* is an in-depth study of a single occupational group: women who had tended cattle at the summer mountain dairies of a particular Norwegian district. He inquired into all aspects of their life – tools and techniques, hardships and pleasures – as well as their stories, which naturally revolved round the dangers and mysterious occurrences that cow-girls were exposed to, as can be seen from 'Good Neighbours' (p. 216), 'Bad Neighbours' (p. 217), and 'Anne Rykhus' (p. 219). Danish collections of the twentieth century are represented by Laurits Bødker. I have drawn all my Swedish examples from Bengt af Klintberg's *Svenska Folksägner* – a most valuable selection taken directly from among the thousands of legends in the four great folklore archives of Sweden, with only minimal editing of the verbatim records. All were collected in this century, some as recently as the 1940s, but, since the informants were old and were recalling tales they had known all their lives, the tradition they imparted was firmly rooted in the nineteenth century. The same is true of Christiansen's and Grimstad's informants. Since we can safely assume that in the 1840s Faye and Thiele were similarly seeking out the oldest informants available, and that these too were drawing on childhood memories of what their elders had told them, the stories given here represent over 200 years of stable, homogeneous tradition.

Although the legend as a genre has attracted less attention from scholars than the fairy-tale, there are several books available in English offering translations and commentaries on legends from Scandinavia. These are: Reidar Th. Christiansen, *The Folktales of Norway*, RKP (1964); John Lindow, *Swedish Legends and Folktales*, University of California Press (1978); Jacqueline Simpson, *Icelandic Folktales and Legends*, B. T. Batsford and University of California Press (1972), and *The Master Magicians of Iceland*, Mistletoe Books, The Folklore Society (1975); John F. West, *Faroese Folktales and Legends*, Shetland Publishing Company, Lerwick (1980). There is no comparable collection of translations from Danish. In compensation, however, there has appeared Joan Rockwell's biography of a very remarkable Danish folklorist: *Evald Tang Kristensen: A Lifelong Adventure in Folklore*, Aalborg University Press, Copenhagen (1982). It is very much hoped that this will soon be followed by the same author's translations of some of the many thousands of tales Kristensen collected.

ABBREVIATED REFERENCES

The following abbreviated references are used throughout the book. Each source-reference gives relevant page numbers and where appropriate the volume and folktale number. Cross-references include the title and code number of the comparative folktale. Subdivisions of types of folktale are sometimes indicated by asterisks.

NINETEENTH-CENTURY SOURCES

Jón Árnason, *Íslenskar þjóðsögur og Aefintýri*, vols. I & II, Reykjavik, 1862–4. — Árnason

Andreas Faye, *Norske Folke-Sagn*, Christiania, 1844. — Faye

J. M. Thiele, *Danmarks Folkesagn*, vols. I & II, København, 1843. — Thiele

George Webbe Dasent, *Popular Tales from the Norse*, Edinburgh, 1859; translated from P. C. Asbjörnsen & J. I. Moe's *Norske Folkeeventyr*, Christiania, 1842. — Webbe Dasent

TWENTIETH-CENTURY SOURCES

Laurits Bødker, *Danske Folkesagn*, København, 1958. — Bødker

Reidar Th. Christiansen, *Norske Sagn*, Oslo, 1938. — Christiansen

Edvard Grimstad, *Etter Gamalt: Folkeminne frå Gudbrandsdal*, Oslo, 1948. — Grimstad

Bengt af Klintberg, *Svenska Folksägner*, Stockholm, 1972. — Klintberg

CODED CROSS-REFERENCES

Reidar Th. Christiansen, *The Migratory Legends*, Helsinki, 1958. — *Migratory Legends*

Antti Aarne & Stith Thompson, *The Types of the Folktale*, Helsinki, 1961. — *Types of Folktale*

PART ONE

LEGENDS OF THE LANDSCAPE

INTRODUCTION

To country-dwellers there is, quite literally, 'no place like home.' Their village and its surrounding mountains, lakes and forests are unique in their eyes, and indeed in past generations, many of them might never have had occasion to travel more than a few miles from home. In such circumstances, local pride may well express itself in traditional stories which cluster round notable natural features or unusual buildings in the district. Their origins, names and histories are a matter for speculation; their exceptional nature makes them fitting scenes for dramatic or eerie events, and thus they become the focus for legend-building. Sometimes, the tales are told simply for their entertainment value. It must be many centuries since anyone in Scandinavia seriously supposed that giants hurled rocks at each other, or at churches, yet stories purporting to explain the presence of a huge boulder as a *jættekast* ('giant's throw') are still much enjoyed, in a humorous spirit. Nor is anyone likely to take very seriously a claim that a Danish village named Benløse ('Legless') was so called because the wicked King Valdemar ordered every dog in it to have one paw cut off, to punish the villagers for setting their watchdogs on him when he arrived there incognito. Many legends, however, drew upon supernatural beliefs which were part of the normal assumptions of the community, such as the existence of ghosts, or the effectiveness of curses; others were plausible and realistic, and alluded to known facts in regional or national history. Such stories were accepted and passed on in good faith, and no doubt to this day there are still plenty of people in Scandinavia (as in Britain) who like to think that their own local legends contain a core of truth, even if they do not credit every detail in the traditional account.

The first story given here – 'A Tale about St Olav' – shows many features typical of the genre. It is exciting, describing amazing feats and supernatural events; its hero is one of the best-known personages in Norwegian history; it is tied to place-names and landscape features which serve as 'proofs' of its veracity and keep the tale vividly present in communal memory. Interestingly, the narrator who sent it in for Christiansen's collection in 1938 began by explaining how he had first learnt it in childhood from his father, while passing the places concerned. Whether the father himself had any degree of belief in the story cannot of course be known; probably he was merely entertaining his son, and enjoying the child's innocent acceptance of a very tall tale. Such mild hoaxing is not resented. When, in later years, children no longer believe the tales adults have told them, they still recall them vividly and with affection.

The notion that rocks are large trolls turned to stone is common in Norway and Iceland; and in these two countries (though not in the rest of Scandinavia) a troll is imagined to be a huge, malevolent giant. It may be a saint's power that destroys him, or as in 'Hag's Rock', the sun's rays may do it. Giants and trolls are also often credited with forming islands and lakes, as 'A Turf to Tread On' and 'Tissø Lake' show. Generally the activities of giants and trolls are motivated by their hatred of men, whom they wish to drown or crush, but they are always thwarted by luck, by human cunning, or by God's providence. The implication seems to be that all God's creation is by definition 'good' – of obvious usefulness to man – and so anything unproductive or inconvenient can only have resulted from the activities of some hostile superhuman being who is, however, fated to be defeated in the end. Small-scale deficiencies, as in 'The Lake That Has No Trout', may be explained as effects of human wickedness.

Turning from the landscape to the village itself, we find legends clustering most thickly round the church – the focal point of community life. Normally it is the oldest building in the area, unique in its architecture and its contents; always it is numinous, yet also the place most intimately linked to the high points in each villager's life. Many legends describe the building of a church. Some try to account for the choice of one site rather than another and, in doing so, draw on popular Christian beliefs, such as that a miraculous fall of snow is a sign from God, or that his purposes are revealed by the behaviour of animals, especially cattle – an idea based on the biblical account of the cows drawing the Ark of the Covenant (Samuel 6:7–14). Occasionally, as in the story of 'The Floating Logs', a pre-Christian motif is used; it is known that some of the first heathen settlers in Iceland threw sacred posts into the sea and set up home where they drifted ashore. A very common motif involves supernatural beings disrupting the building of a church by tearing down its walls every night; usually the problem is solved by changing the site, but in the Danish story 'Hadderup Church' the interfering troll requires a human sacrifice.

Foundation sacrifice – the immuring of a victim to ensure a building's safety – is mentioned in several Danish legends. In the one selected here, 'The Bloodstained Church', the action is justified on the grounds that the victim was guilty of devil-worship, but most variants simply state, as a matter of course, that someone (generally a child) was walled up alive so that the church would stand firm. Even more common is the belief that at one time animals had been regularly immured, so that their ghosts would guard the church and churchyard. Whether this is true, or mere rumour, is now impossible to discover. In Denmark the ghostly animal was called a Hell Horse or a Church Lamb; in Sweden it was a Church Grim in some districts, a Church Colt in others. Besides guarding the church, the animal was said to roam the village as an omen of someone's imminent death. There may be some confusion here with Death's pale horse in the Book of Revelations, and similarly the Church Lamb may owe something to the religious concept of Christ as the Lamb of God and as 'the Church's one foundation'. At the same time, these church guardians are linked to the much broader category of spectral animals, which are common in folklore and by no means limited to churches.

The death of the young carpenter in 'Our Lady's Tower in Copenhagen' is tragedy of a different type, so plausible one might well take it as reliable oral tradition. It is more likely, however, to be a warning legend about the danger of vertigo. It also approaches, though it does not quite fit, a widespread story-pattern about how an older craftsman murders a brilliant young apprentice out of jealousy.

In Norway and Sweden, the most famous church legend is 'The Church-Building Troll', also known as 'The Finn Legend' – not that it has any connection with Finland, but because in many Swedish variants the troll's name is 'Finn'. It is told of Trondheim Cathedral and Seljord Church in Norway, of Lund Cathedral in Sweden, and occasionally of lesser churches too; the oldest versions are those set at Trondheim, with St Olav as the hero. In Denmark it is also popular, being attached to some twenty village churches. It has interested many scholars, partly because it illustrates an old belief that supernatural beings can be defeated by using their real names (compare the fairy-tale of Rumpelstiltskin), and partly because it resembles a pagan Norse myth recorded in Snorri's *Edda* (c. 1220). The Eddaic myth tells how a giant builds a fortress for the gods, on promise of being given the sun, the moon, and the goddess Freyja. He fails to finish the work on time because the horse on whose help he is relying is distracted from its work by the arrival of a mare, which is really the god Loki in animal form. Thus the giant loses his reward, and is killed by the gods. However, since Loki's trick has nothing to do with guessing the giant's name, scholars generally hold that the 'Church-Building Troll' legend has borrowed this element from 'Rumpelstiltskin' and fitted it on to an updated and Christianized version of the Eddaic myth.

Churches are often said to have been built in fulfilment of a vow, usually in thanksgiving for deliverance from danger, or for sudden wealth. The Danish tale 'Ribe Cathedral' will be immediately recognized by English readers as an analogue to the story of Dick Whittington. As is so often the case, its veracity is allegedly supported by various objects – the arms of the town and, according to some accounts, a painting of a cat and four mice formerly kept in the cathedral. The legend of 'The Church at Erritsø' incorporates another international motif – that of a man who obeys a dream and thus, despite an apparent initial false trail, is led to a treasure.

The last of the church stories, from Heddal in Norway, ('Heddal: The Church in the Woods'), concerns a very remarkable building – one of the surviving wooden stave-churches of the twelfth century, whose architecture is quite unlike that of normal medieval churches. Its timbers are richly carved, and it contains various pre-Reformation objects, including a statue of the Virgin, an incense-burner, and a reliquary casket shaped like a little church, which must be the model 'in bronze' referred to in the legend (p. 31). Possibly such reminders of Catholic ritual were regarded with embarrassment in later times and one function of the legend was to excuse their presence by supplying an alternative provenance for them – these rarities, and indeed the church itself, so the legend implies, belonged to the Otherworld and were won from it by a time-honoured magical rite of disenchantment. It is also worth noticing how a picturesque site such as this attracts tales of many different types. Faye's account of 'Heddal: The Church in the Woods', which was compiled about 1835, combines motifs each of which readily occurs in isolation: the depopulation caused by the Black Death; winning an Otherworld treasure; a hunter's exploit; a guiding bell; a stolen and sunken bell. Presumably Faye was weaving together information from several people, to convey the wealth of traditions surrounding this one site.

Bell legends are frequently found. Bells were formerly regarded as very holy and capable of repelling demons, trolls and thunderstorms. They were given names, and even baptized; they were said to call out in human voices, to fly through the air and to have strong wills of their own. Some tales concern the skilful and expensive task of bell-casting. In these we meet again the theme of the brilliant apprentice and his jealous master; others tell how a dishonest craftsman substituted base metal for the bronze and silver entrusted to him, only to find that the completed bell denounced him and flew from the spire, generally plunging into a lake. By far the most popular bell legend, common throughout Scandinavia and all Europe (including Britain), tells how a church bell is lost in deep water, usually after being forcibly removed from its church. Attempts to retrieve it fail because some magical taboo is broken, but its notes can sometimes still be heard. Such tales teach listeners not to tamper with sacred objects; they are also akin to treasure legends in that they concern a precious, inaccessible object, protected by supernatural powers from humans seeking to possess it.

Buried treasure figures largely in popular tradition. Belief in hidden wealth is a universal wishful dream, but it must be added that in Scandinavia the discovery of buried gold and silver from Viking times was common enough to encourage optimistic expectations. The legends themselves, however, are about failure more often than success: the treasure-seekers are thwarted at the last moment by the supernatural guardians of the hoard, or by their own folly in breaking some taboo. These guardians may be human ghosts, spectral animals, trolls, or demons. Whatever they are, their apparitions terrify or distract the treasure-seekers. Occasionally they can be outwitted; Swedish traditions include stories in which someone, by overhearing the secret instructions given to a treasure-guardian, manages to fulfil the unlikely conditions for obtaining the gold (see 'The Blood of Seven Brothers', p. 37).

The homely landscape also harbours occasional monsters, notably dragons and water-serpents. Until fairly recent times many people took it for granted that such creatures really existed, both because they were mentioned in the Bible and in works by early naturalists and because there was apparent evidence for their existence – fossil bones and strange visual effects of waves and currents which might be interpreted as 'sightings', as at Loch Ness. In Scandinavia there were also many curious beliefs about ordinary land-snakes. It was thought that they could be lured into a fire by magic (see p. 144); so-called 'wheel-snakes' could chase a man faster than a horse could gallop, by seizing their tails in their mouths and bowling like a hoop; there were particularly cunning and dangerous snakes called Lindorms, very like dragons in their ways. From this background of belief sprang dramatic, entertaining legends. Some tell how a land-monster was slain, often by an ingenious trick, as in 'The Lindorm and the Glazier' (p. 39), a type of story closely paralleled by British dragon-slaying legends. But those about water-serpents usually stress that even if one or two have been slaughtered, there are still plenty lurking in the depths where, according to the story-tellers, they guard gold or church bells, and from which they occasionally arise to seize a human victim.

A TALE ABOUT ST OLAV

Norway

Once, in my schooldays, I went rowing with my father up along Framvar Fjord. As we drew level with Horse Leap Point (Hestesprangnes), father stopped rowing and pointed up at the crags with his oar, and showed me plainly the tracks of a horse in a rock about a man's height above the level of the water. There they were, and there they are today – the clear prints of a horse which has come hurtling down at a gallop. The hoof-marks are exactly those left when a horse lands after a big leap. And it looks as if his force had been so great, or the rock so soft, that the horse's feet sank in about three inches down. The size and shape of the prints are quite normal – even the underside of the hoof is clearly shown. The one thing is that the prints of the hind feet are slightly smeared, as if the ground were soft clay.

I asked how such a thing could be, and he answered: 'I can't explain it, my boy, but the story goes that it happened like this. St Olav came riding down from Hira through Kjerringdal, on his way to Lista. On both sides of the valley there are high mountains, and the trolls from up there chased after him, and wanted to kill him, because he was Christian. Olav fled from them. When he got to Bøensnes, which you can see on the other side of the fiord, he spurred his horse so that it leapt from the top of the cliff over there, right across the fiord, and landed here. These are the prints of his horse. The fiord is two or three hundred metres broad at this spot. From then on, this headland and the little crofter's farm you can see up there on the slope have been called Horse Leap Point.'

He also told me: 'Away over by Haugenes, near Bøensida, you see a large rock shaped like a tower some fifteen or twenty metres high. That was one of the trolls who wanted to catch Olav, but he turned him into a rock. It looks a bit like a priest wearing a cloak and shoulder-cape, and that's probably why some people have called it 'The Priest'.

Nowadays The Priest doesn't look anything much, because, later on, when they were building a new road over Bøensfjell, they blew up most of him.

Christiansen, pp. 33–4.

HAG'S ROCK

Iceland

In the neighbourhood of Kirkjubœr on Hroarstunga there are some curious crags called Skersl. There is a cave in them, in which there once lived an old troll and his wife. His name was Thorir, but her name is not remembered. Every year these trolls used magic to lure either the priest at Kirkjubœr or the shepherd there to come to them; this went on, with either priest or shepherd disappearing, until a priest named Eirikur came to that church. This Eirikur was a man of great spiritual strength, and he managed to protect both himself and the shepherd by his prayers, so that all the trolls' efforts were in vain.

So things went on until Christmas Eve. As the evening wore on, the troll hag realized there was no hope of luring either the priest or the shepherd into her power, so she gave up, saying to her husband: 'I've tried as hard as I can to bewitch the priest or the shepherd, but I can't do anything, because every time I cast the spell I feel as if a hot breath were coming at me and burning me to the bone, and I have to stop. So now you must go and find us some food, because there's nothing to eat in the cave.'

The giant said he didn't want to go, but he let himself be talked into it by his wife. He left the cave and went off westwards along the ridge that is now named after him, Thorir's Ridge, and out on to the lake, since then known as Thorir's Lake. There he smashed a hole through the ice and lay down beside it with his fishing line, and caught a great many trout through the ice-hole. It was freezing hard. When he thought he had caught enough he wanted to get up and go home with his catch, but he was frozen so firmly to the ice that he couldn't stand up. He struggled hard and long, but in vain, and so there he lay on his chest on the ice, and there he died.

The hag thought her husband was slow coming home, and she grew hungry. She ran out of the cave, taking the same path as the giant, over the ridge, and found him there, lying lifeless on the ice. She tried for a long time to lift him off the ice and when she saw there was no hope of doing so she clutched the string of trout, slung them over her shoulder, and said: 'This word I say and this curse I lay, that from now on no fish will be caught in this lake.' And these words have come true, for there has never been anything to catch there since then.

The hag set off home to her cave, but as she came up on to the ridge two things happened at once: she saw the sun rising in the east, and the sound of the churchbells rang in her ears. Then she turned into a rock, there on the ridge, and that rock has been called Hag's Rock ever since.

Árnason, I, pp. 153–4.

THE HAG'S BED

Iceland

A little way up the valley from Mælifell in Skagafjord there is a swampy hollow between two gravel banks, which is called The Hag's Bed. It is said that a she-troll went to sleep there on the gravel bank and that the hollow is the mark of her lair. One can see clearly where her head lay. The hollow is deepest where her shoulder and hip rested, for she must have been lying on her side with her knees a bit drawn up; one can even see the marks of her shoes. This depression in the ground is over a hundred fathoms long, which shows how large men imagined a troll to be.

Árnason, I, p. 217.

A TURF TO TREAD ON

Sweden

In the old days there were giants living inside Vistakulle Hill. One day this family of giants was invited to a feast with their kinsmen in Västergötland. But the giantess was so far gone in pregnancy that she could not step across Lake Vättern in a single stride, as she usually did, unless the giant dug up a turf and threw it out into the middle of the

lake for her to have something to set her foot on. And that turf became
the island called Visingsö.

Klintberg, no. 97, p. 122. Collected in
1927 from an informant born in the 1860s.

TISSØ LAKE

Denmark

At Kundby, which is in the district of Holbæk on Zealand, there used
to be a troll living inside the high bank where the church stands, but
since the people in those parts were pious and eager to go to church,
the troll was horribly plagued by the fact that the bells in the church
tower were ringing almost all the time. Eventually he was forced to go
away, for there was nothing more effective in making troll-folk leave
the country than the fact that people grew more pious and the ringing
of church bells increased.

The Kundby troll left the district, went over to Fyn, and lived there
for a while. Then it happened that a man who had recently settled on a
farm in Kundby came to Fyn, and met this troll on the road.

'Where's your home?' the troll asked him.

As this troll looked exactly like a human being, the man answered
truthfully: 'I'm from Kundby.'

'Really?' said the troll. 'I don't know you, yet I know everyone in
Kundby! Will you carry a letter back to Kundby for me?'

The man willingly agreed, and the troll tucked a letter into the
depths of his knapsack, telling him not to take it out before he got to
Kundby Church. There he was to toss it over the churchyard wall and
in that way the person it was meant for would certainly get it. With
this they parted, and the farmer forgot all about the letter. But after he
had crossed back to Zealand he was sitting in a meadow, just where
Tissø Lake is now, when the troll's letter suddenly came into his mind.
He took it out of his knapsack and sat for a while with it in his hands,
when all at once water began to dribble out from under the seal; the
letter unfolded itself – and it was touch and go whether that farmer

could get away with his life! The troll had sealed up a whole lake inside that letter, in order to be revenged on Kundby Church; but God prevented that, and so the lake poured out into the big hollow in the meadow, where it still stands.

Thiele, II, pp. 4–5.

THE LAKE THAT HAS NO TROUT

Iceland

In the middle of Refa parish, in the district of Hunavatn, there is a certain lake called Langavatn; there is a deep gully running out on the west side of this lake which is called Hell Gully, and this is the story they tell about it. In the old days there used to be lots of fish to be caught in that lake, and among the people who had the right to fish in it were two women – Svana, who lived at Svangrund, and Sida, who lived at a place that was also called Sida. There were constant quarrels between them arising out of the fishing rights over this lake.

One day the two of them happened to meet on the west side of the lake, and they started arguing, as so often before, but on this occasion it ended in them solemnly cursing one another. At this the earth opened up and swallowed them both, and then it split and formed the gully which is called Hell Gully to this day. From that time there has been a curse on this lake, with the result that there are no trout in it, nor any other edible fish, even though there are said to be some in other lakes thereabouts. On the other hand, it does have plenty of sticklebacks – which nobody would ever dream of eating.

Árnason, I, p. 477.

THE TWIN STEERS

Sweden

Before the building of the church at Västra Harg was quite complete, it all collapsed in a single night. So then they took a pair of twin steers and loaded four building beams on to a cart, and the steers were allowed to go wherever they chose with this load, and wherever they would come to a halt, there the church would be built. Finally, the cattle did stop. You see, it was not meant that they should stop at the first place they came to. And it had to be twin steers only – no others would do.

Klintberg, no. 371, p. 258. Collected 1926
from an informant born in 1855.

THE FLOATING LOGS

Sweden

When people were planning to build churches at Skillingmark and Järnskog, there were some who wanted to have the churches sited further up in the parish. So then they chopped down two tree trunks, near the border with Norway. They hammered a shilling into the end of one of them, and to the other they fastened a horseshoe. They threw the logs into a current and wherever they stopped of their own accord, there the churches would be built.

One log ran aground between Asksjön and Björklången. Here they built Skillingmark Church, since it was the log with the shilling (*skilling*) in it that had run aground there. The other log with the horseshoe (*järn*) in it floated on, past Björklången and Vadjungen and on down to a place called Stommen. That's where they built the first Järnskog Church, probably in the fifteenth century or perhaps even earlier.

Klintberg, no. 373, pp. 258–9. Collected in 1932.

MIDSUMMER SNOW

Sweden

When a church was to be built at Vintrosa, they began it some way away from where it is now. But there must have been a troll there, or something of the sort, because whatever was built by day was pulled down by night. In the end there was someone – maybe it was the priest, or the parishioners, or whoever it was – who prayed to be given a sign as to where the church should stand.

Then, on Midsummer's Night, snow fell on a hill near there, and that's where they then built the church. And at first the parish was called Vinteråsa ('Winter Ridge'), but now it is shortened to Vintrosa.

Klintberg, no 374, p. 259. Collected in 1923 from an informant born in 1900 at Vintrosa. *Migratory Legends* 7060 'A Disputed Site for a Church'.

HADDERUP CHURCH

Denmark

It is said of Hadderup Church, as of so many others, that when it was being built the trolls would smash down, every night, whatever men had built up by day. The first plan that was tried was to hitch two red cows to a heavy load of stones, so that the church could be built wherever they halted with the wagon. But when that idea, and others, had been tried and found useless, people made a promise to the trolls who had been hindering their work: if only they would let the church stand, then the first woman to come to that church as a bride would be theirs. This did work; the construction went ahead, and in a short while the church was quite ready.

Then one day it happened that a bridal party came driving from Haderis to this church. Just as they were crossing the river which runs between the two villages there came such a thick, black fog that no man could see his neighbour and, when it cleared away, the bride was gone. Since that day, bridal parties much prefer to make a long detour rather than go by that road.

Thiele, I, p. 227. *Migratory Legends* 7060.

THE BLOODSTAINED CHURCH

Denmark

When Bjernede Church was being built, about half a mile from Sorø, the work went very badly at first, for whatever had been built by day was found to have been destroyed by next morning. Eventually it was discovered that among the workmen there was an apprentice mason who had had dealings with the Devil and had made a pact with him. When this became known, this apprentice was walled up alive in the wall of the church, and once that had been done the work went ahead unhindered. In the porch one can still see the red stains left by the blood crushed out of him by the heavy blocks of stone with which this church is built.

Thiele, I, p. 204.

CHURCH GUARDIANS

Denmark

In all churchyards in the old days, before any human corpse was laid in the earth, a horse would be buried alive. So the ghost of this horse comes back again, and is known as a Hell Horse. It has only three legs and if anybody meets it, this forebodes death. Hence the expression used when someone has recovered from a dangerous illness: 'He gave Death a bushel of oats.'

There is a Hell Horse in the churchyard of Aarhus Cathedral which sometimes allows itself to be seen. An Aarhus man whose windows overlooked the churchyard was sitting in his main room one evening when he exclaimed: 'What kind of a horse is that, going past out there?'

'It's surely the Hell Horse!' answered someone else who was sitting there.

'Well then, you Devil, I want to have a look at you!' replied the man. As he looked out of the window he grew as pale as a corpse, but he never uttered one word about what he had seen. Shortly afterwards he began to be ill, and it was not long before he died.

When someone goes into a church alone, at a time when no service is being held, it often happens that he sees the Church Lamb running across the floor – for the whole church rests upon a lamb, so that it should not sink. In days gone by, when churches were being built, it was a general custom to bury a lamb alive under the altar, so that the church should stand unshakable. This lamb's ghost is known by the name of the Church Lamb, and whenever some little child is due to die somewhere the Church Lamb is seen to come and frisk on the threshold of the house, as a forewarning.

In Karlslunde Church, near Roskilde, one can still see a lamb carved in stone below the louvres of the tower, which proves that when the part of the church where the altar now stands was added on, a lamb was walled up alive at this spot.

Thiele, II, p. 294.

OUR LADY'S TOWER IN COPENHAGEN

Denmark

When the spire was being built for Our Lady's Church in Copenhagen in 1514, a young journeyman carpenter had an argument with his master and boasted, in his anger, that he was just as skilful a carpenter as he. To settle the dispute, the master laid a beam jutting outwards from the very top of the tower, took an axe in his hands, walked out along the beam, and drove the axe firmly into the far end of it. When he had done this and had got back safely, he ordered the journeyman to go out and fetch the axe back. The lad did not hesitate, but when he was standing out at the far end of the beam and wanted to grasp the axe, it seemed to him that he could see two, so he asked 'Master! Which of the axes is it to be?'

So the master understood what was happening to the lad, and only answered: 'God have mercy on your poor soul!' And at that instant everything swam before the journeyman's eyes, and he crashed down from the beam.

Thiele, I, p. 184.

THE CHURCH-BUILDING TROLL

Norway

Trondheim Cathedral is known far and wide as one of the finest churches in Christendom, and it was particularly splendid in the old days, when it had its sky-high spire. Building the church itself was a task St Olav was equal to, but to set a spire on it was beyond his skill. In his perplexity St Olav promised the sun itself to anyone who would undertake to raise the spire. As no man dared do it, or could do it, a troll who lived near by inside Hlade Cliff offered to undertake the work if he would receive what St Olav had promised. In addition, he made it a condition that St Olav should not address him by his name, assuming he could manage to learn what it was. Now since St Olav had got himself into a fine scrape by his promise, he tried to find some clue as to the troll's name. So at midnight he sailed along Hlade Cliff, and when he came to the place that is still called Old Woman he heard a child crying inside the rock, and its mother hushing it with the promise that it would have 'Heaven's Gold (the sun) when Tvæster came home.' Joyfully Olav went back to the town and got there in the nick of time, for the spire was soaring high in the air and the troll was just fixing the last gold knob on the weather vane. So St Olav shouted: 'Tvæster!

You've set the vane too far to the west!' The very instant the troll heard his name, he toppled down dead.

Faye, pp. 14-15, from oral versions. The first printed reference is in J. Eenberg's *Kort berättelse af de märkvärdigaste saker uti Upsala stad*; 1704. *Migratory Legends* 7065 'Building a Church: The Name of the Master Builder'.

RIBE CATHEDRAL

Denmark

A poor skipper from Ribe sailed abroad one day, and took three cats with him. Now it so happened that he came to an island where the people were terribly plagued with mice. They swarmed everywhere, not just at night but in broad daylight too, and when people were eating they had to spend almost all the time driving the mice off with their spoons.

The skipper saw this, of course, and he explained to the people that he could rid them of these unwelcome guests in a much easier way.

Well, they said, if he could do that, they would give him many barrels of gold.

So he stepped forward with his cats, saying the cats would be able to do whatever they pleased with those mice. No sooner had he set the cats loose than everyone saw this was no lie, and they were so glad that they gave him a whole ship-load of money at once.

He put to sea again, and made a vow to the Lord that if he allowed him to reach home safely he would build so fine a church that one would have to go a long way to find one equal to it. When he reached home safe and sound he did as he had vowed and, since it was thanks to his cats that the church was built, one can see to this day on the coat of arms of the City of Ribe three cats leaping from the tower of Ribe Cathedral.

Bødker, p. 52. *Types of Folktale* 1651, 'Whittington's Cat'.

THE CHURCH AT ERRITSØ

Denmark

Many years ago there were two brothers living in Erritsø near Fredericia, one of whom was very rich and the other very poor. Although at that time the village was in great need of a new church, the rich one would not do anything about it, and so one day the poor one said to him: 'If I had a lot of money, I would build a church for the parish!'

Next night he dreamed that he ought to make his way to the bridge at Sønder near Vejle (about ten miles away), for he would find his fortune there. He followed that advice, and he walked to and fro on the bridge till late in the evening, but saw no sign of any fortune. He was preparing to leave when, just as he had turned away, an army officer came up to him and asked him why he had spent all day on the bridge like that. He told him of his dream, and the officer told him that he had had a dream too, on the previous night, namely that over at Erritsø, in a barn belonging to a man whose name he gave, there was supposed to be a buried treasure. Now the name he gave was this farmer's own name. The farmer kept very quiet about it, went back home, and found the treasure in his own barn.

So now this farmer had got the wealth he had wished for, and so one day he went out walking round the fields to pick a site for building the church he had vowed to raise. There he met his rich brother, who did not know what had happened. When the latter asked him what he was doing there, he answered, 'I mean to build a church for the parish, and I'm just looking for a good site for it.'

'Oh yes?' said his brother scornfully. 'Well, if you're going to build a church, I'll give the bells for it.'

But later, when he saw that the church really and truly was being built, he was vexed to such a degree at having to give the bells that he hanged himself.

Thiele, I, pp. 246–7.

HEDDAL: THE CHURCH IN THE WOODS

Norway

Even in the remote mountain valleys of Valdres the Black Death raged with terrifying force. Many farms, and even whole valleys, lost all their inhabitants, and were quite forgotten by the survivors and unknown to the new settlers who arrived in the region later. Many centuries afterwards, a hunter who was out shooting ptarmigan went wandering through these deserted parts which once had been inhabited. As he shot an arrow at a bird perched in a tree, he heard his arrow strike against something which gave out a strange clang. Curious, he approached the spot, and to his amazement found himself before an ancient church. Obeying a common belief that such things will vanish at once unless one can break the spell or illusion by throwing steel over what one has found, he quickly snatched his fire-steel and flung it over the church. A farm was later built where it fell, and to this day it is called Eiljøinstad, from Ildjarnstad, i.e. Fire-steel-stead, in memory of this event.

The key was still in the church door, which was half open. In the middle of the floor stood a great bell, and at the foot of the altar a huge bear had made its winter lair. It was killed by the brave hunter, and in memory of this marvel its pelt was hung up in the church, where the remains of a large bearskin can still be seen. It is said that the man found various paintings in the church, among other things, and a small model of a church in bronze, and four big bells and one little one. It was one of these that his arrow had hit, thus causing the clang which attracted his attention.

The little bell is still used when anyone is lost in the forest, for people believe that a lost man will always hear it and so get back on to the right path. Some people tried to carry off the biggest of the other four bells for the cathedral, but when they had to cross a certain lake it fell in. 'What else can you expect', people said, 'when they were wanting to separate her from her sisters?' In clear windless weather one can still see the bell in the lake, but to get it up is almost impossible, because to do so would require seven brothers, who must not speak one word during the work. Once, seven brothers did make the attempt; they had already raised it to the water's edge when one of them exclaimed, 'We've got it now, thank

God!' but at that very moment the bell plunged back into the lake.

Faye, pp. 130–2. Heddal is a twelfth-century stave-church. Among various medieval objects it possesses a bronze reliquary of about 1200, shaped like a small church, which probably once contained a relic of St Thomas à Becket, who is represented on it. The bearskin Faye describes is no longer there.

THE BELLMAKER'S APPRENTICE

Sweden

The great bell at Gällaryd is a a very fine one, and in its metal one can clearly see many silver coins which did not melt down entirely. This is how it came about.

It had been intended that this bell should be cast by a travelling master craftsman in Ugglekula, but he was out drinking most of the time, and his apprentice was ordered to keep watch on the smelting vat. The apprentice sent word to his master several times that the metal was ready to be cast, but he did not come, so then he poured the metal into the mould with his own hand. At that moment a certain Lady Wallron was passing by on her way from Kyrkebol, and she dropped an apronful of silver coins into the mass of molten metal, saying, 'As sure as I am a virgin, so surely shall this bell utter my name whenever it is rung.'

The bell was cast, and when it was quite ready the apprentice saw a blood-blister on his hand. Then he said: 'I shall lose my life on account of this bell.'

An hour or so later the master returned, and he struck the bell with his hammer and listened to its note. 'Well now,' said he, 'you're taking away my livelihood, so I'll take your life.' And he struck his apprentice, and killed him. But the bell says 'Wallron' whenever anyone rings it.

In later years, someone knocked a hole in that bell, for her note had been as strong as that of a city church, which is not allowed for country bells.

Klintberg, no. 377, p. 260. Collected in 1908. *Migratory Legends* 7070 'Legends about Church Bells'.

LOST BELLS

Denmark

Once, a girl unjustly condemned to death prayed that, as a miracle to prove her innocence, the bell in Søby church tower should fall into Tis Lake the next time anyone rang it. And so it was; the bell left its tower and fell into the lake, where one can still sometimes hear it ringing.

Before St Knud's Tower stood where it stands now, it used to stand where the market is now. There were fine bells in that tower, but one feast day, when they were being rung very hard, the largest flew out of the tower and fell into the river at the spot still called Bell Pit because of this. Some people say this pit is bottomless; others, on the contrary, say that if one probes with long poles one can feel the bell down there. It is also said that whenever anybody in Odense is about to die one can hear it tolling under water, and that it sounds like the note of a far-off village bell.

Thiele, I, p. 194, pp. 206–7. *Migratory Legends* 7070

The Milk-Fed Steers

Sweden

There's supposed to be a bell from Haråkers Church lying in Black River, just below the church. There were some enemies or other who wanted to steal the bell, and they set out across the ice with it, but the ice broke and the bell sank.

Now, they say that the people were able to raise it a little, just enough to see it. But the Spirit said that if they could rear a pair of steers by feeding them on fresh milk only, they would be able to haul the bell right up. And they did it too, only one day the dairymaid happened to spill the fresh milk and, in order that the steers should not go hungry, she gave them skimmed milk – for surely it wouldn't matter, just for once.

Well then, they took these steers and drove them down to the river, and they got the bell right to the edge of the water, but then the Spirit said: 'Those skim-milk calves of yours, they'll never haul the bell up!'

And so it sank down again, and it may well be lying there still.

Klintberg, no. 382, p. 262. Collected in 1938. *Migratory Legends* 7070. The text uses a very general term, *rå*, for 'spirit', but variant versions indicate that this is probably the 'Church Grim' rather than a river spirit.

Helga's Hillock

Iceland

Beside the farm named Grund in Eyjafjord there is a hillock called Helga's Hillock. It is said that a woman named Helga of Grund had herself buried in this hillock, and that she had been a very rich woman, and covetous too – or so it was said in later years – and the men of

34

Eyjafjord say she lived at the time when the Black Death was raging. It is said that she ordered a great deal of money to be laid in the hillock; but when men went to dig into it, it seemed to them that the church at Grund was on fire. They ran there to put the fire out, but it was simply an illusion, to divert the diggers from their undertaking.

Árnason, I. p. 280. In Iceland the Black Death was 1402–4.

THE GUARDIAN OF BRUSI'S MOUND

Iceland

Brusi's Mound is near Brusastad, a farm in Vatnsdal. There was once a man who went to dig into it, and when he had been digging there all day he dreamt that night that a man came to him – a big, evil-looking man – and told him to stop breaking into his burial mound, or it would be the worse for him. Next morning the man awoke and remembered his dream, but took no notice and went back to break into the mound, as before. The following night he dreamed of the same man again, and this time he looked even more menacing, and he threatened him with all sorts of evils if he didn't now leave the mound alone. But the man went back for the third day, and paid no more attention to his dream than before. All the soil had fallen back into the trench, as indeed it had on the previous day too. So then he dug all day till evening, by which time he had reached something wooden. Then he had to stop; night had fallen. But during that night the people of the farm were awoken because this man was trying to hang himself. He had been dragged from his bed, and he hadn't woken until he found himself outside. After this, the man stopped trying to break into the mound, and nobody has tried it since. But one can still see traces of the man's work to this day, on the east side of Brusi's Mound.

Árnason, I, pp. 279–80.

Queen Margrethe's Treasure

Denmark

Once, during the war between King Albrekt of Sweden and Queen Margrethe of Denmark, the latter encamped with her army on Gammelstrup Heath, a few miles west of Viborg. While she was peacefully resting there, she suddenly got news that Albrekt was marching against her from the east. She thought it wisest to avoid battle, so she gave orders to march westwards. There was a river on this route which they had to cross, but they had no time to have a bridge built, so they had to ford it. Queen Margrethe was carrying her money with her in a little copper cauldron. While she was riding through the river she dropped her cauldron in the middle, and it sank to the bottom. She had no time to get it fished out, for King Albrekt and his army were not far off.

From that time on, there has always been a little light hovering over the spot where the cauldron sank. Once, there were some men who wanted to try and fish it up, but they knew that none of them must speak a single word until they had got it well and truly up on to dry land. They began to fish for it, and in fact it was not very long before they got a hold upon it. They carefully raised it to the surface of the water, where they managed to pass a pole through the handle, so now all they had to do was to draw it to the bank. But the pole happened to slip a little, so that it looked as if it would come out, and at that one of the men exclaimed: 'Look out!' No sooner had he spoken than the cauldron lay at the bottom of the river again, after which it was impossible even to get a hold on it. Since then no one has tried to fish up the copper cauldron.

Bødker, pp. 40–41.

The Miser and His Son

Norway

A few generations ago, an old man called Jørgen lived in Skatvik. He had a lot of money locked away in a chest but he lived like the poorest of the poor, and even though his son said he couldn't bear living like that, it made no difference. The old man took it into his head that his son wanted to get hold of his money, and to make sure that that did not happen he simply buried the whole chest in a little mound on the hillside above the farm. The son followed him to see what he would do with it, arriving in time to see the spot. He heard his father pledge himself to the Evil One, and swear that this treasure would never be found unless his own hand held the handle of the spade. He must have intended to dig the chest up again, but he died shortly afterwards. The son went off to get the chest but returned empty-handed, for there was no chest at the place where the old man had buried it. The reason must have been that unless Jørgen's own hand was on the handle of the spade, that treasure could never be found.

Christiansen, p. 244.

The Blood of Seven Brothers

Sweden

There was a man, once, who buried a treasure on a mountain. And there had been a child close by who had seen and heard it, while he was gathering berries. 'Well now,' this old man had said as he was burying the treasure, 'you are to keep this safe until the blood of seven brothers has flowed over it.' The child talked of this to his parents. Then they took seven cockerels and an axe and went up there. They cut their heads off and let the blood flow over the spot, and then they were able

37

to dig up the treasure. My grandmother used to tell us about it, and she was born here in Tving.

Klintberg, no. 387, p. 264. Collected in 1924 from a woman born in 1866. It is implied that the old man has set a magical guardian to keep his money — the ghost of an animal he has killed, possibly, or a demon, or a magic bone.

THE OLD TROLL TRICKED

Sweden

Once there used to be a light which shone at night at one spot in the outfields by Nordre Bäck. There was treasure buried there, of course, and there were many who tried to get hold of it. When one sees a troll-light burning far off in the outfields one should walk straight towards the light and keep one's eyes on it all the time without blinking. A farmer from Tyft tried to do this, they say, out at Nordre Bäck. But just as he was jumping across a ditch he blinked, and at that very moment the light vanished.

Now not far off there lived another farmer, who was more cunning. He took a big cooking pot and crammed it full of old horseshoes and other bits of scrap iron. Then he carried it to the outfields at Nordre Bäck and put it down a little way from the place where the light used to burn. Then he built a fire and set it burning over his pot. At this the old troll grew jealous and curious, so he simply couldn't stay hidden but had to go and see what this farmer had in his pot. He crept up to him and peeped, but when he saw what was in the pot he snorted and said: 'Oh, that's nothing worth burning a light over! Now, you come over to my place, and you'll see something very different!'

The farmer went along with him, and the old troll showed him a huge pot full of gold and silver coins. Then the farmer seized his chance and threw a drawn knife into the pot. Thus he got power over the pot and could carry it home with him. He became rich enough to last him the rest of his life.

Klintberg, no. 391, p. 266.

THE LINDORM AND THE GLAZIER

Denmark

It happened once, many years ago, that corpses which were buried in Aarhus Cathedral were removed, time after time, and nobody knew what the explanation could be. Sothen people kept watch and saw how a Lindorm, which had its lair in a hole under the church, used to go inside every night and eat the corpses. Besides this horrible affair, they also realized that the creature was undermining the church so much that it would certainly soon crack and collapse, and so everyone was in great distress and searched in vain for help and good advice.

Then a travelling glazier came to Aarhus, and when he heard of the trouble the town was in, he promised to help them. Thereupon he made himself a chest out of mirror glass, making it so that there was only a single opening in it, and that no bigger than was necessary for him to thrust his rapier through. He had the chest carried into the cathedral and laid on the floor in broad daylight. When midnight came he lit four wax candles which he placed at the corners of the chest, and then he laid himself inside it.

Then the Lindorm came crawling up the nave, and when it became aware of the chest and saw its own reflection in the mirror, it thought it was its mate. But the glazier stabbed it through the neck, so that it died at once. However, the blood and poison which gushed out were so destructive that the glazier died of it, there inside his chest.

It is said that there is still [1843] an old picture to be seen in the cathedral showing this remarkable event.

> Thiele, II, pp. 287–8. A Lindorm, literally 'Heath Snake', was imagined as a kind of super-snake closely akin to a dragon, but flightless.

A Flying Dragon

Sweden

When I was a child I saw a dragon one evening. He came from the east and was going westwards, to the mountain. He was as long as a boat and all black. A mass of fire was coming from him. He was so horrible, I'll never forget it. My father thought he must have some treasure up on the mountain which he was going to mount guard over. It was Satan who sent him, said my father.

Klintberg, no. 385, p. 263. Collected in 1933 from a woman born in 1845.

Water Serpents in Norway

Norway

In both freshwater lakes and rivers and along the coasts of Norway one hears tell of monstrous water-serpents, which, however, are varied in size and appearance. According to widespread belief, they are born on dry land and make their first lairs in forests and on rocky screes. Once they are fairly big, or once they have had a taste of human blood, they make their way down to the lakes or the sea, where they grow to an astonishing size. They seldom show themselves, and when they do they are regarded as portents of great events. In most lakes and rivers of any importance in this country, so it is said, these monsters have been seen on some past occasion rising up out of the depths, thus announcing some great event or other. They have not been seen in fresh water in living memory, but, on the other hand, one does still [1844] sometimes see them in the fiords when there is a dead calm.

In Lake Snåsa there is a great snake which demands a human life every year. In Lake Selbu there is one which has lain there since Noah's Flood; if ever it turns over it will break the rocks which hold in the waters of the lake, with the result that Trondheim will be drowned . . .

The serpent of Lake Gonsbu sometimes attacks horses, and leaves a bloody trail which one can see in the water; the serpent of Lake Lunde never lets itself be seen unless the king is about to die, or some other great event is going to occur.

Of all the serpents in Norwegian lakes, none is more famous than the one in Lake Mjøsa. Among the many signs which foretold the downfall of Hamar Cathedral, says the old *Hamar Chronicle* of 1540, was a terrible, huge serpent which seemed to stretch from Øland to the Royal Estate, but then disappeared at once. Also many great serpents could be seen out in the lake day after day, twisting themselves into huge coils and sending water high into the air. Next, the first serpent reappeared, but because of its rushing speed it ran itself aground on a rocky ledge just outside the cloisters. Its eyes were as big as the hoops of a barrel, and it had a long black mane hanging from its neck. Since it could not get off the rocks, but simply lay there lashing its head against them, one of the lads from the Bishop's household, who was something of a dare-devil, took a crossbow and shot so many bolts into its eyes that the water all around was dyed green with the stuff that gushed out. It was a fearsome-looking serpent, sparkling with many colours. It died from these shots but afterwards its corpse gave off such a stink that the Bishop ordered all the peasants of the area to join forces to get it burnt, which they did. For many more years its skeleton lay on the shore; even the smallest vertebra could only be lifted by a full-grown man. The Bishop's lad was well paid by the peasants, who also had to burn many hundreds of cartloads of wood before the terrible stench ceased.

According to another account, it was a monk who shot an arrow into the serpent's eye; it then drifted away, dead, to Helgø, where a man pulled the arrow from its eye. The place is called 'Arrow Stead' to this day, in memory of it. And even so there is still one serpent which lurks in Mjøsa Lake; it has coiled itself round the great bell from Hamar Cathedral, which, as everybody knows, sank in the Akersvik during the Seven Years' War. In clear weather one can still glimpse this bell, but all attempts to raise it have been in vain.

Faye, pp. 59–61.

41

The Water-Snake of Lagarfljot

Iceland

It happened once, long ago, that there was a woman living on a farm in the district near Lake Lagarfljot. She had a grown-up daughter, and she gave this daughter a gold ring.

Then the girl says, 'How can I make the most of this gold, mother?'

'Lay it under a Heath Snake,' says the woman.

So then then the girl catches a Heath Snake, lays the gold underneath it, and puts it in her trinket box. There the serpent lies for some days. But when the girl goes to take a look inside the box, the snake has grown so big that the panels of the box have begun to split open. Then the girl grows frightened, snatches up the box, and hurls it out into the lake, with everything that's in it.

Now when a long time had passed, people began to become aware of the serpent in the lake. He began to attack men and animals that were crossing the lake; sometimes, too, he would crawl up on to the banks and snort out poison, most horribly. All this was causing a great deal of trouble, but no one knew any way to remedy it.

Then two Lapps were sent for; they were to kill the snake and take the gold. They dived down into the lake, but they soon came up again. These Lapps said they had met their match, and more, down there, and that it would not be easy to kill the snake or take the gold. They said there was a second snake under the gold, and this one was far more evil than the first. So they had tied the snake down with two fetters; one they had placed just behind the fins, the other near the tail.

Therefore the snake cannot harm anyone now, man or beast, but sometimes he happens to thrust a hump of his back above the surface, and whenever that is seen it is thought a sign of dire events to come — for instance, bad seasons or a great shortage of grass. Those who do not believe in this serpent say that it is only a trail of floating foam, and they repeat stories of how some priest, not long ago, rowed right across the spot where it looked as if the serpent was, to prove his assertion that there was nothing there at all.

Árnason, I, pp. 638–9. Collected in 1845. Árnason also describes repeated sightings of this monster in 1749–50 and again in 1819; there were more in 1860, described

in Sabine Baring-Gould's *Iceland, its Scenes and Sagas* (1868). The first mention of the Lagarfljot snake is given in the ancient Icelandic chronicle *Skálholts Annáll*, in the entry for 1345. For more details about Lapps (the nomadic race of northern Scandinavia) see Part Five.

THE MONSTER IN VESTURHOP LAKE

Iceland

In the eighteenth century there was a man called Kolbein living at Bjarghus in Vesturhop. He was extremely poor, but he was an honest man, so many people were willing to be generous to him. On one occasion he walked across the ice of Vesturhop Lake, in calm weather and bright moonlight, to go to Vatnsend and get some food for Christmas from the farmer there. This was on the eve of St Thorlak's Day. The farmer let him have a fine sheep's carcass. Kolbein set off for home, carrying the carcass. When he got to the middle of the lake, he heard a rumbling sound behind him; the ice split, and up came a most extraordinary beast, which for size and shape looked like two horses joined together at the rumps, and one could see two heads on it. This monster set off in pursuit of Kolbein. He saw he could not outrun it, so he dropped the carcass and ran home as fast as he could. Next day he went to look for the carcass, but all he could find was some broken bones. He led his neighbours to the spot and showed them this, and he was so well liked that they made up to him for what he had lost.

Árnason, I, p. 139. St Thorlak (d. 1193) was Bishop of Skalholt in Iceland; his feastday is 23 December.

Part Two

HISTORICAL LEGENDS

INTRODUCTION

Legends which cluster round locally or nationally famous personages and events, embroidering the known facts of history with picturesque elaborations, are as common in Scandinavia as anywhere else. Unfortunately, by their very nature most can only interest people already familiar with the historical framework within which they are set, and so have little appeal to foreign readers. Certain themes, however, can impress any audience, since they do not depend for their effectiveness on detailed knowledge of individuals or particular events. The most striking legends in Scandinavian oral tradition are those about the Black Death in the 1350s – a national disaster to all four countries. The memory of it, vivid enough in itself, was reinforced by further outbreaks of plague as late as the nineteenth century, and also by epidemics of cholera and typhus which could be almost as destructive.

Some of the plague legends seem to preserve reasonably accurate memories of events, for instance when they record which districts were depopulated, or describe how the disease was brought from one village to another by an infected beggar. But there are others which give their theme a supernatural colouring, notably those in which the plague is personified as an old woman or a pair of children roaming the countryside and marking out the doomed by a symbolic gesture. Like the personified Death of the late Middle Ages, the Plague Hag kills by a glance or a touch and grants only one form of mercy – a swift, rather than a lingering, death. In Icelandic tradition, the Plague Hag is said to have been defeated in one region by magical means, twelve wizards having combined to send out a spectral bull against her.

On a more realistic level, some legends celebrate the courage of the men (and the horses) who carried the dead to burial. Others describe how a solitary survivor managed to find another, of the opposite sex, and so begot new families to repopulate a district. The legend of the rediscovery of Heddal Church, given in the previous chapter, also draws upon memories of the Black Death for its setting. But the most tragic and haunting of these tales is undoubtedly 'Earth on the Bread and Butter' (p. 53), a type well known in the southern districts of Sweden and also in Denmark. Its horror is increased by the fact that there is evidence from both countries that people were indeed occasionally buried alive in an attempt to halt the spread of epidemics; a Danish instance is known to have occurred in 1603. The procedure is the same as was used quite frequently to combat outbreaks of cattle-disease by burying an infected animal alive, still sometimes practised as late as the twentieth century, but the rationale underlying it is unclear, and several theories have been proposed. Hans-Egil Hauge argued that the ghost of the dead person (or animal) was expected to become a powerful protector, just as the ghosts of sacrificed animals were believed to guard churches or treasures; this explanation is endorsed by Klintberg. Carl-Herman Tillhagen, however, considered that the victim was believed to be literally inhabited by a plague-demon, which would be trapped underground if its human carrier was buried alive, thus preventing it from infecting others. It must surely also be relevant that the victims in 'Earth on the Bread and Butter' – and often elsewhere too – are vagrant beggars; such people did indeed often carry infection, and being strangers to a community were obviously suitable as scapegoats. As Klintberg has shown, there is a logical progression from legends in which the arrival of beggar children merely precedes the arrival of the plague, to those in which the children's symbolic actions reveal that they can foretell, or even control, its progress; to select such persons as victims carries the logic to its conclusion.

Anecdotes about historical leaders and their wars are very numerous, and fresh ones are constantly produced. In his 1964 collection, *Folktales of Norway*, Reidar Th. Christiansen remarks: 'Even the German occupation is reflected in legends gradually adapted to the traditional patterns: rivers flowing red with blood, and so forth.' The tales I have chosen from this category have themes which will recall familiar British traditions. Thus 'Dyste Drum' resembles the belief, current in Devon in the 1860s, that Sir Francis Drake's drum in Buckland Abbey had rolled during the Napoleonic Wars – a belief enshrined, and publicized, in Henry Newbolt's celebrated ballad 'Drake's Drum' in 1895. The Norwegian tradition, however, is not linked to a specific hero but to a place-name, for *Dyste* means 'battle'.

'The Sleeping Horsemen in Ålleberg' is a Swedish variant of the widespread European theme of the sleeping king who will leave his cavern to save his country; in British legends, this is of course King Arthur. 'The Battle at the Danevirke' tells how the ghost of a famous Viking queen returned to lead her country's army centuries later. The picturesque apparition recalls the story of the Angels of Mons in World War I which, despite its literary origin in a short story by Arthur Machin, was instantly accepted as true and remains well known to this day. The final variation on the theme of supernatural defenders is a Danish one, telling how the fairy-folk of Bornholm became visible to scare off Swedish invaders in 1645. There is nothing quite like this in Britain; its best parallel is a tale from medieval Iceland, telling how Norwegian ships sent to capture that country for their king turned back when they saw the coast swarming with 'land-spirits' led by giants and monsters.

A very widespread theme for historical legendry is the activities of celebrated outlaws and robbers. This material can be treated in two ways: as a glorification of the bandit's courage and trickery, or as an expression of the dread and reprobation felt towards him by law-abiding folk – his potential victims. It is the latter type that predominates in Scandinavian folk-tradition of recent centuries, though the brave and noble outlaw is of course a familiar figure in medieval Icelandic sagas. One extremely popular story found throughout Norway and Sweden (see 'The Twelve Robbers') concerns a girl who is working alone in a dairy high on the mountainside when a robber band arrives, threatening to rob and rape her – a situation which the system of summer pasturage made all too likely. The anecdote is set in many different places, with slight variations; the fixed central feature is the girl's resourcefulness in disabling her captors and summoning help on the *lur* – a large horn which dairymaids used in the mountains to call the cattle home, scare wolves, and summon help from the valley. The verse incorporated into the tale varies slightly in different versions; its tune is a simple one, which could indeed be played on a *lur*.

The Danish traditions of 'Thyre Battleaxe' and 'Jens Long-Knife' illustrate how robbers and their womenfolk can be transformed into monsters in popular imagination. Thyre, it is alleged, is guilty of repeated incest with her eldest son; Jens's wife is described as a cannibalistic gypsy-witch who eats children's hearts. Yet both tales also convey admiration for courage during torture and execution; Jens in particular shows a defiant humour worthy of saga heroes. The last of the robber tales, 'Ram's Mound', is also from Denmark. I have chosen it for its neat dramatic irony, and also because it has about two dozen exact parallels in English local traditions, generally linked to boulders called 'The Hangman's Stone'.

Finally, as an example of the fears and rumours surrounding minority groups even in fairly recent times, comes the Swedish story of 'The Servant and the Freemasons'. Masonic lodges reached Sweden in the 1730s, and were greeted in many quarters with intense suspicion. Masons, it was alleged, drank human blood at their gatherings, and sold the corpses of children from their orphanages and of travellers they had kidnapped as meat for the 'Hound-Turks'. Accusations of murder and cannibalism have been hurled at heretics and similar secretive minority groups from Roman times onwards, but who or what are 'Hound-Turks'? The term reflects a grotesque blending of two notions, one medieval and one based on eighteenth-century history. The first was a belief, common among learned writers of the Middle Ages, that somewhere in Asia or the Middle East lived a race of dog-headed men who preyed on normal humans. The second arose from the heavy taxes levied in Sweden to pay off the nation's debt to Turkey after the wars of Charles XII; the Turks came to be popularly identified with the man-eating dog-heads, about whom many tales were current, especially among Lapps. Soon the secretive, unpopular Masons were said to be trading human flesh to them. The rumour, and the legends incorporating it, now seem fantastic and implausible, yet they are scarcely more outrageous than those current in nineteenth-century London about murderous butchers, barbers or innkeepers who sold their victims' flesh as meat pies. Interestingly, the Swedish story is set in Karlskrona, a seaport which was the second largest town in the country in the eighteenth century, and seems to reflect the fear which servants fresh from the country would feel in such a place; it is an example of the narrative genre which folklorists term an 'urban legend', 'contemporary legend', or 'rumour legend', which is readily believed because it echoes fears or resentments already actively present in a community.

THE PLAGUE CHILDREN

Sweden

Before that terrible sickness came to our region, so I've heard say, there were two beggar children who went round the district asking people, 'Shall we sweep, or shall we rake?' The reply was, 'Yes, it will be best if you sweep, because then everything will be cleaner.' You see, people took it just as a joke, but later on it didn't seem so funny, because then the Black Death came, and it swept men and women away right enough, and so our parishes were almost emptied of their people.

Klintberg, no. 355, p. 251. *Migratory Legends* 7080 'Tales of the Great Plague'.

THE BLACK DEATH

Iceland

When the Black Death was raging in Iceland, it never reached the West Fjords, because twelve wizards from the west country joined forces and made a Sending to go out against it, and they put strength into this Sending.

Now the Black Death was sweeping across the country in the form of a vapour, which reached half way up the mountain slopes and out as far as the fishing banks. This vapour was being guided by an old man who strode along the mountains, and an old woman who strode along the shore. The pair of them lodged one night with a tenant-farmer on Svalbardsstrond, who thought they seemed rather suspicious-looking, so he stayed awake that night, though he pretended to be sleeping, and he heard them planning how to arrange their journey next day so as to lay waste the whole district. By morning, they had disappeared. The farmer was troubled, and went to Helga of Grund, who owned the land, and told her what he had observed. She decided that the thing to do was to move herself and all her household high up into the mountains, and this plan worked, as is well known.

When the vapour and the death-toll began moving westwards, the wizards had the Sending ready; it was a great bull, flayed to the knees, and it dragged its flayed hide behind it. It met the old man and woman on the beach at the foot of the Gilsfjord Cliffs, where their paths were bound to converge. Men with Second Sight saw their encounter, and the end of it was that the bull caught them both in its hide, forced them down under it, and crushed them to pieces.

Árnason, I, pp. 347–8. *Migratory Legends* 7080. A 'Sending' is a ghost or a spectral animal acting under a wizard's orders to destroy his enemies, according to Icelandic traditional belief; see Part IV.

TALES OF THE BLACK DEATH

Norway

The Black Death did not rage in the coastal districts alone, as other epidemics have often done, but found its way into the most remote and secluded mountain districts. It even came to Vinje in Telemark.

There, the plague went from farm to farm in the likeness of a tiny little woman. She always carried a little broom, and wherever she walked in and swept in front of the door, everybody in the house died; but at farms where some were fated to survive, she knocked as many times on the door with the broom handle as there were people due to die in that house.

In due course, this woman came down to Lake Totakvatn; she wanted to go on to Rauland, but the lake was in her way. So she turned inland, to a farm called Kålos, and got a man from there to row her over. By the time they were some way from land, the man guessed pretty well who it was that was sitting in his boat, and he started to beg for his life, asking whether he might be spared from death. The plague-woman said it was not for her to decide; it depended on whether his name was written in her book. They reached the other side. The plague-woman stepped ashore, paid the man for her passage, and then

52

opened her book, but said nothing. The man had to row home again, and as soon as he stepped across the threshold he fell to the floor, dead.

The plague went further and further, and in the end even reached Mjøsstrand Parish. People died there in great numbers, but the bodies had to be carried all the way to Rauland churchyard to be laid in holy ground. Everyone wanted to have their dear ones laid in consecrated ground, but it was a long way, and the snow was five or six feet deep. As for horses, there were not many in the district, but one man at Førnes had a very fine strong one known as the Førnes Bay. They took him and harnessed him to a wagon loaded with the dead, but they had to set it on sleigh-runners, or he could not have moved it at all. Once he had made the trip there and back, he made the same journey again and again, without a driver. But one day one of the runners jammed in the snow about half a mile from the churchyard, and the horse could not go on. Then he neighed so loud that the grave-diggers heard him from the churchyard, and went to help.

There is a tune called 'Førnes Bay', and old folk say it imitates the sound of the horse's hoofs as he went to and fro to the churchyard. At the place where the runner came off, there is supposed to have been an inscription on a rock, which shows it must all have happened just as the story tells.

Christiansen, pp. 36–7. From information sent to Faye in the 1840s, but not published at that time. *Migratory Legends* 7085 'Ferrying the Plague Hag'. Some versions of the second episode say that the horse died, exhausted.

EARTH ON THE BREAD AND BUTTER

Sweden

There was great poverty while the plague spread, and so at that time there were two children wandering about begging for food. Now, people had got the idea into their heads that it would help to stop the plague if they buried somebody alive, and so they dug a grave and told these children that if they would get down in there and sit inside the grave, they would each get a slice of bread and butter. The children climbed down into the grave, and they shovelled earth on top of them. But the children pleaded with them not to throw earth on the bread and butter, which was so good.

Klintberg, no. 358, p. 252. *Migratory Legends* 7080. Collected in 1931 from an informant born in 1871.

SURVIVORS OF THE PLAGUE

Sweden

Lurberg – 'Horn Mountain': Well, my mother's grandmother used to tell the tale of how it came to have this name. After the Black Death, they say, there were only two people left alive here in the whole district of Nora, and one was a man and the other a woman. And she wanted to call to someone and let people know that she was here, so she climbed the mountain and blew a cattle-horn as hard as she could. The man was away over by the northern boundary of Nora, but he heard the horn-call and followed it to reach her, and that's how they married, and that's how the mountain got the name Lurberg. And the Black Death promised not to return to the district of Nora until every bit of woodland had been cleared for habitation.

Klintberg, no. 360, p. 253. Collected in 1935. *Migratory Legends* 7095 'The Fate of Plague Survivors'.

DYSTE DRUM

Norway

At the far end of Kolbu lies a farm called Dystegard ('Battle Farm'). The story goes that there was a strange drum on this farm, and people believed that it was the Underground Folk who owned it, for no one could see or hear it unless there was war. But if war did come, then one could hear that drum from a long way off, and also hear the Underground Folk talking and laughing, and the drum would always give a groan before a war began. It was called the Dyste Drum, and it was quite certain that when anyone heard the Dyste Drum there was going to be a war.

Christiansen, p. 38. 'Underground Folk' is a term for fairies.

THE SLEEPING HORSEMEN IN ÅLLEBERG

Sweden

Inside Ålleberg, a mountain near Falköping, a whole army lies asleep. In the days when my father was a boy, it happened that a farmer from Leaby had to drive a cartload of oats to Falköping, but when he came to Ålleberg an old man met him on the road and offered to buy the oats from him. It did certainly strike him that the old fellow looked a bit odd, but he agreed to sell him the oats, and he even went with him to help carry them into the mountain.

Inside, it was full of soldiers just lying there, and it was terribly crowded, what with the horses and the hussars and all kinds of weapons. The old man had strictly told him that he must take care not to stumble against anything, and he did the best he could, but somehow or other he happened to stumble over a cavalryman's spurs, and this cavalryman raised himself a little from the place where he lay and asked, 'Is it time for us to get up?' But the old man said, 'Oh no, not yet!' and the cavalryman lay down again.

Then the farmer asked the old man how long they were destined to lie there. And he answered that they would lie there till a battle was fought at Nyckelängen, near by.

And then the old man told the farmer, 'Now, when you get home, you must be sure to get these coins you've been paid for the oats exchanged for others.' And so he did, with the exception of one eighteen-shilling piece which he kept – but next morning he had only a little wisp of moss instead of the eighteen-shilling piece.

Klintberg, no. 398, p. 269. Collected in 1906.

THE BATTLE AT THE DANEVIRKE

Denmark

Once, many years ago, a bloody battle between Germans and Danes was being fought beside the earthworks known as the Danevirke. It was a hard fight and on both sides men fought with great courage, so for a long time it was uncertain who would have the victory. However, the Danish king, who was leading his troops himself, was young and inexperienced and, since he was also rash and hot-headed, he paid no attention to the movements of the enemy, and would not accept the advice of his more experienced commanders. After several hours of fighting, it looked likely that the Germans would win.

Then suddenly a tall, slim lady sprang into view in the van of the Danish army. No one saw where she had come from, nor had anyone ever seen her before. Her face was half hidden by a veil, but golden hair hung loose over her shoulders. She rode a snow-white horse, but she herself was dressed in coal-black clothes. Without saying a word she snatched the standard from the hands of its astonished bearer and, turning back towards the army, shouted 'Shame on him who will not follow me!'

As if by magic, courage returned to the disheartened Danes. Those who were already fleeing returned to the fight, and now the battle did not last much longer, for wherever the majestic leader advanced, the enemy fell back. The Danes won a glorious victory, but the woman they could thank for it had suddenly vanished. The soldiers believed it was Thyra Danebod herself who had saved her country, and her ramparts, from defeat.

Bødker, pp. 125–6. The Danevirke is a chain of linked earthworks across the base of the Jutland peninsula; parts date from the 730s, others from the ninth and tenth centuries. Thyra was the wife of King Gorm the Old (died c. 940), who set up a memorial stone for her, on which he called her *Danebod*, 'Glory of the Danes'.

THE UNDERGROUND FOLK DEFEND BORNHOLM

Denmark

Once, the Swedish fleet was lying off the port of Neksø on Bornholm Island, and the senior Danish officers there had let themselves be bribed by the Swedes to allow them to seize the place unopposed. So all the troops had been ordered to muster at Rønne, on the opposite side of the island, except for one old man who, for appearances' sake, had been set to keep watch on the beach.

Now the Swedes began coming ashore, and naturally the old man could not stop them. He was heartbroken about it, but there was nothing to be done. Then he heard something like a whisper: 'Load and shoot! Load and shoot!'

Well, he looked round but he couldn't see anyone. Yet the sound went on, and grew more and more distinct. All around him it rang out without pausing: 'Load and shoot! Load and shoot!'

So in the end he thought he might as well try it. He loaded his gun and fired, and now there came a crackling of shots from all around him, and the Swedes were falling like flies, and they had to beat a hasty retreat from the shore – as many of them as could – while from their ships other Swedes could see that the whole place was swarming with little goblins in red caps. It was the Underground People, of course, but they had no power to oppose the enemy until a person from the Upper World had fired the first shot, so that was why they had urged the old man to load and shoot.

From that time on, the Swedes have never tried to capture the island. It would have been an easy matter to take Bornholm if those red-headed devils had not been there, say the Swedes.

Bødker, pp. 118–9. See also Thiele, II, p. 194, who dates the event to 6 February 1645, when two Swedish warships threatened Bornholm but retreated. In 1645 the Danes were driven out of much territory they had previously ruled in Sweden and the Baltic islands, but did not lose Bornholm.

THE TWELVE ROBBERS

Norway

To the north-west of Lake Sjusjø are the mountain pastures called Storkvandal, and many years ago a bold fellow named Tove lived in that district and owned a summer dairy high up there. One day, while the dairymaid was busy scalding out her milkpans, there came a heavy knocking at the dairy door. She thought it was some folk from the village coming up to visit her, and went to open the door and welcome them. But it was twelve robbers who had come there; each had a sword at his belt, and one was carrying the head of a young goatherd whom they had come upon in the forest. The girl was terrified, for she guessed it was the same robbers as had plundered other mountain dairies round about.

They ordered her to give them some creamy porridge, and be quick about it. She brought the pot over and served out the porridge for the robbers, who sat down at a table in the corner and ate. She herself remained standing and carried on with scalding her pans, and then, while the robbers were busy eating, she suddenly threw the boiling water over them so that they were quite blinded. Then she made for the door, but one of the robbers caught hold of her apron. She untied the string, let the apron fall, and so got through the door. Then she seized an alp-horn and blew it, to call the people of the district to her rescue. This is what she blew:

Tilly tilly Tove,
Twelve forest rovers,
Twelve thieves that harry,
Twelve swords they carry.
Sheepdogs they're beating,
Children they're eating,
Me they'll rape against my will
Far away upon the hill.

People came up from the valley, and the robbers were killed. The old dairy was pulled down long ago, but the mound where the robbers were buried is still called Robber Mound to this day.

Christiansen, pp. 41–2. *Migratory Legends* 2085 'The Robbers and the Captive Girl'. *Types of Folktale* 958 'The Alp-horn and the Robbers', where a captured shepherd boy (or girl) asks the robbers for permission to play a horn, and so summons help. The first line of the verse is a nonsense jingle similar to those in some Scandinavian nursery rhymes; 'Tove' is not a normal Christian name.

THYRE BATTLEAXE

Denmark

The road alongside one branch of the Isefjord passes through Borrevejle Forest, where one can still see what is called 'Thyre's Hole'. This Thyre, nicknamed Battleaxe, was an old robber-woman who by mating with her own eldest son became mother of eleven more. These twelve robbers lived underground and, by using various cords which were stretched across the paths and had bells hung on them, they always knew if someone was travelling through the forest. Generally Thyre Battleaxe sat at the mouth of the cave smoking a short clay pipe, but sometimes she would wander around in the forest, and if she met anybody it was her habit to say to them: 'People do say, sure enough, that there are robbers here in this forest, but Devil take me if it isn't a lie!'

One day she came across a farm-hand who was at work grubbing up tree-stumps, and asked him, 'Can you give me a light for my pipe?' Although he had recognized her easily, he did not panic, but agreed to give her a light, and she calmly sat down on a stump. But as she sat there, all unsuspecting, this fellow took his iron-spiked staff and with a single blow he drove it through her skirts and into the ground, so that she couldn't move. She pulled out a whistle to signal to her sons, but the man tied her hands, hurried to Lindholm, and returned with a large band of farmers, all armed with pitchforks. They surrounded the entrance to the cave, and the farm-hand took the whistle and started blowing it, and so all twelve sons came creeping out, one by one, and were caught and taken to Roskilde. Afterwards the cave was searched, and twenty-five cartloads of stolen goods were found.

Thyre and eleven of the sons were condemned to death, but the twelfth, who was only fifteen, was offered a pardon. But since he obstinately maintained that he wished to die with the others, they were all broken on wheels in the forest, just outside Thyre's Hole.

It sometimes happens when someone is driving past the cave at night that the horses suddenly break into a sweat and can hardly draw the wagon past it. One farmer who got out of his wagon when this happened and looked through the halter of the left-hand horse saw that he had Thyre Battleaxe and her twelve sons in the back of his wagon. There was only one thing to do: take off one of the rear wheels and lay it inside the wagon, for to do this forces the ghosts to run along behind the wagon to support the axle.

Thiele, I, pp. 361–2.

JENS LONG-KNIFE

Denmark

Jens Long-Knife was a robber who used to live at a place between Klode Mill and Vejle. He had a knife eighteen inches long, which was tied to his belt by a cord several fathoms long, so that when he had thrown it at his victim he could pull it back again. His wife's name was

Long Margrete, and she was a wicked gypsy-woman who was determined to obtain the means to fly. If she could have gathered together the hearts of seven unbaptized baby boys she would have got what she wanted. As it was she had already got far enough to be able to flutter along, for she had managed to find six, though she never did get the seventh.

One day a pedlar was crossing the heath where Jens Long-Knife lived. He had of course heard tell of the robber, but hoped to avoid him. However, he had only gone a few hundred yards when Jens stood up from behind one of the hillocks and headed straight for him. The pedlar recognized him, and realized that escape was impossible. While Jens was crossing a dip in the ground, the pedlar lay down on his belly and started moaning miserably, as if he was very sick. So along came Jens, and the pedlar begged him, between his groans, to do him the kindness of carrying his chest of wares to the nearest inn, for he had been taken so ill that he didn't think he could live and, in any case, if he was lucky enough to recover, he could always go and fetch it from there.

Yes, Jens was willing enough. He picked up the chest and walked off with it; but he hadn't gone far before the pedlar lifted his head, got up, and came creeping up behind him with long, silent strides. He was carrying a very thick oak cudgel and, when he got near, he gave Jens such a blow across the shins with it that his legs were smashed under him, and he went head over heels in the heather. 'Well,' said the pedlar, 'how are you now, my little Jens? Me – I'm beginning to feel better.'

He hurried off to get hold of the sheriff, who came out from the village with many men. They had a lot of trouble overpowering Jens, for he could still use his long knife. They set his legs for him, but as they could not get him to confess his crimes they had to break them again. In the end they were broken three times, since he would not confess, and so he was condemned to be broken on a wheel. But first his guts were cut out through his side and one end of them tied to a stake, and he was forced to run the gauntlet round and round the stake as long as there were any guts still in him. When he had finished with that, someone there asked him if he had ever suffered anything worse, and to that he answered: 'Yes, I've had the toothache, and that was worse!'

Bødker, pp. 112–13.

RAM'S MOUND

Denmark

In a field at Rolfsted there lies a great stone on top of a small mound which is called Vædderhøj, 'Ram's Mound', and the following story is told about it.

There was a man living in Rolfsted who stole a ram one night from the next village. It was a bad-tempered beast and would not let itself be led, so he was forced to carry it. He tied it firmly across his back like a pedlar's pack and set off for home, but when he got as far as this mound he had little strength left and badly needed a rest.

'This will suit me nicely,' said he. 'I can rest against the stone up there for a minute, but I must keep the ram on my back so that I can get away fast if anybody comes after me.'

Now when he sat down, this fellow was so top-heavy that he was dragged backwards across the stone, which was so narrow that the ram ended up dangling over the far side of it, while the thief was instantly choked by the rope with which it was tied to him. The ram luckily slipped free, and was found there quite safe and well when people came along next morning, and since then everyone calls that mound Ram's Mound.

Bødker, p. 28.

THE SERVANT AND THE FREEMASONS

Sweden

One can find Freemasons in Kalmar and Karlskrona, and everywhere else too, come to that. A gentleman in Lessebo (I've forgotten his name) had a servant that he sent off to Karlskrona with a letter. When the servant reached town he went into a bookshop, and there he chatted with the shop assistant about where he was going and what his errand was. But this fellow warned him, and hid an iron bar up one of his sleeves, and said: 'Now you'll have to defend yourself with all your might, if you want to get out of that place alive.' And, above all, he must not tread on the rug!

The servant went to the house he'd been sent to and handed over the letter, so they offered him a drink. The bottle stood on a table at the far end of the room, and they said he should walk across and take it. 'My feet aren't clean enough for me to walk on such a fine rug,' says he. 'I'll go round the edge of the room, on the bare boards.' But they said no, he must walk over the rug. Then in rushed three roughs, and they tried to push him on to the rug, but he fought back and hit them on the head with the sleeve in which he had the iron bar, so they were all stunned, and he ran out into the street.

You see, under the rug was a trapdoor, and if anyone stepped on it he tumbled down into a cellar under the floor, and there they would chop his head off. Then they would cut him into joints and salt the meat down, and sell it to the Hound-Turks. A Hound-Turk would eat this meat so that he could become a Christian. And the Freemasons were obliged to send them enough of it every year, otherwise they'd lose their own lives instead.

Later, when the servant came home alive, his master was very worried, I can tell you, for he'd never expected that! The servant was angry and wanted to kill his master, but instead he ran up into the attic and hid. If it hadn't been for the fact that the master's wife used to pray for her husband, the servant would certainly have killed him. But the servant ran away from there that very day.

There was also a girl from these parts who was in service in Stockholm, and as she was walking down the street a gentleman came up to her and told her to carry a letter to a certain place; she took the letter and went off. But before she got there it struck her that it was odd that anyone should send a letter by hand like that in Stockholm, where they have so many post-boxes, and she took it and opened it, but there was nothing written in it at all. It was one of those Freemasons, who wanted to trap her so that they could take her life.

But how these Freemasons become Freemasons nobody knows; it's such a secret that even their own wives know nothing about it.

Klintberg, no. 422, pp. 283–4. Collected in 1933 from an informant born in 1858.

PART THREE

MORALITY: FATES AND PUNISHMENTS

INTRODUCTION

Legends are often used in order to define and reinforce a communal code of right and wrong, generally by recounting the dire punishments which are believed to have befallen people who broke it. Such stories may inculcate specifically Christian rules, for instance the right observance of Sunday and proper respect for sacred places or sacraments; they may also be concerned with more general principles of good behaviour towards supernatural beings, towards the dead, or towards one's fellow men.

The first five tales in this chapter are concerned with fate, which is represented as ruling over death, birth and marriage. The first, 'The Man Who Drowned in a Washbasin', is a widespread story which has been known throughout Europe since the early thirteenth century. Folklorists have chiefly been interested in it for the grim concept it embodies of a bloodthirsty water-spirit calling out for a human victim. The narrator of the present version, however, is not primarily concerned with this; as his opening comment makes clear, to him the main point of the story is not the voice from the lake but an implacable, amoral, semi-personal fate which contrives, in an unforeseeable way, to outwit all human efforts to save the doomed man. This is the usual way the legend is presented in Sweden; the Icelandic version which follows omits the voice and substitutes a human prophecy.

'Twelve Children on a Platter' is more closely linked to old-style Christian morality. Told by a woman, it stresses how wicked it is to try to avoid the childbearing which is God's will for women, and how God fittingly punishes this sin. It also reflects some deep-rooted prejudices widely found in European peasant communities. There, multiple births were traditionally regarded as disgraceful, and the greater the number of children the worse was the shame, since this reduced the mother to the status of an animal. Often, she was also suspected of adultery, it being thought that multiple births must necessarily imply multiple sexual acts with different men. Klintberg remarks that 'Twelve Children' was usually told by mothers to their daughters, as a stern warning against interfering with nature in sexual matters. Some variants also, as a secondary feature, serve to explain place-names; a few tellers even present the story as a humorous one. The final detail of the present version is rather ambiguous. The narrator interprets it rationally, as an attempt to save the weak babies by putting them in a homely 'incubator'. However, it is more likely that, as John Lindow suggests, the intention is to eliminate all but one baby, the 'real' one, subjecting the others to a procedure borrowed from beliefs about changelings, as described on pp. 192–5. In most European analogues the horrified father takes the babies away to drown them, but their lives are saved by the intervention of a charitable stranger, who adopts them all. These alternative endings seem to express uncertainty as to the right attitude to be taken towards unusual births – a theme which will be met with again in Part Six, in connection with changelings.

The next two legends ('The Girl Who Kept Vigil on Christmas Eve' and 'The Destined Husband's Knife') form a pair, expressing contrasting attitudes towards attempts to discover one's future, especially as regards marriage. They centre upon a divinatory ritual widely practised in Sweden: a girl who wants to see her destined husband must sit alone and in silence in the kitchen at night, with one glass of water and one of brandy in front of her, until a man's spectre appears and drinks from one of them. His choice indicates whether their marriage will be prosperous. The brandy is an omen of wealth, but the water means poverty. In the first story, which is notable for its subtlety and dramatic force, the girl is regarded as blameless and destined for unexpected good fortune; the other, however, is a terrible warning against such magical procedures. This attitude of suspicion and reproof was common; a Norwegian recipe for a divinatory rite similar to this one ends: 'NB: The person who evokes the figure often falls into a serious illness.'

Christian morality is the motivation for the remaining stories in this chapter, which all show God punishing sinners in various dramatic ways, either directly or through the agency of the Devil, who is both tempter and destroyer. In such stories, the Devil is by no means the comic, gullible figure he appears in topographical legends and jocular folktales; he is as sinister and as powerful as in any medieval sermon.

One tale-type, represented here by the Icelandic 'The Dance in Hruni Church', is known to have developed out of a famous *exemplum* used by many medieval preachers, 'The Dancers of Kölbigk'. According to this story, in the year 1212, at Kölbigk in Germany, some peasants were cursed by a priest for dancing in a churchyard on Christmas Eve. They were doomed to dance without stopping for a whole year, after which some fell dead, while the rest, repentant, became wandering beggars. The story spread swiftly through Europe, and became localized in several new places. Sweden has a famous version, 'The Hårga

Dance', telling how the Devil came to Hårga while the villagers were dancing on a holy day, and led them up into the mountains, 'where they danced till only their skulls were left.' Some said they wore a groove in the rocks by their dancing, just as in Germany some versions of the Kölbigk story claimed that the sinners 'danced themselves into the earth up to their waists and hollowed out a deep hole, which can still be seen there'. The Icelandic version develops to the full the idea of the ground swallowing up the doomed; it also acts as an ætiological landscape legend, for there really is a hollow in the ground at Hruni which looks like church foundations.

In these stories, the dancing is regarded as sinful because it occurs in a sacred place, or on a holy day when all should be at prayer. It is thus a sacrilege, as well as being open to the usual accusations of encouraging drunkenness and sensuality which dancing often incurs in traditionally moral communities. Other forms of blasphemy are punished in 'The Sunken Castle' and 'The Parson Who Could See Where Souls Go'. In 'The Girl's Ford', the girl is not merely selfish and proud, but is guilty of misusing bread – a food formerly regarded as almost sacred, so that to waste or defile it was reckoned a sacrilege. In 'The Evil One as a Magpie', the Devil in the guise of a magpie ensures that a mock-suicide becomes a reality – suicide being the most irretrievable and deadliest of sins.

'The Devil Plays Cards', a Danish version of a story well known in Scandinavia and northern Europe, is more optimistic in that a priest drives Satan away before serious damage is done. However, card-playing was certainly disapproved of, and so was swearing, for to speak of the Devil might summon his presence.

Perhaps the eeriest in this group of stories is the Danish 'The Christmas Goat', which exploits the ambivalent fear and fascination created by masked figures in folk rituals. The 'Goat' was a traditional masquerader, similar to the hobby-horses used in some English and Welsh customary mumming rituals; it consisted of a goat-head with clacking jaws carried on a pole by a man hidden under draperies, and was taken from house to house around Christmas time. Such figures can seem sinister to some onlookers, funny to others; moreover, their primitive, non-Christian quality, and the associated rowdiness and drinking, must often have incurred disapproval from the Church and from respectable members of the community. A horror-story such as this could therefore be used to argue that the Christmas Goat is an evil creature, and the custom a wicked one. On the other hand, and equally plausibly, one might interpret it simply in terms of the girl-victim's behaviour; her fearlessness leads her to show disrespect to a supernatural visitant and to behave with unfeminine bravado, for which she pays the penalty. The narrator's comments show that she holds this latter view.

In general, as these stories amply demonstrate, the morality implied in folk legends is conservative, repressive, and based upon fear. The duty of charity, in the sense of alms-giving, is, however, often stressed, and there are even a few tales in which folk morality sets itself up in opposition to certain legalistic Church doctrines, and shows a more compassionate attitude. Thus, 'The Greedy Priest' is punished for his ruthless insistence on claiming his tithes without regard to the poverty of his parishioner. Similarly, 'A Painting in Halsted Church' illustrates a clash between the rule that unbaptized babies must not be buried in consecrated ground and the natural instinct of a grieving mother, and endorses the latter; appropriately, this priest's rigidity is punished by the loss of his own offspring. In folklore, as in the Bible, the sins of the parents are commonly visited upon the children.

Finally comes a less clear-cut story, 'The Roadside Cairn'. Is the rude and boastful young man's death simply due to his own folly, or to a magical revenge by the 'rather heathen' old man he tormented, or to a divine punishment? The presence of the saintly Bishop Gudmund (a famous person in Icelandic medieval history) tips the balance in favour of the third interpretation; certainly the young man's final fate – to be buried where he fell, not in Christian ground – indicates strong religious condemnation of his behaviour.

Concern with morality, fate and punishment naturally extends beyond this life to the world of the dead, and many ghost stories could logically have been placed in this chapter. However, tales about the dead are so numerous that they must be given a section to themselves.

70

The Man Who Drowned in a Washbasin

Sweden

It's my belief that what a man must go through, he will have to go through. It's laid down in advance.

In Bäckseda Lake, one day, there was a voice heard crying: 'The hour has come, but the man has not yet come!' Some people from Bråtåkra were on the shore. A little while later, along came a man and asked the way to Drakulla. He wanted to cross the lake.

Then these people said: 'You mustn't cross the lake. You must stay here for tonight.'

'I can't do that,' says he.

'You must not cross over, not on any account, for if you do, you'll drown.'

They forced him to stay, so he broke his journey there. They prepared a separate room for him, and in the evening they carried a basin of water up to his room for him to wash in. Next morning, when they went upstairs, he was lying with his face in the washbasin, and he was dead. There was no help for it – he had to drown in that water, come what may. The hour had come.

Klintberg, no. 2, p. 79. *Migratory Legends*
4050 'The Hour has Come, but Not the
Man'. For another version, see 'The Nökk',
p. 203.

What Will Be, Will Be

Iceland

A certain farmer was told by someone with the Second Sight that it was fated that the sea would be his death. He was also the owner of a fishing boat and used often to row out fishing. In order to escape his fate he vowed never to go to sea again, and he kept his word, though he still used to send his boat out, manned by others. This went on for many years, and nothing noteworthy happened, and the farmer grew old.

One day his hired men rowed out to sea. The weather turned rough during the course of the day, and their boat took in a great deal of water; however, they managed to get safe home that evening, tired out and soaked to the skin. The path from the shore to the farm was only a short one, so they went up to the house still wearing their sea-clothes, and stripped them off on the kitchen floor, and the clothes were hung up in the kitchen to dry.

The farmer had been very gloomy all that day; he wandered in and out, took no notice of anything, and yet he did not complain of any pain. When the men had got their clothes off, they went up into the warm loft above the kitchen, and so the farmer was there in the kitchen by himself. He had been walking up and down in silence while they undressed. Not long afterwards someone came into the kitchen carrying a lamp. The farmer was lying flat on his face, with his head in a puddle of water that had trickled from the clothes and collected in a dip of the floor; and he was no longer breathing.

Árnason, I. pp. 427–8.

Twelve Children on a Platter

Sweden

What one must go through, one must. That's what she learnt, that girl who refused to marry before she was fifty, so as to avoid having any children! She got twelve, all at one go. That was because she would have had that many if she had married when she should and had had what she was meant to have. They looked as if the whole lot of them were dead, but someone laid them on a platter and put them in the oven and, as it was nice and warm in there, one of them came to life and began to move. And so that child, he did live, and grew up and became a fine man, so they say.

Klintberg, no. 4, p. 80. Collected in 1923
from a woman born in 1871.

The Girl Who Kept Vigil on Christmas Eve

Sweden

Long ago, it happened that a girl in Björna sat up late and kept vigil on Christmas Eve to see the man she would marry. The rest of the household all slept in other rooms, so that she would be left in peace to keep her vigil in the kitchen. But all at once they heard her make a noise by speaking sharply to someone and throwing something, after which she went back to her bed and lay down.

Next morning they asked her how she had got on, at which she got angry and said that they had all promised to let her keep her vigil in peace, and yet the master of the house himself had behaved most annoyingly – he had come into the kitchen, and drunk from one of the glasses. She'd been so angry at this that she had thrown a stool at him.

But the mistress of the house simply said: 'I can see how things will be before next year.' And she died soon afterwards, and the girl married the master. It was simply a vision of him that she had seen.

Klintberg, no. 5, p. 80. Collected in 1926,
from a woman born in 1864.

The Destined Husband's Knife

Sweden

There was a girl who kept vigil on Christmas Eve with a slice of bread and butter and a glass of brandy in front of her. Towards midnight, in came a man who was quite a stranger to her. He took out his pocket-knife, cut the bread and butter and ate it, drank from the glass of brandy, and went out. But he left the knife behind.

In due course this stranger really did come to that place, and they did marry. Everything went well until their first child was born and they had to lay steel in the cradle, and, as it happened, it was that very knife. The husband recognized it and was amazed, for he had lost it years before, so now his wife had to explain how she came to have it. The man got so furious that he snatched the knife from her, saying that now she would find out what pain he had had to bear that Christmas night when she had forced his soul to tear itself from his body and travel on so long a journey. And he stabbed her to death.

It is said that there is never any peace or affection in a marriage where either partner has made use of such means as this.

Klintberg, no. 6, p. 81. Collected in 1930 from a man born in 1852. Laying a steel blade in the cradle is a protective device to prevent the child being bewitched or stolen by fairies.

THE DANCE IN HRUNI CHURCH

Iceland

Once, long ago, there was a priest at Hruni in Arnesysla who was very fond of merry-making and pleasure. When people came to church on Christmas Eve, it was always his custom to hold no service during the first part of the night, but rather to hold a great dance inside the church with his parishioners, with drinking and gambling and other unseemly sports going on far into the night. This priest had an old mother called Una; her son's ways were not at all to her liking, and she often rebuked him for them. But he paid no attention, and for many years he kept to the customs he had adopted.

One Christmas Eve the priest went on longer than usual with the dancing and fun. Then his mother, who had the Second Sight and the gift of prophecy, went out to the church and told her son to stop the fun and start saying Mass.

But the priest says there is still ample time for that, and says: 'One more round-dance, Mother!'

So his mother went back from the church to her house. Three times over the same thing happens – Una goes out to her son and tells him to take heed of God, and to stop while things are as they are and no worse. But he always answers in the same words as at first. But as she is walking through the church, on the point of leaving her son for the third time, she hears someone speaking a rhyme, and catches the words:

> Loud the mirth at Hruni,
> Lads sport beneath the moon-o;
> They'll dance to such a tune-o
> Men won't forget it soon-o.
> There'll be none left but Una,
> There'll be none left but Una.

As soon as Una gets outside the church, she sees a man standing outside the door. She did not know him by sight, but she disliked the look of him, and felt sure it was he who had spoken the rhyme. She was most upset by the whole affair, and foresaw that things were now taking a dangerous turn, for this might well be the Devil himself.

So then she takes her son's best horse and rides off in great haste to the nearest priest, and begs him to come and try to help them in their trouble, and save her son from the danger he is in. This priest goes with her at once, bringing many men with him, for the people who had been hearing Mass at his church had not yet left. But by the time they reached Hruni, the church and the churchyard had sunk down into the earth, with all the people inside it, and one could hear them shrieking and howling from deep underground.

One can still see traces showing that a building once stood on the high ground at Hruni, and the name is still given to a hill there and to the farm at its foot. But the story goes that after this the site of the church was moved further down the valley to where it is now, and moreover it is said that there was never again any dancing on Christmas Eve in Hruni church.

Árnason, II, pp. 7–8, from accounts by two clergymen.

THE SUNKEN CASTLE

Denmark

Not far from Lindenborg, by Aarhus, there is a lake whose bottom no one has ever found, and going round the district there is an old story about it. Long ago, a castle used to stand on the spot where the lake is now – a proud, ancient castle. But now there is no trace of it left, except for a carriage road which in those days led to the castle gate but now disappears into the waters of the lake.

The story goes that once, on the eve of some church feast, when the master and mistress were not at home, the servants there were drinking heavily and making merry. Things got so wild in the end, when they were drunk, that they took a pig from the pigpens, wrapped it in a sheet and pillowcase, put a cap on its head, and laid it in the master's bed. Then, having arranged all this, they sent word to the priest to come quickly to minister to their master, who was at death's door and wanted to receive the Sacrament. The priest set out at once for the castle, and as he did not spot the trick he read prayers over that pig and did all that his calling required. But just as he was about to administer the Sacrament all the bystanders burst out laughing, and the pig snapped the Host out of his hands – and he rushed away, in horror and dismay, and forgot to take his prayer-book with him.

Now the castle clock was just striking twelve as he passed the outer gateway, and all at once a great creaking and cracking began to be heard from every nook and cranny of the castle. And, when he turned round, the castle had sunk into the ground and the lake waters were welling up out of the depths. He could not move one step for terror and astonishment, but as he stood there, a little stool came floating up on the water and drifted to the bank, and there on that stool lay the book he had forgotten in the castle.

Thiele, II, pp. 7–8.

THE PARSON WHO COULD SEE WHERE SOULS GO

Sweden

Here in Vissefjärda, many years ago, we had a parson who was quite outstanding as a preacher and in other ways too. He was a proper parson, sure enough – so much so that he could even tell whether people had gone to Heaven or Hell. 'I see this soul in the torments of Hell,' he would say during a funeral, or else 'I see him in Heaven'; and then you could be quite sure that it was so, because he could see things like that.

Well, there were some practical jokers who thought he didn't know what he was talking about, and they wanted to catch him out. So they went and made a coffin, and got everything ready for a funeral. But there was a live man lying inside the coffin, and they had bored a small hole in the coffin so that he could get some air. Then they went to church and carried the coffin out to the grave, and they were all agog to hear what the parson would say, because he wasn't dead at all, this fellow inside the coffin.

The parson stepped forward, and he looked up to Heaven, and then he said: 'Where shall I find this soul? Neither in Heaven nor in Hell do I find this soul.' They all stared at one another and were absolutely amazed. Then all at once the coffin fell into the grave, and there came a sound like a loud crash. 'Now this soul has gone to the torments of Hell!' said the parson in a loud voice.

And what had happened was that the coffin had fallen in such a way that the air-hole was quite blocked, so that this other man, he couldn't breathe, and he died. And all the others were scared out of their wits, so much so that they did not run and lift the coffin out when this happened, but just shovelled the earth back into the grave.

Klintberg, no. 275, p. 211. Collected in
1933 from an informant born in 1858.

THE GIRL'S FORD

Denmark

On the island of Mors there is a shallow little pool on the road between Tøving and Flade which is called the Girl's Ford.

A poor girl from Tøving took service with some well-to-do people who gave her fine clothes and treated her in every way as if she was their own child. As a result, she gradually became very proud and would scarcely consent to recognize her own poor family. On one occasion, however, she did want to visit her parents for once in a way, and she put on all her best finery so as to show herself off properly.

When she was half way there her way was blocked by a pool. She saw that she could not get across it dry-shod, so she took some loaves which she meant to bring for her poor parents and threw them out into the pool to serve as stepping-stones. But as soon as she set foot on the bread it sank right down, and she went down with it, and nothing was left except the place itself, which has been called The Girl's Ford ever since.

Thiele, II, p. 17. Types of Folktale 962**
'The Girl Who Trod on Bread'.

THE EVIL ONE AS A MAGPIE

Sweden

There were a couple of men busy threshing in a barn early one morning, while it was still dark. They began talking about hanging oneself, and what that must feel like. They agreed that one of them would try to hang himself, and the other would cut him down. So then they did just that, but while one of them had his head in a noose, in came a magpie and snatched up their lamp and flew up on to the stack of corn with it. The other man had to chase the magpie and get hold of the lamp, for he was afraid it would start a fire. But the magpie flew hither and thither with the lamp, and by the time he had finally got hold of it and gone back to the other man to cut him down, he was quite dead. As for the magpie, she laughed, which showed pretty plainly what sort of a magpie it was – it was the Evil One himself who had changed into a magpie to get the man who was in the noose.

Klintberg, no. 267, p. 206.

THE DEVIL PLAYS CARDS

Denmark

Once, there were some fellows sitting in an inn in Southern Jutland, playing cards and swearing pretty dreadfully. While they were sitting there, in came a stranger, and he came over and played cards with them, but in such a way that he was winning all the time. In the middle of the game one of the lads dropped the ace of clubs on the floor, and when they took the lamp to look for it, they noticed that the stranger had a horse's hoof. So now they knew well enough who it was that was playing with them, and so they contrived to send a servant girl out secretly to fetch a priest, while they went on playing as if nothing was wrong.

Soon after, the priest walked in at the door with a Bible under his arm and said: 'Good afternoon to you all, except one!'

So the stranger asked which one he meant, and the priest answered: 'You, you filthy brute!'

The stranger started pleading to be allowed to go out by way of the chimney, since he was now bound to be chased away.

'No,' says the priest, 'that's much too wide a place for you to pass through.' And he cut a little hole in the crossbar of the window, close up against the glass, and said he must go out through there.

The Devil (for of course it was him) turned himself into a puff of smoke and went out through this hole, but he left such a stink behind him that they could hardly bear to stay in the room. From then on, those men gave up swearing and playing cards, and the inn got the name of 'The Ace of Clubs'.

Bødker, pp. 146–7. *Migratory Legends* 3015 'The Devil and the Card Players'. The ace of clubs is a lucky card because of its cross-like shape; in this story it seems to have the power of enabling people to see through magic disguise, as a four-leafed clover is said to do.

THE CHRISTMAS GOAT

Denmark

One of the farms at the village of Vinten, west of Horsens, has long been badly haunted, and old folks say things can be so unpleasant there that sometimes one can get no peace on account of it.

There was once a girl who worked as a servant on that farm, and she had the reputation of being afraid of nothing, not even the Devil himself. One Christmas the farm lads had carved a Christmas Goat and dressed it up, according to the old custom. When everyone had eaten their Christmas Eve dinner, the lads said to this girl: 'Would you dare to dance with the Christmas Goat tonight, out in the barn, when the clock strikes twelve?'

'Yes,' answered the girl. And when the time came she took the Goat in her arms and skipped and jumped about with it out in the yard, and then danced into the barn with it, singing:

> The ploughman is dancing,
> The cowman is dancing,
> And I'm dancing too.

She repeated this a few times, but then another voice began singing, and it came from the Goat, and sounded horribly hollow and gruff:

> Yes, the ploughman is dancing,
> The cowman is dancing,
> But the Devil's dancing too,
> He's dancing with you!

The Devil had taken on the appearance of the Christmas Goat, for everybody who makes mock of the Goat is mocking at Christmas itself, and they belong to the Devil, which is why he had transformed himself in order to get hold of this girl. So now, having sung this verse, he gripped the girl, and a horrible dance began, with a loud uproar. The girl was uncommonly strong, and she fought against the Devil, but she could not break free. She shrieked aloud, and people could also hear the Devil saying something.

On the morning of Christmas Day, some people decided to go into the barn and look for the girl. When they opened the barn doors, there was such a stench of sulphur inside that they could hardly bear to be there. The girl had gone, but a few shreds of her clothes, blood, and bits of her flesh were sticking to the walls and even to the roof beams along the whole length of the barn. In fact, while he was dancing with her the Devil had battered her against the walls and beams until she was dead, and then had carried her off with him.

From then on, the farm was haunted in a very frightening way, and it was particularly bad at festival times. As it grew dark, one could not go into any of the out-buildings because of the haunting, and even in the farmhouse itself it was pretty unpleasant to go up into the loft at night.

Eventually, a priest who had thoroughly learned the Black Arts came to this parish. He laid the girl's ghost, driving it down in the north-west corner of the farmyard, under an apple-tree which grew there. Now the worst of the haunting was over, but from then on the apple-tree only bore 'ash-apples', which are full of a yellow ash when one cuts them open, and smell bad. And on the eve of great feast-days something would still go rummaging about in the farm.

'I myself heard tell how the Devil and the girl danced out in the barn, when I was in service on that farm,' said the old woman who told this story. She also said that blood could still be seen on the roof-beams.

Bødker, pp. 147–8.

A PAINTING IN HALSTED CHURCH

Denmark

In the church at Halsted on Lolland Island there is a painting which shows a priest with his wife and one living child, and eight others lying dead in their swaddling clothes.

The story told about this picture is that there was once a woman who earnestly begged the priest, kneeling at the church door, to cast earth on her stillborn baby. But he kicked her, and said he did not cast earth on puppy dogs. So the woman called down a curse on him and his house, that his wife would never bear him a living child. This came true, for the priest's wife bore eight dead children, one after another. The curse was only lifted when the priest later on allowed himself to be persuaded to cast earth on another stillborn child in his parish; his wife then bore him a living child.

Thiele, I, p. 217.

THE GREEDY PRIEST

Iceland

On Mulaness, in the west of Iceland, there is a great rock midway between Muli and Ingunnarstadir. At one time, there was a priest living at Muli, while at Ingunnarstadir there lived a woman called Ingunn. She could not pay her tithes to the priest, she was so poor. Ingunn owned one cow, and it was the most precious thing in the world to her. Now this priest would never lose one penny if he could help it, for he was very strict in exacting his tithes; so when he saw that he was receiving nothing from Ingunn, off he goes to Ingunnarstadir, takes away Ingunn's cow, and sets off home again, taking it with him. But when he came to the spot where that rock is now, the rock came hurtling down from the mountain, from Mulaness Fell, and the priest was crushed under it, and there he lies to this day. But the rock never even touched the cow, and she made her way home to Ingunnarstadir.

Árnason, I, p. 480.

THE ROADSIDE CAIRN

Iceland

One day when the holy Bishop Gudmund was at Reykholt a farmer from further up that valley came to see him. His name was Grim, and his farm was at Skaney; he was an old man, and rather heathen in his ways. The Bishop's servants thought him ridiculous, and made fun of him. There was one who jeered at the old man even more than the rest; he was a very conceited fellow. Old Grim tells him that something will happen before very long to put a stop to his arrogance, and that it would be better for him to quieten down a bit. But the man turned a deaf ear to Grim's words.

Now when the Bishop left Reykholt, he and his company rode along the valley. The man who had been jeering so much at Grim was amusing himself by bracing his spear against his chest as he rode. The Bishop told him not to do it, but he paid no attention and said he knew how to take care of himself. But at that very moment his horse stumbled, and the spear went right through him, and he fell dead from his horse. The Bishop ordered that he be buried just there, beside the path, and that a pile of stones be heaped over him as a warning to all conceited people who pass that way. It is at the north end of the gravel-banks, not far from Kleppjarns-Reykjar.

Nobody should ever ride past that cairn without throwing three stones on to it, otherwise some misfortune will befall him on his journey.

Árnason, I, p. 479. Bishop Gudmund Árason died in 1237 and was canonized by local acclaim; for another tale about him, see pp. 224–4.

PART FOUR

THE DEAD

INTRODUCTION

The dead play a major role in folk traditions throughout Scandinavia, and have done so as far back as written records stretch; anyone familiar with the medieval Icelandic sagas will remember their accounts of fearsome *draugar* – malevolent 'living corpses' who defend their burial mounds against intruders, or emerge to harry the living. This concept of the active corpse still persists in more recent lore, not merely in Iceland (as in 'Isn't It Fun in the Dark!' and 'Grey is My Skull, Garun, Garun') but in the belief, common to all three countries of mainland Scandinavia, that when bodies of the drowned are washed ashore they will plague the living in the hope of being granted Christian burial. In Norway, the old word *draug* is still used, with a specialized meaning. It now refers to a drowned man who has remained unburied; he is believed to turn into a sinister, grotesque monster, covered in seaweed, which lurks alongside fishing boats in the hope of overturning them and killing the crew, and shrieks at sea before disastrous storms.

The various words for 'ghost' in the Scandinavian languages offer interesting insights into distinctions which are blurred by our all-embracing English term. Icelandic has, besides the powerfully physical *draugar*, a wraith-like spectre called a *svipa* or a *vofa*, and the destructive *sending*, which is a ghost raised from its grave by a wizard and acting at his command. This last type is non-material in its mode of action, being capable, for instance, of changing its shape or becoming invisible, but it always originates from a corpse, or at the very least a bone into which the wizard has 'put strength' by magical means. The gruesome procedure involved is described fully by Jón Árnason in 'How to Raise the Dead'. If such a ghost remains attached to a particular family and persecutes them, it is called a *fylgja* – 'follower'.

The Swedish had many local terms for ghost; the chief ones have been analysed by Klintberg as follows: a *gengånger*, literally 'one who walks again', is a ghost which returns to its own family or friends because it has a specific request to make or message to give; a *gast*, 'ghost', is the spirit of some unknown person which haunts a road, forest, or some other open-air site, usually at night and always in a terrifying way; *spöke*, 'spook', is a term chiefly used when the speaker wishes to stress the way in which the spirit is manifesting its presence, for instance by a visual apparition, noises, cries or poltergeist activities. The *spöke*, like the *gengånger*, is the spirit of someone whose identity is known; its haunting may be due either to the sinfulness of its previous life, the violence of its death, or to some message it wants to give to the living.

Folk traditions offer what at first seems to be a bewildering number of explanations as to why hauntings occur, but all are based on the basic notion that a haunting is a symptom of something that has gone wrong and needs to be put right. The first possibility is that the funeral has not been properly carried out, for the dead are held to be unable or unwilling to depart peacefully unless this essential rite of passage has been performed. In the interval between death and burial, therefore, a corpse may be dangerously active, as is shown in the Icelandic tale 'Isn't It Fun in the Dark!' It is important to observe traditional customs regulating how it should be treated; for instance, it must not be left unattended, and lights should be kept burning near it at night. The burial must be correctly done; there is an Icelandic tale about a man who haunted the grave-diggers for laying his coffin north-and-south, instead of the customary east-and-west. The *whole* corpse must be buried (see 'The Dead Woman's Plait'), and the grave must remain undisturbed for ever; there are numerous accounts of ghosts revenging themselves because bones or coffins have been callously dug up to make room for later burials. Yet even when everything has been carefully done, a dead man of evil character may still play truant from his own funeral and begin haunting (see 'A Clever Woman').

Naturally, the dead who have had no Christian burial at all are thought to be in a terrible predicament. The Church has at various times refused the funeral rites to several categories of people: stillborn and unbaptized infants; suicides; executed criminals; persons dying while excommunicated. All these were buried on waste ground, without any prayers or ceremonies. Others were given curtailed rites; for instance, Swedish clergy were formerly unwilling to give full funeral rites to women who died before they had been 'churched' (that is, had attended a service of purification and thanksgiving after childbirth), despite Luther's dictum that to die in childbirth assured a woman's entry into heaven. Others lacked burial because their bodies had never been found, they having died in the mountains or at sea.

Drowned men whose bodies were washed ashore posed a particularly difficult problem: if they were not taken to the churchyard, they would become ghosts; but if they were, there was a fear that the sea would be angry at 'being cheated of its own', which might lead to more shipwrecks or floods. There was even the horrible possibility that the body was not human at all, as in the story of 'The Merman at Nissum' in Part Seven (p. 240). Despite these risks, however, most legends teach that it is a charitable duty to give these 'strand-ghosts' a resting-place in holy ground, and that those who do so will be rewarded. On the other hand, according to some of Thiele's informants, the 'Church Grim' may try to reject the newcomer, hurling the corpse back over the churchyard wall, and inflicting sickness on those who had brought it in. Taken as a whole, the corpus of legends on this topic conveys great anxiety, guilt and ambivalence in communal attitudes towards those who die at sea.

Another major category of ghost comprises unbaptized illegitimate babies murdered or abandoned by their mothers, who are buried, if at all, in some secret place in unhallowed ground. They are known by various special terms – *útburðir* in Icelandic, *utboren* in Norwegian, *utböling* or *utkasting* in Swedish – all of which mean, roughly, 'cast-out'. Their deprivation is a double one: not only have they been denied a Christian funeral, but the fact that they are unbaptized and unnamed means that they have never been integrated into the human community, and so, through no fault of their own, they have no status in this world or the next. The legends often describe how such a ghost brings punishment on its guilty mother by publicly revealing her shame, by driving her mad with remorse, or by the gruesome physical vengeance of sucking her to death. The effectiveness of such stories as moral warnings is obvious. But the *utböling*'s activities are not limited to punishing its mother; being barred from heaven yet undeserving of hell, it remains earthbound, wailing and screaming near its burial-place, to the terror of passers-by. It is said also to lead people astray in the dark, or jump up on their backs. In Iceland it was thought that if a baby's ghost, crawling swiftly on one elbow and one knee, could make three circles round anyone, he would go mad. The only way to lay the spectre was to baptize it, as is shown in the vigorous Norwegian tale of 'The Lapp Who Baptized a Baby's Ghost'; so important was this rite that it alone, even without Christian burial, would suffice to restore the wronged child to its proper status, and so lay it to rest.

Many earthbound ghosts are sinners whose guilt, undiscovered or unpunished in life, is the cause of posthumous torments that are generally being acted out in the places where they lived. Such stories satisfy a deep-seated longing for justice, and are frequently told against persons whose rank or official position put them out of reach of punishment by the outraged community – cruel landowners, for instance, or lawyers who were (or were assumed to be) dishonest in their work. Some of them can be released from their torments by being given a chance to repair the wrong done in life; thus misers who have buried their money (a dire sin in popular morality, since it deprives the heirs of it) will be laid to rest once they can tell somebody where it is. A common notion is that a farmer, or a land-surveyor, who steals land by shifting the marker stones which established the boundary between one field and the next is doomed to wander around carrying the stone until someone tells him where to put it. This story reflects a pre-occupation with a problem vital to villages where farmers owned multiple small parcels of land scattered through the surrounding area, each carefully marked off. It would be only too easy to shift the markers secretly at night for one's own profit, or to bribe a surveyor to measure wrongly. In Denmark, the theme is particularly associated with a large-scale redistribution of peasant land-holdings which began in 1820 and left a bitter legacy of suspicion and resentment. The biblical text 'Cursed be he that moveth his neighbour's landmark' must have strongly reinforced the message of warning implied in legends such as 'The Boundary Stone' and 'Lady Ingebjorg of Voergård'. The latter, a vigorous, detailed ghost story, shows how folklore can dramatically express the repressed anger of small farmers against overbearing aristo-crats by devising fantasies about their posthumous punishments.

Many tales end by explaining how the ghost was finally laid. Thus, a priest imprisons Lady Ingebjorg's ghost in a local pool, from which she is said to be slowly returning at the rate of one cock-stride per year – a motif found in Britain too; the ghost of the girl who danced with the Christmas Goat was confined under an apple tree; in Icelandic tales ghosts were often said to be trapped in bottles or hollow bones. The usual exorcists were priests, who might also be magicians, and some layfolk too could be credited with great knowledge, as in the Danish story 'A Clever Woman'. Those who, like Macduff, could be called 'unborn' because they had been cut from their mother's wombs, were particularly powerful against troublesome spirits.

In Danish tales, the ritual of ghost-laying often ends with a stake being driven into the ground to pin the ghost down at a chosen spot, not necessarily the grave – the latter might well be unknown, or inaccessible. This custom, which to English readers is probably most familiar in connection with the vampire beliefs of the Balkans, has a long and well-documented history in Denmark. Several of the famous prehistoric corpses recovered from Danish peat-bogs in a well-preserved condition had been staked in this way, or held down by wooden crooks, or covered with a lattice of branches; another later bog-corpse, which can be dated by its clothing to about 1360 AD, similarly had an oak stake driven through its heart. In 1839, during the excavation of a staked bog-body at Haraldskjær, a local newspaper commented:

Every countryman will immediately recognize in this corpse the body of someone who when living was regarded as a witch and whom it was intended to prevent from walking again after death. Many of us have either ourselves seen, or have heard old people speak of, stakes standing here or there which have been driven in in earlier times, since men first recognized the existence of such restless spirits, by those who, having read of these matters in magical books, thought that by this means they could get the better of the ghosts. Our forefathers believed that so long as the stakes stood the ghost remained pinned in the ground. If the stakes were removed, however, trouble would start all over again.

Several internationally famous ghost legends are found in Scandinavia. One, 'The Mass of the Dead', has been current since the sixth century and is known in virtually every country of Europe. It tells how ghosts gather in church by night on the eve of some major religious festival, in some versions to expiate their laxity in church-going when alive. In Scandinavia, the date is almost always either Christmas Eve or New Year's Eve, times when all types of supernatural beings were held to be active. Sometimes it was added that not only the dead, but also the spectral images of anyone due to die within the year would appear in church that night. To spy on them was thought wicked and dangerous; legends on the topic stress that any living person who is present at their service, however innocently, will be lucky to get home alive.

The Icelandic legend 'Grey is My Skull, Garun, Garun!' is an impressive local variant of an international tale-type, 'The Dead Bridegroom', also known as 'Lenore' from the title of a famous German romantic ballad based upon it. In the German version it is clear that the girl's terrible experience is her own fault, for her excessive grief has summoned her lover back from the grave – folklore often discourages prolonged or passionate mourning. This moralistic message, however, was dropped in Iceland; there, the lover conforms to the native tradition of the spontaneously active and ruthless *draugar*.

It was held, in general, that one must act bravely when confronted by a ghost, but also be ready to show compassion by carrying out any reasonable request it might make. Yet the encounter always entailed some danger, so some stories teach caution, implying that it is best never to answer a ghost or try to help it. All agreed that anyone who deliberately sought out the dead in a spirit of bravado or frivolity was risking a great deal. The bold girl in the Swedish tale 'Are My Eyes Red?' would have been killed if she had turned round, as other versions make plain; even so, despite her prompt retort which nonplussed the ghost, she still 'fell seriously ill and kept to her bed for three days'.

Such was the power ascribed to the dead that bones, coffin-nails, churchyard earth, scrapings from gravestones, and other such objects often figure in traditions about black magic. In Iceland there was a particular stress on this aspect of witchcraft, and also many legends about necromantic wizards who raised the dead and controlled them for their own ends. Jón Árnason compiled a general description of nineteenth-century beliefs on how to raise the dead (see pp. 110–12), and collected many illustrative legends about 'Sendings', four of which are included here. The theme may have partly grown out of older myths alluding to Odin's necromantic arts, but in its fullest development it belongs to the seventeenth and eighteenth centuries, as part of a whole complex of beliefs in black magic prevalent in Iceland at that time. Often when illness and misfortune repeatedly struck a family, this was blamed on a *fylgja* – a malevolent ghost (usually originally a Sending) which 'followed' the family members from generation to generation. Indeed, in its concepts of the *draugar* and the Sendings, Icelandic folklore has created figures as grimly powerful as the well-known zombies and vampires of other lands.

'Isn't It Fun in the Dark!'

Iceland

In the old days, and right into the nineteenth century, it was customary for someone to keep watch beside a corpse, and this was generally done with a light burning, unless the night was very bright. Once a certain magician died; his mind had been full of the old heathen ways, and he had not been a pleasant person to deal with, so there were not many people willing to come and keep watch by his body. However, one man was found to do the job; he was a very strong man, with a fearless heart. His vigil went well.

On the last night before the body was to be put in its coffin, the light went out a little before dawn broke.

Then the body sat up and said: 'Isn't it fun in the dark!'

The watcher replied: 'You won't gain much out of it!' and then recited this verse:

> All the earth is shining now,
> Night has fled away;
> The candle's out, but dust art thou –
> Be silent for today!

Then he flung himself on the corpse and forced it down on its back, and it stayed quiet for the rest of the night.

Árnason, I, pp. 226–7.

THE DEAD WOMAN'S PLAIT

Sweden

In Nydala, at the time when I was being prepared for my Confirmation, the priest's wife had uncommonly fine hair. When she piled it up, her head seemed twice as big, and when she wore it in a plait, the plait was as thick as my arm. When she died her children wanted to have a keepsake of her, so they cut the plait off and kept it.

However, when the time came to bury her it proved impossible to close the grave up properly, for there was always a hole in it at the head end, so big one could put one's hand down it. I've been there myself, many a time, and I've thrown pebbles down the hole and heard how they rattled on the coffin lid as they fell. The priest's farm began to be haunted too; there were rumblings and bangings there at nights.

In the end, they called in an old soldier called Plym, who had been pensioned off. He knew a bit more than most people. When he came to the priest's farm he asked out loud: 'What do you want?'

'I want to have my plait back,' sighed a voice in the air.

So then they took the plait and stuffed it down into the hole in the grave, and it seemed as if something dragged it under. After this they managed to close the grave up for good. It was obvious, of course, that she had to have her plait back so that she could stand before Our Lord on Judgement Day.

Klintberg, no. 206, p. 178. Collected in 1932 from an informant born in Nydala in 1849.

THE SAILOR'S BUTTONS

Sweden

There was this girl at Bökebol, and she had to go and milk the cows which were grazing near the shore early one morning. There she happened to see a dead body lying on the shingle. It was a drowned sailor who had been washed ashore. He had handsome gold buttons on his clothes. The girl was keen to have those buttons, but she couldn't pull them off. In the end she crouched down and bit them off, and took them home with her.

But that night there was a terrible commotion at Bökebol. No one in the house could get any peace to get to sleep, so in the end the girl had to go out and throw the buttons away. Afterwards, everything was quiet once more.

Klintberg, no. 246, p. 197. Collected in 1939 from an informant born in 1863.

BURNING THE COFFINS

Iceland

In the north of Iceland there was a priest named Ketill Jonsson, who lived at Husavik in the 1530s. He once ordered some coffins to be dug up from his churchyard, and said that he was doing so because there was so little room left and these coffins took up space but served no useful purpose since the bodies were quite rotted away.

One day it so happened that three old women were at work in his kitchen, busy burning these coffins, when a spark jumped from the fire and landed on one of them. It quickly set her clothes on fire, and those of the other two also, for they were all very close to one another. The fire was so fierce that they were all dead before anyone could come to put it out.

That night the priest dreamed that a man came to him and said: 'You'll never succeed in making a clear space in the churchyard, however much you smash our coffins up. I've just killed your three old women for you, in revenge for what you did to us, and they'll take up some room in the churchyard. And I'll kill plenty more, if you don't stop these ways of yours.'

And so this man went off; but the priest woke up, and he never dug up coffins from the churchyard again.

Árnason, I, p. 237.

'ARE MY EYES RED?'

Sweden

It happened once at the farm called Kantigårn, here in Veddige, that they'd got the tailor and the shoemaker staying at the house, both at the same time, so you can guess what a lot of chatter went on in the evenings during that time. It was in autumn, when the nights are dark.

One evening they got round to talking about ghosts and suchlike, and about people who are afraid of the dark. Now there was a girl who was a servant there, and she maintained that she had never been afraid of the dark in her life. This the craftsmen didn't believe, but she insisted that it was true. So they made a bet that she wouldn't dare go into the churchyard alone. The girl said she would certainly go. And so they agreed that she must bring back a knob from a grave-fence. It used to be the custom here in Veddige to put a low wooden fence round each grave, and there were lathe-turned knobs on top of the poles in these fences. The knobs sat loosely, so it wasn't hard to take one off.

Off went the girl straight away. Everything was quite all right as she came into the churchyard and took a knob, but when she had come out again and was on the path, she heard someone behind her calling: 'Are my eyes red?'

'Is my arse black?' the girl replied, and away she went, without turning round.

But it came closer, whatever it was that was after her, and then she began to run.

When she came into the living room at Kantigårn, she threw the grave-knob on to the shoemaker's table and said: 'Well, you can all see that I wasn't afraid of the dark!'

Later, there was a terrible commotion outside. There was something beating against the walls, crashing into the log-pile out in the yard, and shrieking. The girl fell seriously ill and kept to her bed for three days.

Klintberg, no. 202, p. 176. Collected 1927 from an informant born in 1852. A coarse word or gesture, in Scandinavia as elsewhere, can protect against supernatural evil.

The Corpse Washed Ashore

Denmark

There once was a girl working as a maid at the vicarage on the island of Bøgø, and her lover worked on a farm some way away. One Saturday evening when she went out to meet him, she noticed that there was a man lolling right across the low wall of the churchyard, so that his head even overhung it a little. She assumed it was her lover, but she couldn't understand why he was lying there. To play a trick on him she crept up behind him, grabbed him by the legs and threw him over the wall, so that he fell into the churchyard.

'Put your hand in my pocket,' shouted a voice from inside the church-yard.

She was sure it was her lover, so she answered cheerfully: 'Yes, and you can put *your* hand wherever you like, but you won't get anything from me!'

'Put your hand in my pocket!' the voice shouted again, and she answered the same as before. So too a third time. Then she ran round to the churchyard gate to get at him, but the gate was locked, so she went home. She thought that if he was trying to play tricks on her she wouldn't let him make a fool of her.

Shortly afterwards her lover arrived at the house, and she was angry with him for having wanted to make fun of her. But she soon discovered that it was not him that she had been fooling around with outside, so she was quite frightened.

Early next morning she went and told the priest all about it, and they went out to the churchyard together. There they found a dead man, his clothes still dripping wet. Then they understood that this was one of the living dead from the sea, who had been washed up on the shore and could get no peace until he lay in Christian ground, for at that time the sea had not yet been blessed. But since he had died in the heathen sea, he could not get more than half way into the hallowed ground without a Christian to help him. The girl had help-ed him without knowing it, and that was why he had shouted: 'Put your hand in my pocket!' In fact, in his pocket they found a lot of gold coins, which now by rights belonged to the girl. So she was able to marry the man she loved. They bought themselves a farm on the island with the money, and lived there happily ever afterwards.

Bødker, pp. 26–7.

THE CORPSE THAT WOULD NOT ROT

Iceland

One day a dead man was washed up by the sea at Selvog beach, and nobody knew where he came from. He was buried at Strönd. Later, another man was to be laid alongside him in the same grave-plot, and the sextons found that the man who had been washed ashore had not rotted, and was lying face downwards. He was turned back the right way round. Then, many years later, this same grave-plot of his was dug up again, and he still had not rotted and was lying face down again. Once again he was turned the right way up, and Eiríkur the priest set a wooden post upright on his grave, and declared that nobody must dig into this grave-plot for as long as the post still stood, but that once it had fallen there would be no danger. This post fell a few years ago, in 1859.

Árnason, I, p. 579. Eiríkur Magnússon (1637/8–1716), the priest in whose parish this story is set, was reputed in later tradition to have been a very powerful but wholly benevolent wizard.

'MOTHER MINE, DON'T WEEP, WEEP'

There was once a girl who was a servant on a farm. She had become pregnant and had given birth to her child, and had put it out in the open to die, as was not uncommon in Iceland, even though harsh penalties of outlawry or death were imposed for such crimes. Some time after, it so happened that there was to be one of those parties with dancing and mumming which were once so common in Iceland and were called *vikivaki* dances, and this girl was invited to the *vikivaki*. But she did not possess any showy and expensive dresses good enough for such a merry gathering as an old-time *vikivaki* used to be, and as she was a girl who was fond of finery she was very upset to think she would have to stay at home and miss the dancing.

One day, at the time when this dance was being held, the servant girl was busy milking ewes in the sheepfold with some other women, and began telling another milkmaid how she had no clothes fit to go to the *vikivaki* in. No sooner had she stopped speaking than they both heard this verse, spoken by a voice from under the wall of the sheepfold:

> Mother mine, don't weep, weep,
> As you milk the sheep, sheep,
> I can lend my rags to you,
> So you'll go a-dancing too,
> You'll go a-dancing too.

The girl who had put her child out to die thought she had had a message from it, and this verse impressed her so deeply that for the rest of her life she was never in her right mind.

Árnason, I, p. 225. A *vikivaki* was a party lasting several days, usually at Christmas or the New Year.

SUCKED TO DEATH

Sweden

This happened on an island. There was a group of people coming back from a fair, and among them was this girl, and she was most unwilling to stay on the island at all when the others wanted to pass the night there. When they had been resting for a while, they saw a tall, strong fellow come and carry her away, and no one in the company was able to prevent him. What he said was: 'Well, I couldna suck 'ee this eighteen year, but now I be going to suck 'ee, Devil take 'ee!'

Next morning they found her dead. You see, she must have borne a child secretly and then done away with it, there on that very island.

Klintberg, no. 238, p. 193. Collected in 1931 from an informant born in 1895. The ghost's words are in strong dialect.

KARL ERSSON'S BURDEN

Sweden

One time, Karl Ersson, the brother of Anna over at Nergård Farm, was going along a road which wound along the edge of a bog. Out in this bog one would sometimes hear something whining, whimpering, and screaming. Karl Ersson amused himself by imitating the noise, and in a trice there was a whistling and crackling sound all around him, and he found a load on his back, so heavy that his legs folded under him. Well, he struggled on towards the village, and as soon as he reached the first farm he was free. But his clothes were soaked with sweat. He wasn't properly himself again for many days. It was the ghost of a murdered baby.

Klintberg, no. 225, p. 188.

THE LAPP WHO BAPTIZED A BABY'S GHOST

Norway

There was an old Lappish fellow called Petter Nilsø who used to travel round between Folda and Fanske, and lived in a turf house away to the north of the pastures. But in the north, in Røsvik Valley, the place was so badly haunted that it was almost impossible for anyone to go that way. Something wailed in the undergrowth; it whimpered and whined and wept most pitifully, just like a sickly little baby will moan and cry.

And sometimes it would make a noise fit to wake the dead; it would screech and scream among the mountains round about, and then tree-roots, earth and stones would come crashing down on people's heads.

It was bad enough for anybody, but it was especially bad for this Petter Nilsø. He could never pass that way without hearing it moan and groan, and sometimes it would become a child's voice speaking to him: 'Petter Nilsø, Petter Nilsø, free me from the pit of torment; baptize me, let me lie in consecrated ground!'

So it would go on and on moaning and lamenting, feebly at first, but as it came nearer and nearer it would grow stronger and stronger, till in the end it was like a howling gale and a peal of thunder. Now Petter Nilsø was a man who knew rather more than the Lord's Prayer (or so people used to say), otherwise, on more than one occasion, he would scarcely have got away from this thing alive.

Well, it happened one moonlit autumn night that Petter Nilsø was on his way home from Røsvik. Coming up into the valley, the performance began, at first softly lamenting and moaning, but then it grew and grew. In the end it echoed to and fro among the mountains, with thunderclaps and crashes and howls that split the sky. Also, he thought there was a black shadow flitting between the steep sides of the valley. Then he glimpsed something like a huge rock breaking loose high up on the mountainside, and with a crash like a great landslide this rock came rolling straight at him. He jumped to one side, hoping to escape. But it was no use; whether he jumped forwards or backwards – straight towards him it came. But gradually it got smaller and smaller. In the end, it was just a baby's head which came trundling down the snowy slopes and came to rest at his feet.

There it turned into a tiny, chubby little child which clung fast to his overcoat and scratched and clawed its way up until it was sitting on his shoulders, wailing and crying in his ear: 'Petter Nilsø, baptize me! Save me, Petter Nilsø!'

'So be it, in God's name, then,' said Petter Nilsø, and he took the child in his arms and went down to the brook. There he took water in his hat and sprinkled it over him, giving him the name Jord-Mattis, said a prayer and made the sign of the cross – and the child vanished away, and everything was as quiet as in a church. After this, nobody ever saw or heard anything at that place again.

Christiansen, pp. 83–4. Collected c. 1930.

THE BOUNDARY STONE

Denmark

South of Tæbring, once, there lived a man who moved a boundary stone, and so he could find no peace in the grave but wandered about by night in the field he had stolen, shouting: 'Where shall I put it? Where shall I put it?'

For a long time people heard this shout, but there was nobody who dared give an answer. Now one evening there was a party, and when the young folk were going home that night and heard the man shouting, there was one of them who was bold enough to say: 'Put it back where you took it from, in God's name!'

'Thank you – now I will have peace,' said the ghost. And since then nobody has seen or heard him.

Bødker, p. 150. To answer the call of a supernatural being or ghost was normally thought to bring misfortune.

THE DEAD MAN AND THE MONEY CHEST

Iceland

There once lived a tenant farmer in the north. He was married. This farmer was very rich and worked hard to make money, so everyone knew for sure that he must own a great deal of money. He was very harsh, but his wife was kindly and pious, though she had no influence on her husband. One winter this farmer fell ill, and died shortly after. His body was duly laid out and buried. An inventory was made at the farm, but there was no sign of any money that he would have left. The wife was asked if she knew anything about the farmer's money, but she assured them that she knew nothing at all about it, and since everyone thought highly of her she was not questioned any further. Most people's guess was that he must have hidden his money by burying it, as indeed was later proved true.

As the winter wore on, people began to notice that the farm was haunted, and they felt sure that the farmer was walking in order to visit his money. The trouble increased so much that most of the widow's farm-hands intended to leave in the spring, and she was forced to consider giving up her homestead. So time went on, till the customary date for changing one's job, when a certain trader came to the widow and offered to become one of her farm-workers, and she agreed. He had not been there long before he noticed that the place was badly haunted.

One day, the trader asked the widow if her husband had had much money, but she said she did not know. So time passed, till the day of the fair came round. The trader went to the fair and bought, among other things, a lot of sheet-iron and white linen. When he came home he got someone to sew him a shroud from that linen, and he himself set to work at the forge (for he was a good blacksmith) and made himself iron gloves. And more time passed, till the nights were dark.

Then one evening when everyone was asleep, the trader put on the iron gloves, tied a sheet of iron across his chest, wrapped himself in the shroud and went out to the churchyard. He began walking up and down near the farmer's tomb and playing with some coins in the palm of his hand. It was not long before a dead man rises up out of the farmer's tomb, and he soon notices the farm-worker.

'Are you one of us?' says he.

'Yes,' says the farm-worker.

'Let me see,' says the dead man. Then the other gives him his hand, and the dead man finds that it is cold. 'It's true that you're a dead man like me,' says he. 'Why are you walking?'

'To play with my wealth,' says the farm-worker, and at that the dead man stalks out of the churchyard, and the other follows him.

So off they went till they came to a spot at the edge of the home-field, where the dead man kicked open a hillock and lifted out his chest of money. Then they both began tossing their coins about, and went on with that all night long. But as it drew towards dawn, the dead man wanted to leave his money, whereas the farm-worker still tossed his coins and scattered them about. Then the dead man said: 'You're certainly no ghost.'

'Yes I am,' said the farm-worker. 'Test me,' and he gave him his hand.

'That's true,' says the dead man, and starts picking up the coins, but the other hurls them far and wide. Then the dead man grew very suspicious and said that the other must be a human planning to betray him, but he still denied it. The ghost seizes him round the chest and finds that he is cold there too, and says: 'It's true what you say; you're just like me!' And he starts collecting the coins together.

Now the workman dare not stop him from having his way, so he says: 'I want to leave my money alongside yours.'

'Yes, that's quite all right,' says the dead man, and so he left it there, and there is no trace left on the hillock.

Then they go home to the churchyard. Then the dead man says: 'Where's your hole?'

'It's on the other side of the church,' says the other.

'You go into yours first,' says the dead man.

'No,' says the workman. '*You* go first into yours.' They stayed arguing stubbornly about this till dawn broke, and the dead man flung himself into his grave, but the farm-worker went home to the farm.

There he had a large cask filled with water and hid it under the floorboards. He put the clothes he had worn that night in it, and fetched the money-chest, and put that in it too. Evening came, and everyone went to sleep. The farm-worker lay opposite the doorway, and before the night was far gone the dead man came in, stinking horribly, aimed a blow at the bed, and went out, and the farmworker followed. It is said that he then did something to the farmer's tomb, for the ghost was never seen again. The reason he had put the clothes and the money-chest in water was so that the dead man would not smell the earth on them. The farm-worker married the widow, and they lived a long while together, and so ends this story.

Árnason, I., pp. 268–70.

LADY INGEBJORG OF VOERGÅRD

Denmark

At Voergård, many years ago, there lived a certain Lady Ingebjorg. She was the widow of a nobleman who had cheated the village of Agersted out of some meadows – indeed, those fields are still called Agersted Meadows to this day, and yet they belong to the Voergård estate. But if the lord of the manor had been hard on the farmers, Lady Ingebjorg was even worse.

One day, as she was driving to church on the anniversary of her husband's death, she said to the coachman: 'I wish I knew how things are now with my late husband.'

The coachman, whose name was Claus, was a cheeky devil; he replied: 'Well, my Lady, it's not right to know that sort of thing, but he's not freezing, that's for sure – it's certainly warm enough where he is!'

The lady was absolutely furious at this reply, and said that if Claus didn't bring a message from her late lamented husband himself to say how things were with him, before three Sundays had passed, he would lose his life. Claus the coachman knew she meant it, so he went off to see the priest at Albæk, who was as clever at his books as any bishop, and could both lay ghosts and raise them. However, the priest thought that this job was beyond his power.

Now Claus, as good luck would have it, had a brother who was a priest in Norway and would certainly be able to help him, for Norwegian priests are cleverer than any others at that sort of thing. He sailed across to Norway, and the first thing his brother said when he arrived was: 'Welcome, Claus! Things must be hot for you if you're coming to me.' Claus gathered from this that he already knew why he had come, and when the priest had thought for a while about how to help his brother, he said: 'I can certainly compel your dead master to appear, but you'll have to state your errand yourself, so I hope you're not afraid of him.'

It was arranged that the following night at midnight the priest would raise the ghost at a crossroads in a great forest. The coachman's hair stood on end when his brother began to read the spells aloud, and almost at once they heard a terrible noise, and a red-hot coach, drawn by horses which snorted flames on every side, came galloping through the woods and drew up where they were standing. Then Claus recognized his old master, even though he was glowing red-hot.

'Who wants to speak with me?' roared the lord from his coach.

Claus took his hat off and said: 'I am to give her Ladyship's greetings to your Lordship, and to enquire how things have been with your Lordship since your death.'

'Tell her', answered the lord, 'that I am in the pains of Hell, where a seat is being prepared for her too. Only the last crossbar is still lacking, and once it is in place she will be fetched, unless she gives back the Agersted Meadows. And as proof that you have spoken with me I give you my betrothal ring, which you can show her.'

Then the priest whispered to the coachman to hold his hat out, and at the same moment the ring fell into the hat, burnt a hole straight through it, and fell to the ground, where Claus picked it up. Next moment the carriage and horses had rushed away and disappeared.

On the third Sunday Claus was standing outside the Church at Voer as Lady Ingebjorg drove up. When her ladyship saw him she asked at once what message he was bringing. So now the coachman told her what he had seen and heard, and also gave her the ring, which she recognized.

'Very well,' said she. 'You have saved your life. If I am to join my husband when I am dead, then what must be must be – but never will I give back the Agersted Meadows!'

Not long afterwards there was great pomp and ceremony in Voer Church, when Lady Ingebjorg was buried. But soon she started coming back by night, and caused such a commotion in the castle courtyard that the miller and some other people staying at the mill ran to Albæk to fetch the priest, who read over her and managed to exorcize her from the yard and drive her into a nearby pool called Pulsen. But he could not win any further mastery over her, so in the end he had to permit her to move one cock-stride closer to Voergård each year, and people say that if she ever does get back at this rate to the exact spot from which the priest exorcized her, Voergård will be destroyed. At the place where she was forced down into the pool no blade of grass ever grows, and from the scorched lines on the field one can see by how many cock-strides she has drawn nearer.

Bødker, pp. 141–2.

A Clever Woman

Denmark

At Little Værløse, on Zealand, there once lived a farmer who was in league with thieves and robbers, never went to church, and was disliked by everybody because of his wickedness. When he was dead and buried, and the funeral party was coming home from church to drink his burial ale at the farm, they became aware that he was sitting on the roof-ridge glaring down at anyone who dared look up, so nobody was willing to stay there and everyone left that farm as fast as they could.

Eventually the priest came and started reading prayers at him, and conjured him down into the depths of Kalsmose, which is a bog close by Farum Lake; and so that he should stay down there until the end of the world, they drove a sharp stake down into the ground in such a way that it split his head open. Now, while this was going on, there happened to be an old woman present who understood such matters better than the priest himself, and she took a darning needle without an eye and stuck it into the stake. Then the ghost down below shouted: 'You shouldn't have done that, you old witch! If it hadn't been for this, I'd have been home again before you.' But now he had to stay down there, though every night he does fly to and fro until cock-crow, in the form of a night-raven.

Thiele, II, 157–8.

'GREY IS MY SKULL, GARUN, GARUN!'

Iceland

Once there was a couple who lived on a farm, but what their names were, or the name of the farm, is not said. They had two servants, a workman and a maid, whose names were Sigurd and Gudrun. Sigurd had taken a fancy to Gudrun and wanted to marry her, but she would not live with him for anything in the world. One Christmas Eve they both rode to church for the midnight service, and they had just the one horse, which the farmer had lent them, so for part of the way they were both riding it together. And as they rode along like that, Sigurd began to speak, saying to Gudrun: 'We'll be riding together again next Christmas, won't we?' She said that that would not happen. They argued over it for a while, until he said: 'We will ride together on Christmas Eve one year from now, whether you want to or not.' That put an end to their talking, and there is no more to tell about this journey of theirs.

Towards the end of that winter Sigurd fell sick and died, and was carried to the churchyard and buried. And so the year passed on, till the following Christmas. And when it came to the evening of Christmas Eve, the people of this farm were getting ready to go to church and asked Gudrun to go with them. But she does not want to go, and says she will stay at home, and so she does.

When the others have ridden off, she goes round the house and arranges everything as she thinks best; then she lights candles, takes a cape and lays it over her shoulders, but does not put her arms into the sleeves. When she has done all this, she sits down and reads a book. After she had been reading a little while, she hears a knock at the door. She takes a light in her hand and goes to the door; there she sees a human figure standing outside, and a horse saddled and bridled, and she recognizes it as being the priest's horse. The stranger tells her that she must come now and ride with him, and she feels sure that she recognizes him, and that it is her fellow-servant, Sigurd, who has come to her. So now she puts the light down and goes outside. He asks her whether he should lift her on to the horse, but she says she does not need his help for that and mounts alone, but he mounts too straight away, and sits in front of her.

So now they ride off along the path to the church, and neither speaks a word to the other. But when they had been riding for some time, he said: 'Grey is my skull, Garun, Garun!' She answered: 'Be quiet, you wretched man. Ride on!' It is not said that they spoke again until they reached the church. There he stopped, somewhere in the churchyard, and they both dismounted, and he then said:

> Wait here, wait here, Garun, Garun,
> Till I've taken Faxi, Faxi,
> To the east fence, east fence.

With this, he disappeared with the horse Faxi, but she ran across the churchyard towards the door of the church. Just as she was about to go inside the church, something gripped her cape from behind, but it was only loosely slung over her shoulders, and so it was only the cape that was torn away, while Gudrun herself escaped into the church and fell to the floor in a faint. This happened just when the service was at its most solemn moment. People ran to Gudrun and tried to bring her back to life; they carried her into the house and sprinkled her with water. After a while she came to her senses and told them all that had happened, and how she had got there. Then someone went out to the stables to have a look at the priest's horse. It was found to be dead, and every bone was broken in its body, and the skin torn off its back. In front of the church door they found the remains of the cape; it was torn to tatters, and shreds of it were scattered all around. Later on, they reburied Sigurd in such a way that he stayed in his grave after that.

Árnason, I, pp. 352–3. Collected from a woman informant. *Types of Folktale* 365 'The Dead Bridegroom Fetches his Bride', an international folktale which became well known in literature through the German ballad 'Lenore' by Wilhelm Bürger (1773). The ghost distorts Gudrun's name because he cannot say *Gud*, 'God'; the repetitions in his rhyme are intended by the story-teller to produce an eerie effect.

THE MASS OF THE DEAD

Denmark

There was once an old woman in Skodsbøl who had got up much too early one Sunday morning. It was in the days when there were still no clocks. She had got up so very early that she reached church for the early morning Mass before midnight had passed, and she went into the church and sat down. And when she looked about her, she saw that the church was full of people who had long been dead, and a remarkably old priest whom she had never seen before climbed up into the pulpit to preach.

And when she had been sitting there for some little while, she saw among the women seated near her a neighbour of hers who was herself dead, and in the end this woman told her to make haste and get out of the church before the hour was over – and she had barely got outside the church when the door slammed shut, and nearly crushed her heel.

Bødker, pp. 50–1. *Migratory Legends* 4015 'The Midnight Mass of the Dead'. In most versions the dead assemble for a midnight service on Christmas Eve or New Year's Eve, not an ordinary Sunday.

How to Raise the Dead

Iceland

There are many tales about dead men whom those skilled in magic have brought back to life and forced to do them service. Some say that to do this one must take one bone from the dead man and put magic strength into it so that it takes on human shape, and then send it to attack those one wants to harm. If a man against whom such a Sending is sent is clever enough to strike precisely the bone inside it which had been taken from the dead body, or to name it by its right name, the ghost will not be able to do anything against him and will have to leave him alone.

But others say that more than this is needed to raise a ghost. First one must see that it is done on the night between a Friday and a Saturday, and preferably between either the 18th and 19th or the 28th and 29th of a month; but which month or which week it is does not matter. The sorcerer who means to raise a ghost must, on the previous evening, write the Our Father backwards on paper or parchment with a water-rail's quill, using his own blood, drawn from his left arm. He must also carve certain runes on a stick, and go out to the churchyard at midnight, taking both paper and stick, and go to whichever grave he chooses – but it is thought prudent to pick one of the smaller ones. He must lay the stick on the grave and roll it to and fro, meanwhile chanting the Our Father backwards from his paper, and also certain formulas which few people know.

Then little by little the grave begins to stir, and various strange sights appear to the sorcerer while the dead man is being very gradually raised; but it goes very slowly, as the dead are most unwilling to move, and say: 'Let me lie quiet!' But the wizard must not give in to their pleading, nor yet let himself be dismayed by the sights, but must mutter his incantations faster than ever and roll his stick until the dead man is half-way out of the ground. At the same time he must be very careful that no earth falls outside the grave when it begins to heave, for such earth can never be put in again.

When the dead man has risen half-way out, he must ask him two questions (not three, or he will sink down again out of fear of the Trinity); the usual ones are who he was in his lifetime, and how powerful a man he was then. Others say there was one question only, namely: 'How old are you?' If the ghost says he died as a middle-aged man or older, it is not thought safe to proceed any further, because at a later stage the sorcerer will have to wrestle with the ghost, and ghosts can be extremely strong, their strength being half as great again as it was in life, and so proportionate to their age. That is why sorcerers prefer to raise children of about twelve or fourteen, or at any rate people who are not over thirty, and never on any account those older than themselves.

When the dead man has said who he is and is half-way out of the grave, the sorcerer can either drive him down again if he chooses, or can continue the spells till he is quite out. When the dead first emerge from their graves, their mouths and nostrils are all bubbling with a frothy mixture of mucus and mud known as 'corpse-froth'; this the wizard licks off with his own tongue. Then he must draw blood from under the little toe of his right foot, and moisten the ghost's tongue with it. Some say that as soon as he has done so the ghost attacks him, and he will need all his strength to get him under; if he succeeds and the ghost falls, then the latter is henceforth bound to serve the wizard in every way; but if the ghost is the stronger, he will drag the man down into the grave with him – and those who thus come into a ghost's power never return again. But others say it is the sorcerer who attacks the ghost when he is only half-way up, forcing him on to his back while his legs are still caught fast, and keeping him there till the sorcerer is ready to lick his mouth and nostrils and moisten his tongue.

Now if for any reason the sorcerer chooses not to let the ghost come more than half-way, and prefers to send him down again, it is usually enough to speak the name of the Trinity or to say the Our Father the right way round; but if the dead man was himself a wizard in his lifetime, more will be needed. The sorcerer must have with him a cord to which he has tied the ropes of both bells on the lychgate (or all of them if there are more than two, since otherwise the dead man would seize the rope that was still free and ring that bell in opposition to the sorcerer, so that no magic rhymes or formulas could touch him). So while wizards are getting rid of ghosts they ring the bells without stopping, and recite not only the Our Father but also certain magic rhymes, very different from those used to raise them. If the sorcerer does not send the ghost down again, it will haunt him and his descendants for nine generations. So too do ghosts that have finished the tasks their raisers gave them, unless the sorcerers send them on other errands or manage to get rid of them – and he is a good wizard who can do this without danger! For some say ghosts get stronger and stronger for the first forty years they are above ground, stay unchanged for the next forty, and dwindle away during the third forty. They do not normally remain active any longer, unless some word or spell of power causes them to do so.

Árnason, I, pp. 317–19. Compiled from several
informants.

THE NECKBONE ON THE KNIFE

Iceland

A certain widow lived on a farm of her own in the north of the country. She was well-off and very capable, so several people asked for her hand, including a fellow in the same neighbourhood who was skilled in wizardry – and him she refused. This widow had the Second Sight, which made it easier for her to protect herself.

Not long after, she was in the larder one day towards evening, preparing food rations for her household, and she was slicing a black pudding. She saw a spectre making its way in along the passage, and in it came by the larder door. The woman stood there with the knife in her hand, and faced the spectre resolutely and fearlessly. The spectre hesitated and tried to pass to one side of the woman, or behind her, for an unclean spirit never attacks a fearless person from in front. The woman saw that the spectre was quite black, except that it had one white mark. She drove her knife into that spot; there was a loud crash, and the woman lost her grip on the knife, just as if it had been jerked out of her hand. She saw nothing more, and she could not find her knife.

Next morning the knife was found outside, on the flagged court; the top vertebra from a man's back was stuck on the point of it, and yet all the gates had been closed on the previous evening.

Árnason, I, p. 321.

The Sending in a Bottle

Iceland

There was once a farmer in the West Fjords; he was married, and well-off. He had an enemy who hated him. It is said that this enemy of the farmer's was skilled in wizardry, and that he planned to use his magic against him and kill him by his cunning.

One day the farmer was extremely sleepy, and he told his wife that he thought someone must be attacking him and meaning to ensnare him in some way. She said he must go and lie down on his bed, and she would sit by him and keep guard. The farmer did this, and fell fast asleep. While he was sleeping, in comes a tiny little boy. The woman asks him his errand. He says he has come to kill her husband. She says he'll never manage it, being as small as he is. He says he knows how to stretch himself if he wants to. She says it is pretty remarkable if he knows how to do that, and that she would love to see it. So then the boy began to stretch himself, and the woman was goading him to make himself bigger and bigger. In the end he was so big that to fit into the house he had to bend right over, and even so his head was among the rafters. The woman thinks he has now grown big enough, and asks him whether he can make himself small too. He says he also knows the way to do that, and she asks him to show her. Little by little he dwindles, till he is as small as he was when he first came in. The woman asks if he can make himself smaller than that, and he does make himself a good deal smaller. Then she says that he could surely make himself smaller still. He does so. The woman brings a little glass and shows it to him, and asks him whether he could make himself so small that he could get down to the bottom of the glass. This too he says he can do. She says he must let her see it, and do it. He goes down into the glass, but she seizes the stopper, puts it in, and ties a skin bag over it; now the boy cannot come up out of the glass, because of the bag over it. She puts the glass away, with him in it.

Shortly afterwards, the farmer wakes up and asks whether anyone came. She says that a little puny fellow did come in and say that he meant to kill him, and she hands him the glass and says that the creature is in there. The farmer takes it, and says that he had always known he had a fine wife, but had never known or imagined that she was as fine as he now knew she was. Then he destroyed the demon in the glass, and after that he and his wife noticed no more Sendings such as this demon had been.

Árnason, I, pp. 336–7. This tale shows influence from the widespread international story 'The Spirit in the Bottle', *Types of Folktale* 331, where a demonic spirit is first released from a small bottle, box or nut, and then tricked into returning to it.

SKOTTA, THE MYVATN GHOST

Iceland

In her time, one of the most famous ghosts in northern Iceland was Skotta of Myvatn, and people living in the Myvatn district have many stories about her evil deeds. This is the story of her origin.

At one time the man living on the farm of Grimsstadir near Myvatn was a magician, and he had a grudge against a man who lived over at Koldukinn. One Easter Saturday, or perhaps a Whit-Saturday, a wandering beggar girl came to Grimsstadir. The farmer welcomed her kindly and led her to the kitchen, where his wife was busy packing dried meat in a trough. The farmer takes a sheepshank from the trough, hands it to the girl, and tells her to eat. The poor girl snatches the meat eagerly, and eats heartily. When she has eaten her fill, the farmer offers to accompany her to the next farm. But when they come to the river between the farms, he seizes the girl, flings her into the river, and holds her by the feet while she is drowning. This girl was wearing a stiff, peaked head-dress, as was the custom in those days, and now, while he was holding her under water, its curved peak swung round to the back, so that it was hanging down her neck. As soon as he was sure the girl was dead he dragged her out of the water and up on to the bank, and then put strength in her corpse by his magic powers and sent her off to kill the man on whom he wanted to take revenge. Ever afterwards, when this ghost was seen going about, the peak of her head-dress was dangling down her back, which is why she came to be called Skotta, 'Peaky'.

Skotta carried out his errand for him and did what she had been told to do. Then she came back to the farmer and told him she had killed the man, and asked what work she must do now. He told her she must follow all this man's kindred and bring disasters on them, and this she did, causing much harm to the family descended from the man she killed first. She remained in the Myvatn district, since this is where his descendants lived . . . Skotta went about all over the district, and it was said she accompanied members of the Myvatn family wherever they went. Many people with the Second Sight would see her shortly before one or other of this family arrived, while to others she would appear in their dreams.

Árnason, I, pp. 371–2; some genealogical details omitted. 'Skotta' is a regular nickname for female ghosts of this type in Iceland, who are often described as wearing the old-fashioned head-dress back to front.

MORI, THE SOLHEIM GHOST

Iceland

Early in the nineteenth century, a farmer named Finn lived at Enni in Skidunes. His wife was called Gudrun, and their foster-daughter Elizabet. There was a man working on their farm whose name was Hall; he had set his heart on marrying Elizabet, but this was very much against the wishes of her foster-parents. Hall left for Jokull in western Iceland that winter, and before he left he asked for Elizabet's hand, but was refused, and so he left in a grim mood.

In the first week of January, Elizabet went to church at Eyrar, as she usually did. When she comes home that evening she sits down in her usual place at the table, picks up her plate, and is just about to start eating when all of a sudden she hurls the plate away, crying that a reddish-brown spectre is attacking her; then she falls down in an epileptic fit and dies straight away.

From then on, the farm at Enni was terribly haunted. People there began to feel uneasy in their sleep, to fear the dark and so on. The farmer was a brave man and tried to hearten his household, but it was no use. His wife's brother, named Gudmund, was living with them there, and it was he who was most often attacked by the ghost; it appeared to him like a ragged tramp – heavy-built but short-legged, wearing a russet-brown jacket and a lambskin hood, with its peak hanging down behind. Many others too now began to see the ghost in the same form, and so they called him Mori, 'Russet'.

Gudmund found it unbearable to stay at Enni any longer that winter, so he leaves and goes to the west country, where he visits a 'cunning man'. And there he learns that some men had been drowned in a shipwreck at Rif on or just after the New Year, and that one of them was called Fridrek. Hall must have got someone to raise this Fridrek from the dead and send him against Elizabet and her family, and that was how Mori came into existence.

Some time later, Finn and his wife Gudrun moved to Solheim in Laxardal, so from then on the ghost that followed them was called Mori of Solheim. He was generally blamed for any damage to life or limb to anyone connected with Finn, and he caused great trouble to many people, so it is said . . .

The same Gudmund who has been mentioned already was then living at Broddanes. One day he meant to go to Hrutafjord by boat with a cargo of timber, and come back by land with cows and other livestock. He had a dog which had the gift of seeing 'followers'. On the morning he was to leave, the dog was nowhere to be found. They looked everywhere for him, and finally he was found hiding under the floorboards, and Gudmund had to carry him into the boat by force. The weather was good, but when the boat came level with Kollsa it capsized. Two men were seen clambering up on to the keel, and the boat drifted up Hrutafjord, driven by a north wind. All the boats near by were either ice-bound or had no oars. People ran to fetch help, but the drifting boat seemed to be driven back from every beach until it ran aground at Baernes, by which time there was no one on board. This accident was blamed on Mori.

Another time, Finn went to trade at the market at Budar, and on the homeward journey his boat capsized, his goods were lost and one man was drowned. Just before the boat capsized, the men in it were certain that they could see one more man in the boat than ought to have been there, and it was sure that it must have been Mori. It used to be reported, concerning Finn himself, that Mori was never able actually to harm him, and this incident proved the truth of that. Nowadays (1862) Mori seems to have become quieter and much less active. All the same, one cannot be sure that people are safe from harmful attacks at Solheim, even now.

As for Hall, who was mentioned at the beginning, he got married while he was at Jokull in the west, but he was always reputed to be an evil man. It is said that once, when a daughter of his had just died and her body lay on the bier, he quarrelled violently with his wife, and in order to take revenge on her he treated the child's body so roughly that he broke every bone in it.

Árnason, I, pp. 391–2; some genealogical details omitted. Male 'follower'-ghosts were often nicknamed 'Mori' from the russet-brown (*mór*) of their jackets or cloaks, which were the rough clothes of the poor.

Part Five
Magicians, Witches, Shapechangers

INTRODUCTION

Several tales in the previous chapter featured a priest whose timely intervention subdued a menacing ghost. This was but one among various supernatural powers popularly attributed to certain individual priests, though not to the clergy in general. Such men were thought capable of exorcizing the Devil or forcing him to work for them, detecting witches and thieves, seeing into the future or to distant regions, breaking fairy spells, inflicting hallucinations and magical paralysis on wrongdoers, and many other marvels. It was not that they were exceptionally holy; their power was believed to derive from unusual learnedness, particularly a knowledge of prayers and formulae in the ancient sacred languages, Latin, Greek and Hebrew.

A whole series of rather stereotyped legends about clerics who were 'master-magicians' circulated throughout Scandinavia and became attached to various historical personages. Typical are the Icelandic anecdotes about the priest Sæmund the Wise (1056–1133), who was an aristocratic landowner and an authority on the history of his own country and of Norway. This, together with the fact that he attended a French university, gave him a reputation for immense learning; in later generations, it was claimed that he had studied at the Devil's 'Black School' for sorcerers – an institution often alleged to have existed at one or other of the great universities of medieval Europe. The anecdote of his clever escape from there (see 'Sæmund at the Black School') has been told of many other famous magicians in oral tradition; so too the tale of the inexperienced but resourceful pupil who inadvertently calls up demons – 'The Magic Whistle'. These are entertaining tales, but the account of Sæmund's death strikes a graver note: so suspect was magic that even its most pious and benevolent practitioners must fear for their salvation. Next in this group comes a legend about a Norwegian Lutheran priest, entitled 'The Rev. Petter Dass'. Petter Dass (1647–1707) was famous for his poems and hymns. The story that a demon was forced to carry him to Denmark to preach before the king is very well known in Norway, and he is also the hero of other typical anecdotes about magicians' exploits. The Danish anecdote 'Doctor Kongsted of Ballerup' is more homely and, like other anecdotes about Dr Kongsted, shows the learned magician carrying out much the same helpful functions for his community as a simple village 'cunning man' – curbing fires and detecting thieves by scrying in a bucket of water.

It was taken for granted that great magicians owned powerful books of spells, probably acquired in the Black School. In real life, too, collections of magical recipes were common; many handwritten copies have survived. They were given prestigious names, alleging authorship by Solomon, Moses, or celebrated medieval and Renaissance scholars. One very popular one in Scandinavia (still not wholly forgotten) was called *Cyprianus*, after a magician who supposedly lived in the Middle Ages but is probably non-historical. It contained both harmful and protective spells, a feature which gave rise to various explanations. Some said its author had first composed the evil ones, then repented and devised the counterspells; others, that there were two authors – a holy man named Cypri and his wicked witch of a wife, Ani, each striving to outdo the other. Numerous copies collected in the nineteenth century by Evald Tang Kristensen are now in the Danish Folklore Archives.

Besides books, there were various magical objects which it was said could be obtained by anybody who knew how to make or find them – but generally at the peril of his soul. The traditions about them are akin to widespread European notions about the 'luck-penny', the 'spirit in the bottle', the mandrake root, and so on. Noteworthy in Swedish tradition was the *spiritus*: a sort of familiar which looked like an insect, was kept in a box and fed on human spittle, and which would bring its owner as much money each day as had originally been spent buying it. The belief was so general that fairground salesmen exploited it by selling, to the credulous, little boxes containing metal insects mounted on delicate springs which quivered at a touch, as if alive. Icelanders had other recipes for magic wealth: using a mandrake to draw buried silver out of the ground, or a 'tide-mouse' (caught in a net of maiden's hair) to draw it from wrecks on the sea-bed; or making the gruesome 'Lappish Breeches' (see p. 139). They also believed that one could become a seer by trapping a 'speaking spirit' at a crossroads and keeping it imprisoned in a foal's caul; it would foretell the future on demand, but if it got free it would drive its owner mad.

Another way to become a seer is described in 'The White Snake', a sombre Norwegian version of a well-known international story in which the hero gains magical powers by accidentally tasting serpent's, or dragon's, flesh; famous examples are Siegfried the Volsung and the Celtic heroes Taliesin and Finn MacCumaill. The Norwegian story stresses the anguish which Second Sight brings, thus transforming the theme into a warning against magic practices; it is possible, though proof is lacking, that local memories of some mentally deranged girl lie behind the story and account for its pathos (cf. 'Anne Rykhus', p. 219).

In Scandinavia, as in all rural communities until very recent times, there were plenty of local seers and healers, corresponding to the 'wise women' and 'cunning men' or 'conjurers' of Britain. They dealt with any diseases in humans or in farm animals which were considered due to witchcraft or evil spirits; they might also be called on to lay ghosts, get rid of changelings, expel vermin, use the Second Sight to unmask thieves or find missing persons, and so forth. In the Icelandic tale 'Seeing the Ships Come In' a woman is asked to predict the arrival of supply-ships from Denmark, which were vital to the local people. Seers and healers were generally indistinguishable from the rest of the community, except for their special powers, and worked for their living like other countryfolk; their services, which were highly valued by the community, would be rewarded by tactful gifts but never by money payments. A second group of persons credited with abnormal powers were those who, while not 'book-learned', were skilled at certain crafts: blacksmiths, huntsmen, musicians (especially fiddlers), coachmen and others in charge of horses. Such men were sometimes said to use their powers for good, sometimes for ill. The tales about them must have greatly enhanced the prestige of their crafts, and may well have been deliberately exploited to impress outsiders. Finally, there were two ethnic groups whose members were thought to be almost all capable of magic: the gypsies, and the Lapps and Finns. Being semi-nomadic outsiders, linguistically and culturally distinct from the main population, they were viewed with intense suspicion. Some tales show their magic being put to good use (against vermin, in particular), but they were more often represented as dangerous and vindictive, and in popular imagination there is no hard and fast division between them and the wholly evil shape-changers and practitioners of witchcraft.

Many of the tales about such people centred on their uncanny ability to control animals. Stories about expelling rats were common, though without the additional element of child-luring which made the legend of the Pied Piper of Hamlyn so famous in Germany. In Sweden, those who conjure rats are usually said to be Lapps; it is said of one of them that he would simply hold out his knife, and that all the rats of the village would walk up one by one to slit their throats on it, and of another that he would order them to leap into the sea. In Denmark there are similar tales, though in the absence of exotic Lapps 'an old Norwegian' suffices as the hero. As 'A Lawsuit against Rats' shows, it was also believed that rats could be expelled by law – a notion presumably based on memories of the actual trials occasionally held in medieval Europe against infestations of vermin or insect pests. Related to the legendary ratcatchers are the snake-charmers; a story well-known throughout Scandinavia ('The Lindorm of Heilskov') concerns a man – in other versions often a Lapp or Finn – who lures serpents into a bonfire, but is then himself killed by the powerful, dragon-like Lindorm which he has unwittingly summoned.

Tales about huntsmen able to control game animals are represented in this chapter by the Swedish story of 'The Man Who Summoned a Roebuck'; further examples, in which the hunter is explicitly said to owe this uncanny power to the favour of a forest spirit, will be found in Part Seven. Finally, there were said to be men whose powers affected horses or, occasionally, other draught animals. The Swedish instance given here, 'The Coachman Who Stole the Oxen's Strength', concerns a man who uses this ability to his own profit at the expense of others, in much the same way as witches were believed to 'steal' the 'goodness' of their neighbours' cattle or crops for themselves.

Witchcraft has long been a matter of utmost importance in folk belief. It was constantly put forward as an explanation for disease, trouble with livestock, crop failure, poverty and personal misfortunes. Naturally, alternative explanations, both rational and irrational, were often available too; an ailing cow, for instance, might as readily be regarded as the victim of a hostile fairy as of a witch. The psychological advantage in blaming witches is that it offers an outlet for anger. If a misfortune comes from God, one can only submit; if it is caused by fairies, one may try to appease them by offerings or drive them away with counter-charms; but if it comes from a witch, a fellow-member of the community, one can identify her (or him) and exact concrete punishment.

If 'witch' is taken in its broadest, simplest sense, as a person who uses magic to harm others, then there have been witches in Scandinavian belief as far back as recorded texts can reach – the pre-Christian Viking Age, and no doubt earlier too. But the definition of a 'witch' as a member of a secret society of Devil-worshippers who have made a pact with Satan and gather regularly at 'Sabbats' for sexual and cannibalistic orgies is a purely theological notion which arose in fifteenth-century Christian Europe, and was vigorously propagated by the majority of both Catholic and Protestant writers for about 250 years. In

Scandinavia, the witch-hunts reached their height in the latter part of the seventeenth century, when several hundred people, mostly women, were tried and executed. The stereotyped beliefs of the witch-hunters left many traces in the oral tales of the three mainland Scandinavian nations, though not so much in Iceland where the images of the evil corpse-raising wizard and the benevolent magician-priest dominated tradition to such an extent that the female witch was virtually confined to one role, that of milk-stealer.

In their trials, alleged witches were regularly accused of flying to the Sabbat by smearing a magic salve on to a stool, a broom or an animal, and this became a popular theme in story-telling. Often it is handled humorously, the main point being the ludicrous misadventures of a man who tries to copy the witch's flight but gets the magic formula wrong. However, in another story-pattern (see 'The Parson's Wife Turned into a Horse') a man revenges himself on a witch who has turned him into a horse and ridden him. He uses her own magic bridle to do the same to her, and gets a blacksmith to shoe her. When she returns to human form, the horseshoes nailed to her hands and feet prove her guilt. As for the Sabbat itself, it was supposed to be held on a mountain peak; the Swedes called the place Blåkulla ('Black Peak'), but it is not clear which of two real mountains so named is the one meant, or whether it is an imaginary location. Sabbats were thought to be held on the eves of major Christian festivals. A strange Swedish motif, unknown elsewhere, is that witches amused themselves fighting one another at the Sabbat, inflicting wounds which healed by morning. Many scholars think this derives from the heathen belief in an everlasting battle enjoyed by warriors in Valhalla; Klintberg, however, thinks it is no more than an aggressive fantasy. Be that as it may, the legends about flights to the Sabbat and the witches' behaviour there do have an air of exaggeration and even humour which may imply that they were told primarily for their dramatic effectiveness and, by the nineteenth century at any rate, no longer commanded full belief.

Stories about witches' day-to-day activities were more deeply anchored in communal fears and anxieties. Most of them concerned cattle and dairy work, which were of primary importance economically and at the same time vulnerable to unpredictable hazards – cows could fall sick, the milk yield might fluctuate unaccountably, butter-making might be easy one day but difficult the next. All this was woman's work, so it seemed appropriate to blame the difficulties on to another woman: the thieving, hostile neighbourhood witch. Stories about stealing cream and milk by magic are by far the commonest witch-legends in Scandinavia. One magical method is described in 'Milking a Garter'; the other was to send out a familiar known as a 'Carrier', 'Milk-Hare', 'Troll Cat' or 'Puke', which would suck cows dry and bring their milk home to the witch. Unlike the familiars in British lore, this creature was not a gift from the Devil but was made by the witch herself from some common object – a spindle, a bone, a stocking, a hank of wool – and brought to life with magic formulas. It then fed on her blood. Such at least was the belief in Sweden, Norway and Iceland; in Denmark, however, as in the rest of Europe, it was thought that the witch herself could turn into a hare or cat. The existence of Carriers was supposedly 'proved' by the existence of a certain type of fungus found in meadows which looks like clotted cream and appears suddenly overnight; this was said to be the vomit, or the droppings, of a milk-fed Carrier.

The shape-changing witch is not so common in Scandinavian traditions as in British ones, but there are some tales of this type, especially in Denmark. Several describe transformation to bird-form. One instance is the Swedish 'Red Woodpeckers', and there are also Swedish tales where the witch appears as a magpie. A Danish tale, 'The Witch and the Huntsman', illustrates a particularly widespread and persistent belief: if a witch is wounded while in animal form, a corresponding wound will show itself on her own body, causing her to be recognized for what she is. And recognition, it is implied, will suffice in itself to break her power.

Shape-changing may play a minor role in witch-legends, but it is central to the belief in werewolves and were-bears, which was common in Norway and Sweden and is also found to some extent in Denmark; it does not occur in Iceland, naturally, as there are no real wolves or bears there. This belief is very widespread and archaic, being rooted in the notion of ancient hunters that certain large animals can shed their skins and appear as humans (see 'Better the Skin than the Child', p. 241). In Scandinavia, one must distinguish two kinds of werewolf legend: those in which the human deliberately transforms himself for his own malevolent purposes, and those where he is an unwilling victim. In the first group, the central figure is generally a Lapp or Finn. The method of transformation is to put on, or crawl through, a looped strip of wolfskin or bearskin. The Norwegian tale 'Lapp Wizards', collected in 1938, has interesting sociological implications; it shows Lapps exploiting the fear they inspire to extort gifts from unwilling givers, and inevitably arouses in a rationalistic reader the suspicion that such legends arise when people who have refused a request for help retrospectively attribute their later misfortunes to magical revenge. This psychological mechanism of 'projected' guilt is often to be observed in accusations of witchcraft.

The other type of werewolf, the involuntary victim, is credited with a quite different origin and different behaviour. His condition might sometimes be thought due to an enemy's spell, but far more commonly it was blamed upon his mother. It was said that if a pregnant woman wanted to avoid pain in childbirth, she should take the caul of a newborn foal, spread it on raised sticks and crawl three times under it, naked. This would enable her to give birth as quickly and painlessly as a mare, but her baby would grow up to be a werewolf, if a boy, or a Nightmare, if a girl. Werewolves often did not know their own nature and, if they did know it, longed to be rid of it; the only ways to free them were either to address them by their human name while they were in wolf form, or conversely to accuse them of being werewolves while they were human. Either way, recognition would break the spell. This belief is at the root of the very common legend of the Werewolf Husband, exemplified here by a Danish version, 'The Werewolf of Borregård'. It is probably relevant that although involuntary werewolves were harmless to most people, they were a threat to pregnant women, whose unborn babies they would try to rip out – an aspect symbolically hinted at by the wolf's attack on the woman's apron in this legend. The whole complex of belief and story conveys the message that it is wrong for women to hope to avoid the pains of childbirth, ordained by God as their allotted punishment for Eve's sin. Viewed from this angle, the werewolf belief can be seen as yet one more example of the repressive morality in traditional culture.

Like the involuntary werewolf, the *mara* ('Nightmare') is an unwitting victim of her mother's act. By day she is a normal woman; by night she becomes 'an invisible little thing' who can pass through cracks or keyholes into people's bedrooms, where she sits on the chests of sleepers, crushing and smothering them, or 'twisting their hearts within them', as one Norwegian account puts it. Such activities, known in English lore as 'hag-riding', go well beyond the mere bad dreams to which 'nightmare' now refers. The *mara* was also thought to go into stables and cowsheds to 'ride' the animals, making them sick and feverish. The belief in the *mara*, common in many parts of Europe, draws upon actual experience of discomforts felt during sleep: asthma, sinus troubles, heart tremors or oppressive heat could all bring troubles which the sufferer could ascribe to her. Charms were used to keep her at bay; one could recite the Lord's Prayer, or a traditional rhyme against her, or swing a knife round one's body, or hang various plants over the bed and in the cowshed.

Stories about the *mara* develop different aspects of the concept. One very popular tale, illustrated here by a Danish example, 'The Man Who Married a Nightmare', assimilates her to the broader category of the Supernatural Bride captured by a human who eventually resumes her true identity as Swan Maiden, Lake Fairy, etc., and escapes. Then there are tales in which the *mara* is released from her unwelcome condition by a direct accusation, in the same way as werewolves are. Finally, there are stories where the *mara* is hardly distinguishable from a witch; she haunts stables and cowsheds in the form of a feather or straw, and is killed when this is found and burnt. In such tales there is often, as in witch–legends, the surprise of discovering that the guilty person is a respected neighbour, or even a member of the family. The Swedish tale 'Scythes on the Horse's Back' has a particularly dramatic denouement.

SÆMUND AT THE BLACK SCHOOL

Iceland

Sæmund the Wise travelled abroad and went to the Black School, and there he learned strange arts. There was no schoolmaster to be seen in the Black School, but whatever the students might say one evening they wished to learn about, books about it would be provided next morning, or else it might be written up on the walls. Over the doorway, on the inner side, was written: 'You may come in; your soul is lost.' There was a rule in that school that anyone who came must study there for three years. All those who were leaving in any one year must all leave the place together, and the Devil would always keep the one who was last to get out, and so they used always to draw lots to see who would be the last out. More than once the lot fell on Sæmund, and so he remained there longer than the rules laid down. It so happened that Bishop Jon was travelling to Rome and passed near this place. He learned that Sæmund was still at the Black School for the reason we have said, so he went in and spoke to Sæmund and offered to help him get away, provided he would go home to Iceland and live as a good Christian, and Sæmund agreed. Bishop Jon made Sæmund walk out ahead of him, and he himself wore his cloak loose round his shoulders; and just as Jon was going out, a hand came up through the floor and grabbed the cloak and dragged it down, but Jon got away . . .

Others say this was how Sæmund escaped: his fellow-students arranged with him that he would go out last, so now he got a sheep's leg stitched to the bottom of his cloak, and as he followed the group who were rushing out through the school doors something gripped at the cloak and caught the leg. Then Sæmund let the whole thing drop and took to his heels, saying 'He gripped, but away I slipped,' and so rejoined his comrades.

Árnason, I, pp. 485–6, following eighteenth-century accounts. *Migratory Legends* 3000 'Escape from the Black School'. Sæmund Sigfússon the Wise lived from 1056 to 1133; the bishop mentioned is Jón Ögmundsson, Bishop of Hólar 1106–21, subsequently canonized. Most oral versions omit the bishop, giving credit to Sæmund's own cleverness.

The Magic Whistle

Iceland

Sæmund the Wise owned a whistle, and the power of it was such that as soon as anyone blew it one or more imps would come to whoever had blown it, and would ask what work they were to do. One day Sæmund had left this whistle in his bed, under the pillow, where he always used to keep it at night. That evening he told a servant girl to get things ready for him as usual, but he warned her that if she found anything unusual in the bed she must not touch it, but just leave it where it was.

Now the girl went to get things ready, and when she saw the whistle she was more than a little curious. She picked it up eagerly, examined it all round and about, and finally she blew it. Immediately an imp appeared before her and asked: 'What work must I do?'

The girl was startled, but she did not let it show. It so happened that ten of Sæmund's sheep had been slaughtered that day, and their fleeces were all lying outside. So the girl tells the imp that he must count all the hairs on all the fleeces, and if he can do that faster than she can make the bed, then he can have her. The imp rushed off and strained every nerve to count them, while the girl hurried to make the bed. By the time she had finished the imp still had one shank to count, and so he lost his bargain.

Afterwards, Sæmund asked the girl if she had found anything in the bed. She told the whole story, just as it happened, and Sæmund was pleased with her presence of mind.

Árnason, I, pp. 495–6. *Migratory Legends* 3020 'Inexperienced Use of the Black Book', which normally tells of a pupil opening his master's book of spells.

OLD NICK BUILDS A BRIDGE

Iceland

Once, Sæmund ordered Old Nick to build a bridge over Ranga River below Bergvad, since it was often difficult to ford the river, especially for those coming to Oddi to church. As payment, Old Nick demanded to have the first three who would cross the bridge on the first Sunday it was in use; this Sæmund agreed to. Once the bridge was finished, Sæmund, in order to keep his promise, had three puppies carried to the bridge and thrown on to it. The bridge-builder had to be satisfied with this, for he got no other payment.

Árnason, I, p. 487. *Types of Folktale* 1191
'The Dog on the Bridge'.

SÆMUND ON HIS DEATHBED

Iceland

Sæmund had taken in a poor man's child to be his foster-daughter; he thought that some evil fate hung over her, and he loved her so much that he always kept his eye on her and would not be parted from her. When he lay on his deathbed he made her put her couch at the foot of his bed, for it seemed he trusted her most to be the witness of his death. While he lay sick he guessed that this would be his last illness, and as time wore on she observed that he was anxious whether after his death he would go home to Heaven, or to the other place.

On the evening before his death he told his foster-daughter to be on her guard that night, and to be sure not to fall asleep, for he said he had a feeling he would die that night, and that if so one might see some tokens to show what would become of him in the next world. So he bade her keep awake and take good note of everything, so that she would be able to tell his kinsmen, with full proofs, what fitting place was allotted to him. After this he ceased speaking and lay back. But the girl loyally kept watch.

When much of the night had passed, she saw that the room where they were was filling with demon imps. It seemed to her that by their words they were trying to coax Sæmund into some evil, but from Sæmund's words and looks she judged that he would have nothing to do with them. As soon as the imps had failed in this, they tried to threaten Sæmund into doing evil. But he bravely resisted their threats, just as he had their coaxings. After this, the imps vanished, but the room filled again with mosquitoes, which attacked Sæmund. His strength was failing by then, so he could not defend himself or brush the mosquitoes off. But just when their biting was tormenting him most fiercely, the girl noticed a ray of light glide up from his mouth; she realized it must have been his soul gliding up to its blessed home. And indeed, all the mosquitoes had vanished, and Sæmund had passed away.

Árnason, I, p. 502.

THE REV. PETTER DASS

Norway

Petter Dass, the priest in Alstahaug in northern Norway, was pretty clever in most matters, as everyone knows. He owned a Black Book, or so people said, but they also knew that he kept on good terms with Our Lord. He was a very fine preacher, and the fame of his preaching spread all over his own country and even reached Denmark, for one Christmas Eve he received an order from the King saying that he must preach in the Castle Church in Copenhagen on Christmas Day itself. The text would be lying ready for him on the pulpit when he got there, and the King wanted to hear whether he was as good a preacher as people said.

It was absolutely impossible to get to Copenhagen in so short a time (at any rate in those days), but even so Petter Dass swore he would get there, and give his sermon too. He sent for three spirits of the air. They came, and he asked how fast they could fly. The first and second were both rejected because they were not fast enough, but the third one said he could fly as fast as man's thought, which was good enough to satisfy the Rev. Petter. As his payment, the carrier demanded the souls of all who would fall asleep in church that day, and this was promised to him. This carrier was none other than Old Nick himself.

Off they went all at once, out over the sea, and when they had gone a little way, the Carrier began to swoop down low, skimming the surface of the waves. Not surprisingly, the Rev. Petter began to get angry, for first his feet touched water, and soon the waves sent spray almost over his head.

So then the Carrier asked: 'What do people generally say when they're in danger at sea?' He thought he would thus trick the priest into saying some holy word, in which case he would have thrown him down at once.

'Higher up and further on, Satan!' said the Rev. Petter, and so they went on their way and he got to Copenhagen in good time.

In the Castle Church the people had gathered, and the Rev. Petter went up into the pulpit. There lay the piece of paper which would have the text on it, but when he looked at it, it was quite blank. He picked it up, looked at it, and said: 'There's nothing here!' So then he turned the paper over, looked at the other side, and said: 'Nothing here either!' And then he continued: 'And out of nothing God created the world!' With that, he began to discourse upon Creation, and he preached so well that there was not a dry eye in the church.

He did not get much payment, that Carrier!

Christiansen, pp. 53–4. *Migratory Legends* 3025 'Carried by the Devil'. Petter Dass (1647–1707) was the author of hymns and religious poems, and of a book describing his home district; many other typical magician legends are told of him.

DOCTOR KONGSTED OF BALLERUP

Denmark

Doctor Kongsted of Ballerup could extinguish fire. One night, one of the farmhouses in Ballerup was on fire. There were so many people there that they could have put it out, except that in those days there were no fire-engines in the countryside, except on manor estates. They realized very well that they could not put out the fire in the burning farm itself with buckets only, so they were trying to stop the fire from reaching the outlying buildings by covering them with wet carpets and sheets. In the middle of all the hubbub, Dr Kongsted came running up with nothing on but his shirt. He ran three times round the burning house and then jumped into the village pond. When he came up from the water, he said: 'Now the fire won't go any further this time,' after which he hurried home to bed. It proved true, sure enough – the fire slackened, and spread no further.

Dr Kongsted could also scry. Once, a piece of linen, which had been left outside overnight in a garden to bleach, was stolen. The woman who had lost it complained to the doctor about her misfortune. He comforted her, saying it would return to her. Quite right! Two days later it was thrown over her garden wall while people were asleep at midday.

'I was sure it would come, but I didn't think it would come so quickly, for the thief has had to come a long way with it,' said he to the woman when she told him it had been returned.

'Was there anyone who saw him?' she asked.

'No, certainly not,' he replied. 'I can quite well show you the thief in a bucket of water, but it will bring you nothing but sorrow if you see him.'

So naturally she preferred not to see.

Bødker, p. 107.

134

THE BOOK OF CYPRIANUS

Denmark

Cyprianus was a student, a gentle, harmless fellow on the whole, but he had passed through the Black School in Norway, and therefore was forced by the Devil to use his learning and his remarkable powers to do evil. This tormented him for the rest of his life, for in his heart he was good and pious, and so, to make amends for the evil, he wrote a book in which he first teaches how evil can be produced and then how it can be counteracted. The book begins with an explanation of what witchcraft is and remedies against it. It is in three parts: about Cyprianus, about Dr Faustus, and about Jakob Hammel, and the latter two parts are full of weird figures and signs which are supposed to be Persian, or Arabic, or conventional symbols. In this book one can learn all about magic signs and spells, and the Second Sight, and everything the Bible speaks of in Deuteronomy 18: 10–12. Handwritten copies are preserved here and there among the common people like holy relics. Any one who has the Book of Cyprianus will never lack money; he can summon the Devil and dismiss him, and nobody, save the Devil himself, can do him any harm. But he who owns this book can never get rid of it, for whether he sells it, burns it, or buries it, it always returns to him – and yet, if he cannot rid himself of it before his death, things will go badly with him then. The only way of doing so is supposed to be by writing one's name in it in one's own blood, and laying it in a secret hiding-place inside a church, together with four shillings in inscribed coinage.

Thiele, II, p. 92.

How Eirik Learned His Arts at School

Iceland

At Biskupstunga there once lived an old cottager who was heathen in his ways; he did not mix with other people much. He owned two things which he valued more than all the rest of his possessions: a book, of which nobody else knew the contents, and a heifer which he fed lavishly. This old man fell ill, and sent word to the Bishop of Skálholt to come and see him. The Bishop sets out in haste, thinking it would be best to have a few words with the old man, and goes to see him.

The old fellow said: 'The way things are going, my Lord Bishop, I shall soon be dead, and I want to ask you a small favour first.'

The Bishop agreed.

The old man said: 'I've got a book here and a heifer, which I love dearly, and I want to have both of them in my grave with me. If not, it will be the worse for everyone.'

The Bishop says that this would be done, for he thought it only too likely that the old man would walk after death if it were not done. Then the old man died, and the Bishop had him buried with his book and his heifer.

It happened, many years later, that three students at the Cathedral School at Skálholt decided to learn magic. One was called Bogi, the second Magnus, the third Eirik. They had heard tell of this old man and his book, and very much wanted to get hold of the book, so one night they went off to raise the old man from the dead, but no one could tell them where his grave was. They therefore decided to go through the graves row by row, raising the dead from each in turn; by doing this they filled the whole church with ghosts, but the old man did not come. So now they lay them all again, and fill the church a second time, and then a third, and by then there were only a few graves left, and still the old man had not come. When they had laid all the other ghosts they raised these too, and the very last one to come was the old man, and he had his book under his arm and was leading his heifer.

They all set upon the old man, trying to get at the book, but he fought back hard, and it was all they could do to defend themselves; however, they did snatch a few leaves from the first part of the book, but gave up hope of the rest. Then they wanted to lay the dead who were still roaming around, and they managed it with everyone except this old man; they got nowhere at all with him, and in fact he was struggling to take back the torn fragment of his book. But they held their own, though they were hard pressed to do so, and this went on till dawn. When daybreak came, the old man vanished into his grave, and they chanted their spells over it, and the old man never appeared again. As for the leaves from his book, the three companions kept them for their own use, and from them they compiled the manual of magic called Grey Skin which lay for many years on a table in the Cathedral School at Skálholt; Bogi had the most to do with this, for he learned far more than the others.

Later on, these three companions were ordained, and Eirik became the priest of Vogsosar in Selvog, but it is not said which parishes the others got . . .

Though the companions had kept their magic-learning secret, it was not long before a rumour got around that Eirik was versed in witchcraft, so his Bishop summoned him and showed him Grey Skin, and ordered him to state plainly whether he knew what was in it. Eirik flicked the pages and said: 'I don't know a single one of the signs in here,' and he swore to this, and went home again. But afterwards he told his friends that he knew all the signs in the book *except* just one single one, and he told them they could talk of this when he was dead, but not before.

Árnason, I, pp. 554–5. Eirík Magnússon (1637/8–1716) was at the Cathedral School of Skálholt from 1654 to 1658; by the end of the eighteenth century he had acquired a reputation of having been one of the greatest priest-magicians in Iceland, and one who always used his powers for good. The other two boys mentioned here are probably not historical. Both the Icelandic Cathedral Schools, at Skálholt and at Hólar, were rumoured to have manuals of magic in their libraries.

The Spiritus Hatched from a Cock's Egg

Sweden

To make a Spiritus you must take a cock's egg – a cock lays just one egg per year – and lay it in your armpit. When it has hatched, you must put the chick in a glass of alcohol and keep it carefully. From then on, you need only go to it and ask for whatever you want and you will get it at once. If you want to get rid of it, all you need do is sell it to somebody else. But the third person to own it will be unable to get rid of it, and when he is at the point of death the Spiritus will sit itself on his breast, and his soul will be forfeit to the Evil One. There are many people who have had a Spiritus and have grown rich in this way, but it's best not to name names, because all their families are still living round here to this day, some even at our very doors.

Klintberg, no. 333, p. 240. Collected in 1927 from a man born in 1878. 'Cock's eggs' can be either sterile eggs laid by hens which, owing to hormonal imbalance, have acquired a crest and plumage and voice like those of a cock; or fatty concretions found in the bodies of old cocks. Neither, of course, will hatch.

Fishing for a Spiritus

Sweden

I've heard tell about the Spiritus. You could find one on a Thursday evening, if you were willing to serve the Evil One. You must bait a hook with a small human bone and go to a brook and fish there for three Thursdays running. On the third night, you would catch a little, black, creeping thing on the hook, which you must take off and lay in a box. Every time you wanted money, you must spit in the box and close the lid. You could keep it as long as you liked, but it was on loan from the Evil One.

Klintberg, no. 332, p. 240. Collected in 1933 from an informant born in 1858.

LAPPISH BREECHES

Iceland

People who want to gather money that would never run short could get themselves Old Nick's Breeches – also called Lappish Breeches, Money Breeches, Corpse Breeches or Papey Island Breeches – and they are to be obtained as will be described now. He who wants such breeches must make an agreement with someone still alive that as soon as the latter dies, he can have the use of his skin. As soon as this happens, the survivor goes to the churchyard by night and digs the dead man up. He then flays the skin off him from the waist down and slips it off in one piece, for he must take care that there is no hole in the breeches. He must put them on straight away, and they will grow to his flesh until he himself removes them in order to give them to someone else. But before the breeches can be of any use, he must first steal a coin from some wretchedly poor widow, at the moment between the reading of the Epistle and Gospel on one of the three major festivals of the year (or else, some say, on the next day after he puts them on), and put this coin in the pocket of them. After this, the breeches will draw money from living men, so that the pocket is never empty when he puts his hand in it; but he must take care never to take the stolen coin out.

A notable point with Lappish Breeches is that he who has them cannot take them off or get rid of them just when he likes, but on the other hand his soul's salvation depends on his doing so before he dies – not to mention the fact that his corpse will be swarming with lice if he dies still wearing them. His one chance is to find someone who will step into them as he takes them off, stepping into one leg before he has stepped out of the other. As soon as he has done this, the new owner cannot change his mind even if he wants to, for if he tries to take his right leg out he will only find he has put his left leg in, without knowing how this happened. Then he in turn can never get rid of them except by the same method. Lappish Breeches keep their powers as they pass from man to man, and they never get torn.

Árnason, I, pp. 428–9. The men of Papey, one of the offshore islands of Iceland, included several wealthy families who in Árnason's time were sometimes said to have prospered by using magic.

THE WHITE SNAKE

Norway

On a small farmstead in Seljord, long ago, lived an old woman who was skilled in witchcraft of every kind. And good teachers she had too! Every wandering Laplander who came to the district took lodgings with her for weeks on end. She certainly didn't feed them for nothing, that old hag.

One time, she found a white snake. It's a rare bit of luck to happen on snakes of that sort, and they have the power in them to heal all sicknesses. When you cook the white snake, three stars come up on the water it's boiling in. The first makes you wise, the second gives you the Second Sight, but the third drives you mad – and that one whirls round and round like a wheel.

So this old woman began cooking the snake in the usual way, and in the middle she went out to the cowsheds to settle the beasts in their stalls. Her little daughter Margrit went trotting about in the kitchen on her own. She saw the stew standing there, and being just a child she thought it was some broth. She took a hunk of bread, dipped it in the stew, and happened to catch the star which gives one the Second Sight. As soon as she had swallowed that bread, she could see right through thick walls.

So she went down to the cowsheds to her mummy, and cried out cheerfully: 'Now I know just what the calf our Goldie is carrying looks like!'

'Oh Lord help us, child, you've not been at that stew!' **screamed her** mother. She knew Margrit would be bound to suffer through the gift of the Second Sight.

And suffer she did. Everything bad that happened in all the district round about, she saw it all. When a man drowned off Sinnes Point, Margrit saw it. She was almost beside herself with terror, screaming and crying out that they must go out and help this man. She never slept a wink, night or day, because of everything she saw, and in the end she quite lost her wits. But by good luck a wandering Lapp came to the farm. When he found out what was wrong with the girl he took that thing out of her and threw it to the four winds. From that day on, Margrit never had the gift of Second Sight.

Christiansen, pp. 66–7. From a text collected in 1904. *Migratory Legends* 3030 'The White Snake'; *Types of Folktale* 673.

SEEING THE SHIPS COME IN

Iceland

Not so long ago, there was an old woman by the name of Steinunm living in Olafsvik. She had cataracts on both eyes and could hardly see. Every spring, before the first supply-ships reached Iceland, traders used to ask this old woman how long it would be till the ships came in, and what she said generally proved to be right. It was not her way to give the exact number of days one must still wait, but simply to say whether it would take a long time or not. But once this old woman said that a ship was drawing near, it would never be more than a week before it arrived.

On one occasion a merchant came to see the old woman in Olafsvik as usual, and asked whether there was still a long while to wait before any ship arrived. She said she could not tell him, because what she used as a token had not yet come. This happened around midday, and that very evening the old woman said: 'My good friend the merchant came to see me a bit too early, for now I do know that a ship is close – it has reached Ennid.' Now, Ennid is the name of a group of sheer rocks rising up out of the sea at the mouth of Olafsvik Bay. Old Steinunm used to say that in her younger days she had had some kind of dealings with those who live inside the Ennid rocks, but one could never get any clear account of them out of her.

It is also said that there used to be an old woman living at Laugarnes who was in the habit of foretelling when the first ships would reach Reykjavik each spring. The token she used was that a ship belonging to the Hidden Folk had come to Kleppi, the first farm on Laugarnes; usually the first ship to reach Reykjavik would arrive there one week after the old woman foretold its coming.

Árnason, I, pp. 406–7.
'Those who lived inside . . . rocks' might mean either trolls or elves, but more likely the latter, since they are helpful, not hostile. 'The 'Hidden Folk' are elves; see p. 171.

A LAWSUIT AGAINST RATS

Denmark

At one time there used to be so many rats in Viborg that they were a plague to everyone. And while people were wondering how to get rid of them, an old woman came to the authorities there and advised that someone should issue a summons against the rats and prepare a lawsuit against them. This plan was agreed on, so a man was chosen then and there to issue the summons and announce the lawsuit against those rats. And when the suit was brought to court and the authorities gave it as their judgement that they must leave Viborg, they suddenly disappeared, so that for generations Viborg was quite free of them.

Thiele, II, pp. 67–8.

DRIVING OUT RATS FROM RINGKØBING

Denmark

It is very remarkable that throughout the whole district of Hind and Bølling there are no rats to be found – neither in Ringkøbing nor in Varde, nor for four miles more, as far as Schorring Bridge – so that many farmers in this neighbourhood have grown old without having ever set eyes on such a creature. And many men from Ringkøbing can bear witness that rats are often brought ashore among wares unloaded from ships, but that after frantically running round in circles for a little while they all end up by jumping back into the fiord. It is absolutely true that a man from a nearby town once brought a rat to Ringkøbing to make mock of this belief, but when he slipped it out of a bag in the middle of the market square, it turned straight down to the fiord and jumped in.

The reason for this strange state of affairs is said to be as follows. An aged Norwegian once came to Ringkøbing and took lodgings with a skipper who lived alongside the fiord. He left a bag in his house while he went into town on an errand. But when he got back he found the bag had been gnawed to bits by rats, and he was so bitterly angry at this that by using the Black Art he forced all the rats in the town to jump into the fiord. When he noticed, after all his work, that there was still one rat he had overlooked, he started conjuring again, so powerfully that it was forced to run the whole length of East Strand Street in front of many eyewitnesses, and jump into the fiord, where it perished with all the rest.

Thiele, II, p. 68–9. *Migratory Legends* 3016*
'The Pied Piper'.

143

The Lindorm of Heilskov

Denmark

There was once a young woman who refused to settle down and have a home until she found an island where there were no hills, and no inhabitants. So she comes to this region, and builds her house on a little ridge called Kelderbakke. There she found a nut, and inside it there was a serpent, which she put in a little box. Now it grew in there and got big, and in the end it could not stay in the box, so it went into a barrel. When the serpent had grown really big, the barrel would trundle along behind that young woman wherever she went, and she became rather embarrassed about this serpent and thought of getting rid of it. So she put it deep inside a mountain near Heilskove which is now called Lindberg, for it took its name from this Lindorm snake.

Many years now passed, and many settlers had come to live there, but they were terribly plagued with adders. So they sent for a man who was clever at destroying creatures of this sort to come there one day, and he told the people to have a bonfire built on the meadow here, south of the village. He had a flute, and when he blew it all the adders would come creeping to him. At the first note, along they all came, all that really were just adders, but the people there wanted him to play one note more. He did not dare do so, and asked whether there was any Lindorm in the district. No, they assured him, there was none. So then he piped again – and the Lindorm came. Long before it got there they could hear how it roared. So he climbed up into a tree near by, but the Lindorm twined itself round it and pulled both man and tree into the fire.

This was the Lindorm which the young woman had reared.

Bødker, pp. 38–9. *Migratory Legends* 3060 'Banning the Snakes'.

THE MAN WHO SUMMONED A ROEBUCK

Sweden

There was an old fellow called Jens Hulte around here who was skilled in magic. One time, he was at a farm where they were holding a feast. They happened to talk about hunting, and Jens said that if they gave him a quart of brandy he would guarantee to shoot a roebuck before sun-up. Nobody refused, and then they sat drinking and playing cards all night. When it was getting towards day-break, someone told Jens that if he meant to shoot any roebuck before the sun rose he had better hurry up. But Jens said there was plenty of time. Then suddenly along came a roebuck, running at full speed, and came to a halt just outside the window. And then some of them told Jens to hurry and shoot the roebuck. But Jens, he said: 'Oh, let him pant a bit first. He has run all the way from Stenshuved tonight, so he must need to get his breath back.'

Then, after a while, Jens opened the window and shot that buck.

Klintberg, no 292, p. 220. Collected 1943 from an informant in 1883.

THE COACHMAN WHO STOLE THE OXEN'S STRENGTH

Sweden

In the old days there were people who could steal the strength from other people's beasts. At Västanå, one time, there was a heavy millstone which must be moved, and three pairs of horses had been harnessed to the load, and two pairs were heaving and hauling so hard that they were streaming with sweat. But the coachman's pair were quite dry.

Then the estate owner asked him how it could be that his horses showed no sign of the weight they were hauling. 'Well, that's not so strange. They aren't hauling anything; it's the black oxen in the cattleshed that are doing the work for them instead.'

Naturally the other did not believe him, but when they got home he went out to the shed, and there stood the black oxen streaming with sweat, so it was obvious that it had been them that had had to haul the load.

But the coachman lost his job, because the landowner, who was an upright man, did not wish to have people like that in his service.

Klintberg, no. 286, pp. 217–18. Collected 1927 from an informant born in 1878.

'HACKED TODAY, WHOLE TOMORROW!'

Sweden

There was a man who asked for a night's lodging at a certain farm on the evening of Maundy Thursday, or maybe on Easter Saturday. In the course of the night the old woman of the household took out a horn of salve and smeared herself with it, and then she climbed on top of the stove, sat astride a broom, and said:

'Up here and out here,
And away to Snake Farm!'

Then up she went through the chimney, and this man planned to follow her, or so he thought. He took his walking stick and wanted to ride it. 'Up here and down here,' said he. But then the old woman's servant girl came in and taught him the words he ought to say, and so away he went to Blåkulla Mountain.

There all the old witches were amusing themselves fighting, and as they struck one another they would say: 'Hacked today, whole tomorrow!' But then this man, he said: 'Hacked today, hacked tomorrow, and hacked for ever and aye!' And when the old women got home again they were all cut and hacked about, and their wounds never healed.

Klintberg, no. 308, pp. 227–8. Collected in 1943 from an informant born in 1873. *Migratory Legends* 3045 'Following the Witch'. As other versions of this legend make plain, the man's mistake in repeating the formula causes him to fly up the chimney and down again all night, until he corrects himself in a second attempt. 'Snake Farm' is hell, since Satan can take on the form of a serpent.

THE PARSON'S WIFE TURNED INTO A HORSE

Sweden

There was a hired hand working on a parson's farm. And the parson's wife was a real old witch, and she planned to go off to Trondheim on Easter Saturday night. She took this man to ride on, because she had a bridle – the sort of bridle that would turn a man into a horse when she put it on him. And when she got there she tethered him to a fence, but the bridle slipped off him, and so when she came back she wanted to put it on him again. 'No,' said he, 'we'll change over now!' And so he put the bridle on the parson's wife and rode her home and stabled her in a stall with the horses – and a fine big mare she was, too.

But he didn't say a word to the parson till next morning, when he asked him whether he might like to buy a fine mare which he'd got hold of. The parson went to the stables with him, looked the mare over, bought her, and sent for the farrier to shoe her. After that the farm-hand took the bridle off her, and there was the parson's wife standing there. So then they were forced to send for the barber-surgeon to get the horseshoes off her, and then the blood flowed from her, sure enough!

Klintberg, no. 312, p. 229. Collected in 1932 from an informant born in 1847. *Migratory Legends* 3057★ 'The Witch-Ridden Boy'. Swedish witches were thought to be particularly active in Holy Week and to hold Sabbats on Easter Eve.

STEALING CREAM

Denmark

In Stødov on Helgenæs there was once a woman who could work witchcraft. When she wanted to churn butter, she would say to herself: 'One spoonful of cream from each man in the district!' and so she would always find her churn quite full of cream.

Now it happened one day that just as she was about to churn, she had to go into the village on an errand. So she said to her servant girl: 'Now you can do the churning while I'm out, but before you begin that, you must say, "One spoonful of cream from each man in the district!" I'll arrange matters so that enough cream will come.'

The woman went off, and the girl set to work at once to pour the cream into the churn, but as she was about to say the words which the woman had taught her it occurred to her that one spoonful from each man was very little indeed, so she said: 'Half a pot of cream from each man in the district!'

Now she got cream, with a vengeance! The churn was full, and still cream kept on coming, until in the end the kitchen was half full of it. When the woman came home the girl was standing there baling cream out of the kitchen door, and the witch was very angry, for she had exceeded her orders by wishing for half a pot instead of a spoonful. Moreover, every man in the district could now notice that cream had been stolen from him, and the girl was never allowed to churn alone again.

Bødker, pp. 144–5. *Migratory Legends* 3040
'The Witch Making Butter'.

MILKING A GARTER

Sweden

In the old days there was a witch called Elin living at Västbo, and she was so skilled in magic she could milk any cow she chose, simply by hanging her garter from the roof. She taught her foster-daughter to do this too. When this girl went to be prepared for Confirmation, the priest asked her if it was true she could milk a garter, and of course she couldn't deny it. Then the priest hung a garter from the roof-beam and ordered her to milk a cow belonging to a crofter, one of his tenants. She began milking the garter and the milk flowed, but when she had gone on for a while she said: 'Now I mustn't go on any longer, because then the blood will come.'

'Just carry on!' said the priest.

'Now the cow will die if I carry on any longer,' said the girl.

'Just carry on! I'll pay for the cow,' said the priest.

The girl went on milking, and the cow died. Shortly afterwards the crofter arrived, weeping and bemoaning his misfortune, and the priest paid him the worth of the cow.

After that, of course, it was decided to send Elin for trial. The constable came and fetched her away, but when he got back all he had in his cart was a bundle of straw; the old hag was still sitting at home in her cottage between her two pussies, as she called them – they were really two lions, or rather two devils which could change their shapes when any intruder entered.

There was a farmer who offered to go and fetch her. He drove out there, and ordered Elin to sit in his cart. 'Well, you have your reins looped to the left, your whiplash looped to the left, and wind-sown rowan in your harness, so neither God nor Devil nor I can do anything against that,' said Elin, and so she went with him to her trial.

She was sentenced to death by beheading, but just as the headsman was about to strike she turned into three bundles of straw.

'What shall I do now?' he asked.

'Strike the middle one,' said the farmer who had driven her there. So that's what the executioner did, and it was indeed Elin.

Klintberg, no. 320, pp. 233–4. Collected 1908. First part: *Migratory Legends* 3035 'The Witch's Daughter', here linked to anecdotes about a well-known figure in nineteenth-century popular tradition in Sweden, the witch Elin or Eli.

THE CARRIER

Iceland

If people want to grow rich by stealing milk or wool, they have discovered a handy way, which is to have a 'Carrier' or 'Spindle'. These are two names for the same things . . . Learned men say that to get a Carrier a woman must steal a dead man's rib from the churchyard on Whitsun morning, soon after he has been buried; then she wraps it in grey wool or yarn which she has stolen elsewhere (or others say she must pluck tufts from between the shoulders of a widow's sheep which has just had its wool plucked), wrapping it round the rib until it looks just like a hank of wool, and this she leaves lying between her breasts for a while. After this, she goes three times to Communion, and each time she lets the wine (or, some say, both bread and wine) fall on to the materials which will form the Carrier, by dribbling it into her bosom. Some say it need touch only one end of the Carrier, but most say both. The first time the woman dribbles on the Carrier, it lies quite still; the second time, it stirs; the third time, it is so strong and lively that it tries to leap out of her bosom. She must then be extremely careful that it should not be seen; if women were denounced as having Carriers, it is said that their punishment used to be to be burned or drowned with the Carrier on them, so wicked and terrible was this thought to be. To ensure justice, the Carrier would be pursued till it took refuge under the woman's skirt; her petticoat would then be tied up or sewn up below the Carrier, and both of them destroyed like that.

When the Carrier has been given its full strength in the manner described, the woman can no longer bear to keep it at her breast, so then she draws blood from the inside of her thigh, which causes a fleshy growth there, and there she lets it suck. It lives there and feeds on the woman's blood whenever it is at home, and so one can always recognize those who are a Carrier's 'mother' because they are lame and have blood-red warts on the inner thigh. However, it seems some women also kept them in empty kegs or barrels in their dairies, at any rate sometimes. As soon as the Carrier's mother bears a child and has milk in her breasts, it will try to get at her, and if it does manage to suck her breasts her life is at risk, for it will suck her to death.

The reason for having Carriers was to send them to suck other people's cows (or, some say, ewes) out in the pastures. Afterwards they come to their mother through the dairy window while she is churning – for she has so arranged that the churn is standing just by the window while it is in use. When the Carrier comes to the window, it calls out, saying 'Full belly, Mummy!' or 'Churn lid off, Mummy!'

Then the woman takes off the churn lid, saying, 'Sick it up, dear son!', or 'Spew in the churn, little rogue!', or 'Let it go, son!' Then it sicks up all it has sucked into its mother's churn so that plenty of butter forms in it . . .

When the Carrier sucks milk, it sets about it by jumping up on the cow's back and coiling over her croup, and then making itself so long that it can reach the dugs from both sides at once, and it sucks through both its ends at once. But people who say that a Carrier has only one mouth say that it twists round as soon as it has sucked the dugs dry on one side, and then takes from the other side . . . It sometimes happens that Carriers do not know the limits of their own stomachs and suck more milk than they can carry home to their mother at the dairy window, in which case they vomit it up on the way home. People have often thought they saw this 'Carrier's Spew' on the moors in the same season as Iceland moss; it looks yellowish white, and thick . . .

Carriers had other uses besides sucking milch cows, for they could also be used for stealing wool, though this is more rarely mentioned. One spring day all the wool of a certain farm was being washed; the weather was good for drying, and all the wool was spread out in great swathes on the homefield. In the evening the weather looked set to be fine and dry again, so the wool was not even gathered into a heap, let alone taken indoors. When the people got up next morning, the wool seemed to have been all scraped up into a heap, and when they went outside to have a closer look, the first thing they knew was that they saw the whole mass whirl itself into a single huge skein, and thereupon the whole pile set itself in motion, except for a few scattered wisps – and those wisps were all the farmer got, for the big ball of wool rolled off so fast that there was no chance to follow it, and so vanished. People believed that a Carrier must have wrapped this wool round itself and run away with it.

When a Carrier's mother grows old and worn out, the Carrier troubles her so much that she can no longer bear to have him suck the nipple on her thigh. Then she sends him up into the mountains and orders him to gather up all the lambs' droppings from three pastures, and he works himself to death over this, for he will do all he can to bring them all home to his mother, and never let himself rest. In proof of which, men have said that one often finds human ribs among heaps of lambs' droppings up on the pastures.

Carriers are amazingly swift, and go hurtling over hill and dale; sometimes they seem to roll like a clew of thread or a skein of wool, or sometimes they bound along on one end. There are a few examples of men who chased them on horseback, but only on the swiftest of horses.

On one occasion, a farmer had ridden out one morning to fetch in his cows which were out at pasture, and was riding along. As he came up to them, he saw that a grey-coloured Carrier was lying across the croup of his best cow and sucking from both sides at once. The Carrier sprang away quickly when the farmer came up, but the farmer chased him on horseback. But the Carrier went creeping and twisting among the hillocks till he reached the farm which was his home. The people there were out in the homefield, but the Carrier rushed in under the skirts of the farmer's wife. The man who was chasing it dismounted, went up to the woman and tied all her clothes below the Carrier, and so she was burned to death.

Árnason, I, pp. 430–433. Compiled from many informants. Slightly abridged.

THE GUTS OF THE MILK-HARE

Sweden

There was a man who met a Milk-Hare and shot it. When he shot this Milk-Hare, the guts came out of it and tried to twist themselves round his neck. He parried this by taking them on his gun-barrel, and guided them on to a birch-tree instead. They wound themselves round the birch so tightly that its bark was stripped off.

People who kept Milk-Hares used to put tubs out for them in the evenings. During the night the Milk-Hare would come and sick up the milk into these tubs; they say there are some people who have actually heard this.

Klintberg, no. 326, p. 237. Collected in 1938 from an informant born in 1856. In southern Sweden the milk-stealing familiar is generally said to look like a hare; in the north, like a rolling ball. It is often called a *puke*, a word used in Scandinavian languages for various types of 'imp' or 'goblin', and cognate with English 'Puck' and Irish 'poohka'.

RED WOODPECKERS

Sweden

My father was once with some men who burned a Puke out in the forest near here, at Vikbodarna. They'd been having terrible trouble with this Puke round there at the time. He had made a regular trail across the pasture, and there was Puke-shit everywhere. My Dad and a few others got together to try to get rid of the beastly thing. So one afternoon they got things ready, taking seven kinds of wood, seven kinds of flowers, seven differently coloured threads, and seven bits of Puke-dung, and set fire to the whole lot.

When it had burned for a while, a lot of red woodpeckers came out of the forest and began fluttering about in the trees round the fire. Then Dad took a stick and threw it into the thick of the flock, hurting one of the birds. At that very hour an old woman in a neighbouring village broke her leg. People believed that it must have been her who controlled the Puke.

Klintberg, no. 329, p. 238. Collected in 1907 from a woman whose father often told this story, saying it happened to him when he was a boy, early in the nineteenth century.

THE WITCH AND THE HUNTSMAN

Denmark

At one time there were many witches at Østrel, on the road between Aalborg and Thisted. A huntsman who often used to go past Baller Farm would frequently see either a hare or a wild duck thereabouts, but though he shot at them and was sure his aim had been good, he never brought down either of them. On one occasion he saw a duck swimming about on a pool just near that farm and shot at it several times, but it would not rise – it was as if it had noticed nothing. So since neither shot nor ball had any effect, he cut a silver button off his jacket, crossed it three times, and put it in his gun. This time he did hit the duck, and it rose from the water and flew into the farmyard, where it hid in the hen-house.

He ran up to the farm, where people were at supper, told them what had happened, and claimed the duck he had shot. The farmer agreed that of course he could go to the kitchen and tell the maid about it, and she would see about getting his duck for him. But when he came into the kitchen, there was a hideous old woman sitting by the fire. She was wearing only one shoe and blood was streaming down her leg from a wound which she said she had got by falling and cutting herself. But the huntsman knew at once that this was the witch he had shot, and he ran away from there as fast as he could.

Thiele, II, pp. 103–4. *Migratory Legends*
3055 'The Witch Who was Hurt'.

LAPP WIZARDS

Norway

In the valleys of the North Trøndelag district, in the old days, people were plagued by Lappish wizards. These men were wanderers who kept no reindeer themselves but simply went around begging, and used witchcraft when they did not get what they asked for. These

Lapp wizards were particularly dangerous because they would 'run as wolf or bear', that is, they would take on the form of a beast of prey and kill small livestock.

One day, as a farmer's wife at the upper end of Stordal was letting her goats out, a Lapp came by and asked her to lend him a good nanny-goat for the summer. The woman refused, saying she couldn't spare any of her beasts, and the Lapp was very angry when he left. A little while later, the herd came rushing back to the farm, bleating loudly as if terrified, and when the woman went to see what was going on she noticed a huge bear, which disappeared into the woods behind the house. It had slaughtered the two finest goats in the whole herd. The woman burst into tears. Just after this the Lapp came strolling out from the same wood which the bear had disappeared in, and softly and gently he murmured: 'Look you now, mother, now you'll be lending me a good nanny-goat, surely?'

At Åsegg Farm, at the upper end of Steinsdal, a Lapp wizard came begging for meat. The womenfolk wanted to give it him, but the farmer himself was young and heedless and didn't believe in witchcraft, so he flatly said no. The Lapp was spluttering with rage when he left, and he swore that there would be plenty of meat in that farm before evening came. Not long after, people heard shrill squealing from the pig-pen behind the cow-house, and they all ran out to see what was the matter. What they saw was that a horrible brute of a long, shaggy wolf had hurled himself on the finest sow and crouched there, biting her to death. Some ran for sticks, some for guns, but the old pauper billeted on that farm knew a better plan. 'You there, Søfren the Lapp, I know you by your pigtail!' he shouted, and the wolf dropped down, stone dead. A Lapp in animal form must die if anyone calls him by his right name. When they flayed the wolf, they found the sheath-knife of this Sølfren the Lapp underneath the wolf's pelt.

Christiansen, pp. 184–5. It was the custom in Norway for paupers and infirm people to be sent by the parish authorities to live in a prosperous farmer's house in their old age.

THE WEREWOLF OF BORREGÅRD

Denmark

There were once a man and a woman living at Borregård, and they had to go over Aertbølle Heath to fetch a cartload of heather. When they had gathered their load and were ready to go home, the man said to his wife: 'Now, you take the reins and drive, and here's the pitchfork, and if anything comes to attack you, you must beat it away from you, but you must not stab it with the prongs.'

Now, only a little while after the man had gone off, there came a horrible great wolf towards her (for this was in the days when there were werewolves), and she beat at it as hard as she could, but the more she beat it the more it struggled to get nearer her, and it snapped at her apron and tore it to shreds. So then she did strike at it with the prongs of the fork and stabbed it, but as soon as she started doing that it ran away.

Shortly afterwards her husband returned, and he was terribly bad-tempered and snappish, and scolded her sharply. And as she looks at him, she notices suddenly that there are threads from her apron stuck between his teeth. So she says: 'It was just as well that you said I mustn't stab, only beat. You are certainly a werewolf, a devil from hell. And it's just as well that I should say so, too, because now that it's been brought out into the open you will never be able to be a werewolf again.'

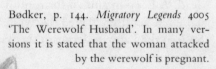

Bødker, p. 144. *Migratory Legends* 4005 'The Werewolf Husband'. In many versions it is stated that the woman attacked by the werewolf is pregnant.

A Mutton Bone for a Werewolf

Sweden

There was a fellow called Ol Annersa who lived at Forsnäs in Åsele, and he told me how his great-great-grandfather had once got into an argument with a Lapp and made him really angry, and the Lapp had threatened him. And then, as bad luck would have it, the old man went skiing in the forest one day and had to relieve himself while he was up there, and this Lapp got hold of it, and used it to cast a spell over him, so that he had to live as a wolf for seven years. And even then he would never be free unless a human being gave him something, quite willingly.

Well, one Christmas morning, when the seven years had gone by, there were seven wolves (and this man was with them, even though he had kept his human fear of other wolves), and they'd gone into a sauna hut. And they were so hungry that they had decided they would hurl themselves at the first horse that came by – the road to the church ran just past there. But in the end they didn't dare, as there were so many sleighs that all came past at the same time.

But this wolf, he took himself off and went back to his own farm, and there he sat down beside the steps. And then out came his old woman to fetch meat from the store-shed, and she felt sorry for him and tossed him a shoulder of mutton, and as soon as he had eaten it up he turned back into a human being again.

Klintberg, no. 347, p. 248. Collected in
1928 from an informant born in 1852.

157

THE NIGHTMARE

Norway

In appearance, Mara, the Nightmare, is like a very beautiful woman, but in her actions she is like a most evil spirit. She passes through locked doors and attacks sleepers, sometimes by sitting astride them and tormenting them with horrible dreams, and sometimes by lying down on them and twisting their hearts within them. Anyone who is visited in this way during the night is said to be 'ridden' by Mara, and often he is almost suffocated. Sometimes she is not content with tormenting humans but rides cattle and horses. In Telemark she is called Muro, and there, as elsewhere, there are many ways of getting rid of her. One of the most effective is said to be to take a knife, wrap it in a cloth, and pass it three times round one's body in the same direction, with the words:

> Muro, Muro, min!
> If you are herein,
> Out you must go!
> Here's a knife, and here's a spear,
> And Simon Svipu is in here.

'Simon Svipu' is a name for the thick growths found on twigs of old birch trees, which are hung up over horses and cattle and over beds so that Mara should not ride there.

There are various descriptions of Mara. One old man explains that when Mara rides him, which often happens, she comes in the shape of a black dog and tries to throttle him, but as soon as he gets to the end of the Lord's Prayer he is free. Others say Mara has to flee if one can speak the words 'In Jesus' Name!', or if one shrieks loudly. Some are of opinion that it is only those who are secretly in love who are liable to be nightmare-ridden, and others say that if Mara has time enough to count all the teeth in a sleeper's mouth in the time it takes to recite the Lord's Prayer, the sleeper will inevitably die.

Faye, pp. 77–8.

THE MAN WHO MARRIED A NIGHTMARE

Denmark

A farmworker had a sweetheart who was a Nightmare without realizing it, and she would come to this man every night, so he soon noticed what was going on. He kept watch and noticed that every night she crept in through a little hole in an oak plank. So then he made a peg which fitted the hole tightly, and when she came in the following night he thrust the peg into the hole, so that now she had to stay in the room. She resumed her human form at once, and the young fellow married her, and they had many children.

Now, when many years had passed and they were both getting on in life, it happened one evening that the man noticed this peg, which was still stuck into the hole in the oak plank. As a joke, he asked his wife if she really knew how she had first come into his house, and since she had no idea at all he told her all about it and laughed a lot about it and, yes, in the end he took the peg out, so that she could see the route by which she had entered. Then the woman peered through the hole, but while she stood there peering, she suddenly grew tiny, slipped out through this hole, and has never been seen again since.

Thiele, II, pp. 280–1. *Migratory Legends*
4010 'Married to a Nightmare'.

SPEAKING TOO SOON

Sweden

It happened once that some tailors had arrived at a farm and were doing some sewing. One evening they were sitting in the main room, together with a girl who was spinning. When they had been sitting at work for some while, the spinning wheel began gradually to slow down, and the girl somehow melted away into a dark mist, until in the end the only thing there was her clothes.

The tailors realized that this girl was a Nightmare, and they decided to wait until she came back. At about half-past ten the spinning wheel began to turn briskly once more, and the girl gradually recovered her human shape as she crept back into her clothes. Then one of the tailors said: 'I do believe that you're a Nightmare!'

'Yes, and thank you for those words, for now I'm free. But you should have waited just a little longer. If you had, I would have got my little finger back too, but now I'm going to have to lose it.'

He had happened to speak to her too soon, so one of her little fingers had not been changed back. People believed that a Nightmare would be free when a male person spoke to her or found out that she was a Nightmare.

Klintberg, no. 337, pp. 242–3. Collected in 1933 from an informant born in 1860. Itinerant tailors and cobblers would visit farms and stay a few days to do whatever work was needed there, staying up late when the farm-workers were in bed.

SCYTHES ON THE HORSE'S BACK

Sweden

This happened at Morskoga in Ramsberg, and it was before I was born, but my father talked a lot about it, and it was certainly true. There was a horse there which was badly troubled by a Nightmare. And the stable lad there, he was so anxious about that horse that he did everything he could to free it from the Nightmare, because the horse would be standing sweating and exhausted in its stall almost every morning. So then this lad took sharpened scythe-blades and tied them to the horse's back one evening to see if that might help, since nothing else had.

When the farmer came out to the stable next morning, the lad was lying dead in the stall beside the horse, all cut to pieces by the scythe-blades. So it was he himself who had been the Nightmare, although he knew nothing at all about it. There must have been someone else, some wicked person, who had forced this lad to go around as a Nightmare, though he was not aware of it himself.

Klintberg, no. 341, pp. 244–5. Collected in 1934 from an informant born in 1853. A rare example of a male Nightmare; other versions of this tale follow normal beliefs by having a female neighbour, or the farmer's own wife, unmasked as the Nightmare. But the dramatic denouement whereby the lad sets a trap for himself necessitates a sex-reversal, since women did not work in stables.

Part Six

Fairies Round the Homestead

INTRODUCTION

In Scandinavia, as in the rest of Europe, popular traditions constantly allude to a category of beings which were believed to exist alongside people on this earth, possessing various superhuman powers including the ability to become visible or invisible at will, and to bestow good or bad luck, while not being purely spiritual entities like angels or devils. The Scandinavian languages do not possess a general, all-inclusive term for them corresponding to 'fairy' or *fée*; instead, they are given descriptive names such as Hidden People, Underground Folk, People of the Mounds; or are referred to evasively as 'They' or 'the Beings' (*vättar*); or have archaic names whose etymology is now obscure. One word needing special comment is 'troll'. In Iceland and in much of Norway this applies exclusively to giant ogres such as were mentioned in several tales given in Part One, but in Denmark it is used of small pixy-goblins, and in Sweden of supernatural beings of approximately human size and appearance. 'Troll' is an ancient word, so it is not surprising that it has developed different applications; its basic meaning seems to be simply 'a magical being', and it may be connected with an archaic root meaning 'to roll, to spin round' – in several folktales we shall encounter rolling and whirling trolls.

During the Middle Ages, it became necessary to devise ways of fitting the concept of fairies (by whatever name these were locally known) into the Bible-based Christian world-picture. Officially the Church classed them as demons, but popular tradition gave them a more ambivalent status. One widespread notion was that they had originally been angels, but that they had refused to join either side in the great war in heaven between God and Lucifer, and so, being cast out from heaven but not welcome in hell, they had fallen to earth and settled there. Other legends ascribed to them a remote kinship with humanity, claiming that they were Adam's children by his mysterious first wife, Lilith; or that they were children of Adam and Eve whom Eve had hidden from God (see p. 171). Many stories state or imply that they are so like human beings as to be easily mistaken for them; the Icelandic *álfar* (elves) and *huldufolk* (Hidden People) can be identified as such only by some minute detail like having a ridge rather than a groove in the upper lip, or no division between the nostrils. But other tales emphasize the *non*-human aspects of supernatural beings; some are said to have cows' tails or mossy backs, others to be hairy, others to have oddly shaped feet.

Whatever their alleged origins and status, they were always considered morally ambiguous and unpredictable; even the friendliest would take revenge if offended, while even the most dangerous might occasionally bestow gifts on some favoured person. One can roughly classify fairies according to whether they are predominantly helpful or harmful to man. One can also classify them by their habitat, and the two groupings broadly correspond: those thought to live in or close alongside human habitations are normally fairly benevolent, while those on the outskirts of the cultivated areas are more dangerous, both aggressively and erotically, and those in remote forests and mountains even more so.

At the 'friendliest' end of both scales is the guardian house-spirit corresponding to the British brownie. In Denmark and in some parts of Norway and Sweden he is called the *nisse* (a nickname, from Nicholas); in most of Sweden, the *tomte* (from *tomt*, 'a plot of land for building'); in parts of Norway, *gardvord*, *godbonde* or *tunkall* (all meaning, roughly, 'farm-guardian'). Iceland, oddly, has no traditions about him, his role as protector and luck-bringer being occasionally filled by a family ghost. The account of Norwegian 'Nisses' written by Andreas Faye in 1844 (p. 171) summarizes many typical beliefs, anecdotes and customs related to them. Among other things, he notes the practice of setting out food and drink for them every Thursday night, with special treats at Christmas. Centuries earlier, St Brigid of Sweden had warned: 'Do not give the Tomte sacrifices of first-born calves or pigs, nor of bread and wine and other things.' In our own time the custom is still partially observed in Swedish families where there are children, by putting out a plate of porridge on Christmas Eve, though naturally it is no longer a matter for serious belief.

Anecdotes about household spirits are mostly light-hearted, but there is no doubt that in the days when the belief flourished it served various useful purposes. First, it supplied an explanation why one farm was more productive, or one animal healthier than another: the successful farmer's belief in his Tomte would boost his self-confidence, while a less successful one could comfort himself by claiming that he was not to blame for failures – it was simply that others had Tomtes more powerful than his. A widespread story, 'The Tomte Carries a Burden' (p. 174), dramatically conveys the underlying belief that prosperity and luck are 'limited goods' so that one man's success will necessarily be at another's expense. Secondly, belief in house-spirits had educative value. It was said that they rewarded good work but punished drunkenness, swearing, laziness, neglect of the livestock and similar faults to which young workmen might be inclined. Children were told that the Tomte watched to see if they were naughty. Many anecdotes stressed that he would take revenge on those who cheated him or treated him disrespectfully. Thus the belief could be exploited to control the behaviour of children and subordinates in a farming household.

At the same time, the Nisse or Tomte was imagined as being a kind of farm-servant himself, albeit a supernatural one, giving his services simply in return for food and lodging, not wages, as farmhands were sometimes expected to do in early peasant communities. A curious and very common story, which spread throughout Europe, tells how a house-spirit unpredictably reacts to a generous gift of new clothes by leaving the farm at once. In Scandinavian versions, his motivation is made quite clear: he now considers himself too elegant to work. Thus interpreted, the story reflects the view (not uncommon among employers) that to treat a servant unusually well will make him too 'uppity' for his job.

Finally, the house-spirit was also thought to be a mischievous prankster who might behave like a poltergeist, throwing or hiding objects, making odd noises, hitting people invisibly, and so on. This aspect comes out well in the Norwegian anecdotes about 'Trouble with Nisses'; one of these, about a farmer moving house, is a standard joke told wherever house-spirits are known.

Guardian spirits are not limited to farms. In Denmark it was said that each church had its Nisse, to keep the place tidy and punish misbehaviour; he was thought to live in a bundle of rags in the tower, or among the roofbeams. The tale of 'The Church Nisse at Besser' amusingly exploits the clash between this belief and the more general one that all species of fairies loathe church bells. Then there is the ship-guardian, whose peculiar names Kabbelgatt (Swedish) and Klaboltermand (Danish) come from the German word for a being of this type, *Klabautermann*. Like a farm-guardian, he shares routine tasks like loading cargo and repairing timbers, but he chiefly manifests himself in moments of danger, guiding the ship through fog or using his great strength to steady the mast in a storm. Naturally his helpfulness turns to anger if he is offended; if he leaves the ship, she is doomed. According to Swedish belief, he is a tree-spirit who arrives with the timber from which the keel is fashioned; in Denmark, he is sometimes said to live in the figurehead.

Whether in a farm, a church or a ship, a brownie-type guardian lives in human territory and is not envisaged as having any activities or concerns except in relation to mankind. In this he is unique; all other types of fairy were thought to pursue their lives independently of man. Many are thought to have families, to work at farming or hunting or cattle-rearing, to have feasts, and even sometimes to have Christian rites of their own, with priests and churches. Their hidden realm can be close alongside man's dwellings; they may live in an elder-tree by the farm door, in a mound in its meadows, or just under the cowshed, so that they complain that its muck splashes their house. But such fairies are, even at best, merely 'good neighbours', not members of the human household, and it is dangerous to encroach on their territory. As several stories show, there is commonly a taboo on cultivating, damaging, building upon, or even being too noisy near places thought to be fairy haunts. In some tales they are not explicitly named, as in 'The Birch Tree' and 'Gona Pool', but their presence is implied.

Some legends imply that when fairies and humans are at odds, it is because the humans have acted badly and spoilt a previously good relationship. One Danish story tells how a troll paid a boy the excellent wage of twopence a day, plus a pancake, to herd his cows; but the ungrateful lad soiled the pancake plate, which ended the arrangement. Another tells of a woman who lent her dress to one of the Mound Folk, then impatiently demanded it back; had she waited politely it would have been given back with diamonds on it, but instead it was stained with wax. Other tales, however, assume that Otherworld beings are hostile even when nothing has been done to annoy them. Some informants go so far as to identify them with demons. This is implied in the interesting Swedish tale 'The Troll in the Chimney' (p. 185), since thunderbolts were thought to be God's weapons, as they had once been Thor's. Another similar story of a troll's destruction ends with the informant explaining: 'You see, that's how it is. Thunder kills evil creatures of that sort. Our Lord has the thunder as his weapon against Satan's followers' (Klintberg, p. 142).

Fairies from the countryside were believed to invade human homes at various times and for various purposes. Just as Halloween in British tradition is a night for supernatural incursions, so is Christmas Eve in Scandinavian lore; it was customary for everyone to leave the house to go to a midnight church service, during which time elves, trolls or the like were said to take it over and hold a feast there. In Iceland it was the custom to sweep the house most thoroughly and keep lamps burning in every room and outhouse all that night, and for the mother of the family to go into every room and outhouse, saying : 'Let those who wish to come, come; and let those who wish to go, go; and let them do no harm to me or mine.' For the 'Christmas Visitors' were dangerous to men, as most anecdotes stress; often the point of the tale is that they used formerly to come, but have been frightened off by one of the standard folk exorcisms – gunfire, the throwing of a steel knife, the display of a Bible. One amusing variant on this theme concerns a bear-trainer whose tame bear terrifies the Christmas trolls infesting a farm; a version from the classic collection of Norwegian fairy-tales by P. C. Asbjörnsen and Jörgen Moe is included here in George Dasent's translation of 1859, the freshness and vigour of which cannot be improved upon.

At other times of year, fairies might enter houses invisibly to suck the goodness out of the food, unless this had been protected by charms and religious symbols. This belief forms the background to most Scandinavian versions of a very old story, often called 'The Pan Legend' by folklorists because it resembles Plutarch's account of a spirit voice which called upon human sailors to announce to other spirits that 'Great Pan is dead' ('De defectu oraculorum,' *Moralia* 3:17). In these, news of a death is sent by trolls or *vättar* to one of their comrades who is busy stealing food or beer from someone's farm. A substantial number of variants, however, especially in Denmark, belong to a light-hearted sub-type where the trolls are disguised as cats, and the farmer is amazed to find that his own puss reveals itself as a supernatural being.

Even more threateningly, fairies might come to a house to carry off a woman who had just given birth to a child, replacing her with a lifeless image. Only post-parturition deaths were accounted for in this way, not other deaths by fever or disease, and the woman was held to be at risk until her churching, three or four weeks after the birth. Fairies might also steal the baby, in which case they would not substitute a wooden figure but one of their own species – a 'changeling' which would never thrive, but would remain sickly, fretful and perpetually hungry, and would grow into an ugly, wizened little child. This might happen at any time from birth up until the toddling stage, though baptism was believed to be some protection. Obviously, many congenital physical and mental defects of infants could thus be conveniently accounted for, together with rickets and other deficiency diseases which commence around the time of weaning. Paradoxically, belief in change-lings may have been comforting to parents; it must at any rate have been less distressing to think one is the victim of evil fairies than to wonder whether one's own sins have drawn down God's punishment on one's baby. Moreover the belief indirectly encouraged good nursing, since it was thought that fairies could only kidnap babies or newly delivered mothers if they had been left unattended – a neglect which would obviously be risky on purely practical grounds.

The final stories in this chapter illustrate an interesting theme – the traditional way to identify and expel a changeling. The method described is one constantly found in legends from all over Europe: the changeling must be startled into betraying his true nature by showing him something ridiculous or perplexing, and then he must be physically ill-treated to force the fairies to restore the real baby and remove the unwelcome substitute. The treatments described are brutal; they include beating, burning, putting into a hot oven, throwing on the dunghill. Were such stories purely told for entertainment? It seems only too likely that the methods they recommend were sometimes applied in real life, in which case they would undoubtedly soon have led to the baby's death. If so, the stories would have functioned as a communal justification for infanticide of abnormal infants, for they embody an assumption that if the harsh treatment does kill the baby, this in itself 'proves' he was a changeling and not a true human being at all. A story given here from Thiele's Danish collection is particularly revealing in its description of how an unbroken colt is used for distinguishing a 'real' baby from a changeling, at great risk to the latter. Such stories reveal harsh and disquieting aspects of the peasant societies from which they come.

THE ORIGIN OF ELVES

Iceland

Once, God Almighty came to Adam and Eve. They welcomed him gladly and showed him everything they had in their house, and they also showed him their children, who seemed to him to be very promising. He asked Eve whether she had any other children besides the ones she was just showing him. She said, 'No.' But the truth of the matter was that Eve had not yet got around to washing some of her children and was ashamed to let God see them, and so she had pushed them away somewhere out of sight. God knew this, and said: 'That which had to be hidden from me, shall also be hidden from men.'

So now these children became invisible to men, and lived in woods and moorlands, knolls and rocks. From them the elves are descended, but human beings are descended from those of Eve's children whom she did show to God. Human beings can never see elves unless the latter wish it, but elves can see men and enable men to see them. It is for this reason that elves are also called the Hidden People.

Árnason, I, p. 5. The commonest name for elves in Iceland was *huldufolk*, 'Hidden People', which was thought more polite than the older word *álfar*, 'elves'. Norwegian has the similar term *hulder* (masc.) or *huldre* (fem.).

NISSES

Norway

There were innumerable hordes of Nisses in the old days, as almost every farm had its own. Their numbers have fallen sharply in later times. They are no bigger than little children, dress in grey clothes, wear a red pointed cap, but have only four fingers, since they lack thumbs. Usually they take up their quarters in barns and stables, where they help to look after the horses and cattle, towards which they show as much favouritism as they do to men. One often hears how a Nisse will draw the hay out of the other horses' mangers into that of one he favours and wants to feed up, so that by morning this horse is standing, well fed, in front of a manger which is still full, whereas the rest have had hardly anything.

He is fond of pranks. Sometimes he lets all the cows loose in the byre, or frightens the dairymaids by suddenly blowing their lamps out; often he holds on to the hay so tightly that the poor girls can't pull out so much as a straw, and then, when they are tugging with all their might, he lets go so suddenly that the girls fall flat on the ground. One girl who was fetching hay from the loft once found something in it that felt like a big hank of wool. Being curious, she put it in her apron to see what it was – but how scared she was when out jumped the Nisse, laughing! Such things amuse the Nisse very much, and after his tricks he loves to burst out laughing.

Often one hears the guard dogs barking at night, and one doesn't know why. Sometimes this is the Nisse's doing. He finds it great fun to pull the cat's tail and to tease the guard dogs. He likes sitting on the beam above the hearth and stretching out first one leg and then the other with the words 'Come on, pussy! Come on, pussy!' mingled with hearty laughter.

If he likes the owners of the farm, he ensures the prosperity of the estate. People have even noticed that he tries to drag hay and other crops from neighbours' farms to his own, which sometimes gives rise to quarrels and fighting between each farm's Nisse, so that one sees straws whirling through the air. The Nisse has, in general, an honest heart. If he is treated well, he is a good worker. He helps the dairymaids to put the cows in their stalls, and helps the cook to scour, carry water, and do other heavy tasks, which he often carries out by himself while she is fast asleep. She, however, must never annoy him, and must not forget to give him good food and drink every Thursday night, and especially on Christmas Eve. On that date it is the custom to give him a treat of porridge, cakes, ale and other nice things, which one puts beside the hearth. If he is in a good mood and the food pleases him (for he is fussy), he will gladly eat it up.

Mockery and disrespect he will not tolerate, and since in spite of his small size he is very strong, the person concerned often gets the worst of it. A farmer who met a Nisse in a lane one winter evening and told him in threatening tones to move out of the way was thrown clear over the fence by the infuriated little fellow, into a deep snowdrift.

Even worse happened to a girl who ate up the Christmas porridge herself and gave him the empty bowl as a joke. The Nisse grabbed her and danced with her so energetically that next morning she was found dead on the floor. As he danced he sang:

> Did you eat up the porridge of the Tomte here?
> Then you must come a-dancing with the Tomte, dear!
>
> Oh yes, you ate the porridge of the Tomte here,
> So now you'll come a-dancing with the Tomte, dear!

Nisses are fond of moonlight, and in winter one can see them amusing themselves jumping over fences. Although they are fond of fun themselves, they don't always like other people to make a noise and disturbance near them, especially on Thursday evenings and on the eve of feast days.

In general, the Nisse is a good fellow and is liked in most places.

Faye, pp. 42–5. Besides 'Nisse' and 'Tomte', Faye gives the names *Gardbo* ('Farm-Guardian'), *Toftvette* ('a being on cultivated land'), and *Haugbonde* ('Mound Dweller') for farm-guardians.

THE TOMTE'S FAVOURITE COW

Sweden

I heard an old Lapp woman once telling about an old farmer's wife in Ångermanland who came into the cowshed very early one morning. There she saw the Tomte come in with a big armful of hay and give it to one of the cows.

'Eat it up then, my dear little cow,' says he. 'It's just come from Jön in Hänum!'

Another cow standing alongside got only a little handful. The first of these cows was always nice and plump, but the other remained always sickly and thin.

Klintberg, no. 80, pp. 112–13. Collected in 1914 from an informant born in 1838. The Tomte has stolen the hay from a farm in a district very far off.

The Tomte Hates the New Horse

Sweden

On one farm there was an old fellow who owned some excellent beasts. Among others, there was a big, handsome piebald horse. And there was also a Tomte there, who used to see to the horses. But the old man went and sold the piebald horse and bought another, a miserable-looking creature. And every morning when he came into the stables, he saw this horse sweating and in a sorry state, and it grew thinner and thinner and got quite wretched.

The old fellow thought: 'I'm going to take steps to find out what's at the bottom of this,' and one night he went and hid in the stables. In the middle of the night he saw the Tomte come in and flog the horse with a great whip, saying: 'Just you turn yourself into a piebald, will you?'

Then the old fellow went and bought his old horse back again, after which everything was all right again.

Klintberg, no. 81, p. 113. Collected in
1927 from an informant born in 1859.

The Tomte Carries One Straw

Sweden

A farmer was out in the fields, carting in his rye. Then a little old Tomte came and walked beside him, carrying one straw on his shoulder. When they got to the barn, first the farmer tipped his cartload in – and it was a big load – and then came the Tomte and threw in his one straw, and as he did so he heaved a deep breath.

'Surely that wasn't much to pant over,' said the farmer.

'Well, if that was nothing to pant over, neither will you get anything for *you* to pant over,' said the Tomte, and took back his straw and dragged it away.

From then on, he dragged everything away from that farmer, so that he became so poor, so poor; however hard he worked, it was no use. The Tomte dragged everything away.

I didn't know the farmer myself, but I heard tell that it happened in Brattfors when I was a little child.

Klintberg, no. 77, pp. 111–12. Collected in 1928 from an informant born at Brattfors in 1852. *Migratory Legends* 7005, 'The Heavy Burden'.

THE HEAVY BURDEN

Norway

On a certain farm there was a man called Lars. One day he was in the barn, threshing corn. Then he caught sight of a tiny little man who was struggling along, dragging a single ear of corn, and puffing and sweating all the while. Lars stood staring at him, and at last he said: 'Why d'you pant so loud, when you're carrying so little, then?'

'If this is little, it'll get even less,' said the little fellow, and was gone in an instant. But from that time things started going badly for this Lars. He got poorer and poorer, and in the end he had to leave the farm.

Christiansen, p. 238. *Migratory Legends* 7005. In some Norwegian variants of this, the farmer sees, too late, that all the goodness of his neighbour's harvest is contained in the Nisse's one ear of corn.

THE NISSE'S REVENGE

Denmark

Nisses are sure to revenge themselves if anyone does them an injury. One day, at a farm at Vosborg in Jutland, a Nisse was running about in the loft above the cowstalls when a board split and his foot went through it. One of the farm lads was in the stalls just as this happened, and when he saw the Nisse's leg hanging down he picked up a dung-fork and gave him a hefty blow across the leg.

At midday, when everyone was sitting at table in the servants' quarters, this lad was sitting chuckling to himself all the time. The foreman asked him why he was laughing, and the lad answered: 'Well, I took a crack at our Nisse today, and I gave him one hell of a thwack with my fork when he stuck his leg down through the floor of the loft!'

'No, you didn't!' shouted the Nisse himself from outside the window. 'You didn't give me one, you gave me three, because there were three prongs on that fork. But you'll be paid back for it!'

Next night, as the lad lay asleep, the Nisse came and grabbed him and threw him right up over the house, and then ran round to the other side so fast that he was able to catch him before he hit the ground and throw him back at once. And he kept the game going till the lad had been tossed over the house eight times. The ninth time he did let him fall, into the big pond – and then he burst into such loud peals of laughter that everyone in the farm woke up.

Thiele, II, pp. 271–2. *Migratory Legends* 7010 'Revenge for Being Teased'.

NEW CLOTHES

Sweden

There was a cottager once who had a little old fellow who would come and potter around in the stable, feed the horses, brush them and currycomb them, and tidy things up in general, so that everything was nice and clean when people came in in the morning.

So now the old man – the farmer himself, I mean – he says: 'I'm going out to the stable to have a look, because there must be some sort of a Tomte out there who goes and looks after the horses. I'll go and hide there and watch when he comes in.'

'All right, if you lie quiet and don't disturb him,' says his wife.

And so he did see the little old fellow, how he was currying and patting the horses. But he had badly torn clothes, almost falling to bits, so that he was dressed in rags.

So when this farmer comes back in to his wife, he says: 'It's a shame about the Tomte – he was all in rags. It would be nice to sew a suit for him.'

This they did, and back he went with this suit, did the farmer, and he lays it in the stall, and he says: 'Here's an outfit for my little stable lad, and he can have it because he's been so good and looked after the horses and groomed them so well.' And then off he goes and hides in a corner, to find out what he'll think of these clothes.

During the night, in comes the Tomte and grooms the horses and feeds them as usual. When he had done it all, he put the suit on. When he was quite dressed, he stroked himself and said: 'Oh you fine, fine fellow! You'll never go inside a stable again!'

And he was as good as his word, and never came there again. He had become far too stuck-up once he had been given these fine clothes.

Klintberg, no. 84, pp. 114–15. Collected in 1915 from an informant aged about seventy. *Migratory Legends* 7015 'The New Suit'.

TROUBLE WITH NISSES

Norway

There used to be a Nisse living on a farm called Lamoen. Children from all the other farms round about used to go to Lamoen for their schooling, and once during lesson-time something began to clatter and bang in the chimney, just as if there was a sweep there poking his brush up it. The teacher went to look at the chimney, but at once everything was quiet.

Another time it was as if someone was walking about and dragging a chain along the floor in the passage outside, and this made a pretty dreadful racket. The teacher tiptoed over to the door and flung it open, but everything was quiet and peaceful then; but no sooner had he sat down again than all the racket started up, as loud as ever. When break-time came and the children rushed out to get their coats and caps, there came a noise as if someone had thrown a fistful of peas across the floor.

Another time, towards dusk, somebody saw a little fellow standing outside and peeping in through a window. It was the Nisse, and all at once he began to grow and grow, until he became taller than the whole window, but at this the man got so scared that he ran away and hid.

Christiansen, p. 133.

MOVING HOUSE

Norway

There was once a farmer who was so sick of the Nisse that he wanted to move out from his home, and so he loaded everything he owned on to a wagon and drove off. On the road he met a man who asked him where he was going. 'Oh, we're moving house today, the both of us!' said the Nisse, poking his head out of a tub at the back of the wagon.

Christiansen, p. 133. *Migratory Legends* 7020
'A Vain Attempt to Escape the Nisse'.

THE CHURCH NISSE AT BESSER

Denmark

In the church at Besser lives a Nisse. He has his lair in a bundle of rags in the church roof, but on Sundays and at other times when the bells are being rung he hides in a mound a little way away. Sometimes he may play some trick or other, so as to enjoy scoring off someone who has annoyed him. One evening, when the sexton came in to ring the curfew, Master Nisse played a little joke on him. When he tried to ring the bell it couldn't give a single note. Then the sexton noticed that there was a big bundle of rags tied round the clapper. While he was standing there puzzling over this, he glimpsed a little face grinning, and a red cap above it, up alongside the bell.

Bødker, p. 178.

THE SHIP'S GUARDIAN

Sweden

People think, you know, that the ship's guardian, the Kabbelgatt-Nisse, comes on board with the keel-timber as soon as the keel is laid. Now it happened, one time, that the tree which was going to be used for the keel had two guardians, and this gave rise to a quarrel over which of them would take charge of the ship. When the skipper saw them fighting, he separated them and asked one of them how long he had guarded that tree. 'Since it was as thick as a wagon's shaft-pole,' he answered. But then the other one retorted: 'But I've been guarding it since it was no thicker than a whip-handle.' So then the skipper settled their quarrel by saying that the second one, the one who had guarded the tree longest, should become the ship's Kabbelgatt-Nisse.

Klintberg, no. 94, p. 120. Collected in 1920.

THE SHIP GNOME (KLABOLTERMAND)

Denmark

A certain ship had reached harbour safe and sound after a long voyage, and the cargo was to be unloaded next day. That evening one of the sailors was standing on deck, thinking of his dear ones at home whom he would soon be seeing. Suddenly he heard a tiny voice hailing a ship that was lying alongside, from which an exactly similar voice replied. The voice from the other ship asked whether they had had a good voyage, and so on. The first voice replied: 'The voyage was not too bad, but what work I had! There wouldn't have been much left of the masts if I hadn't propped them up, nor of the sails if I hadn't held on to them, and I also had to stop up the leaky joints down in the hold so that we shouldn't sink. If I hadn't been on board, everyone would have gone down together, man and mouse. But I can't be bothered to stay here any longer, because the captain and sailors think it's all thanks to their own skill that the voyage went so well, and they're so pleased with themselves that they've forgotten me. No, I'll be leaving this ship tonight.'

So now the sailor, who had been standing unnoticed in the darkness, knew that these were two ship's gnomes who had been having a private conversation. He remained in his hiding-place till all was quiet. Next morning he lost no time in clearing out from that ship, whose luck had now gone, and looking for another berth. Some time later that ship put out to sea again, but it never reached its destination; it was wrecked on the way.

Bødker, p. 159.

THE GRATEFUL ELF-WOMAN

Iceland

A woman once dreamed about someone who she felt sure must be a woman of the Hidden Folk; this woman in her dream asked her to give her milk for her child every day for a month, and to put it at a particular place in her house. She promised she would, and when she woke up she did; she put a bowl of milk at the agreed place every day, and the milk always disappeared, and this went on all that month. When the month was over, the same woman appeared to her again and said that she had done well, and that she could keep a belt which she would find in her bed when she woke. Then the woman vanished, and she woke up, and she found a beautifully made silver belt, just as the elf-woman had said she would.

Árnason, I, pp. 7–8.

A HELPFUL ELF-WOMAN

Iceland

There was a couple living at Bakkagerd in Borgarfjord, and they lived alone. One day the man went out, and did not come home at evening. That night, the woman's labour pains came on, so she lit the lamp. Shortly afterwards, an unknown woman came in and offered to help her. The woman accepted the offer, and so she took care of her, delivered the baby, swaddled it, and laid it in bed beside the mother. Then she went out, and came back with a plate of meat. The meat was hot, and she put the plate down by the bed, saying nothing, and went away. The woman did not dare eat the meat, and did not touch it. A little while later the unknown woman came and took the plate, and said: 'There was no danger for you in this plate, and it would have done you no harm to eat from it. If you had, you would have earned great good luck for yourself and your child.' With that, she went away, and people suppose that she must have been living inside an elf-hillock which is very near that farm. But the woman of Bakkagerd never saw any sign of her again.

Árnason, I, p. 26.

MOVING THE COW-HOUSE

Sweden

Just near our church there is a farm called Lenån. In the old days a man called Gullik lived there. He had nothing but bad luck with his cattle. One time, one of his cows got her back broken, and it looked just as if some cart had run over her. Another time he had to have a cow put down, and embedded in her neck there was a little bundle of charred splinters of wood. In the end he was forced to send for a cunning man to find out what was the matter. The cunning man said he would have to shift his cow-house. Until he did, he would never have any luck with his cattle, because the main road of the Earth Dwellers ran straight through his cow-house.

There was also one part of his infield where nothing would grow, however much manure one put on it. The cunning man allowed Gullik to look through a glass he had, and then he was able to see that this whole area was built over. In the end, Gullik moved his whole farm elsewhere, after which everything went well for him.

Klintberg, no. 164, p. 157. Collected in 1908. *Migratory Legends* 5075 'Moving a Building Placed Above a Fairy's House'.

PLOMGÅRDS MOUND

Denmark

West of Vadum Church in Vendsyssel there is a small mound called Plomgårds Mound which is inhabited by the Hill Folk. They always lived on good terms with the farmers around there; however, it did occasionally happen that they revenged themselves if any sort of harm was done to their mound. It is said, for instance, that long ago there were several trees on the mound, and that one of them served as a boundary marker between two men's fields. One day one of these men was at this spot, busy driving a cow home. As the cow was running about wildly he broke a branch off this tree, because he had nothing else at hand to control her with; but this breach of the rules was punished immediately, for as soon as he struck the cow with the branch she fell to the ground lifeless, and never revived.

On another occasion, the parish priest wanted to have the mound levelled, because he was shocked by all the stories people told about it, but no sooner had his servants stuck a spade into the ground than a sickness came over him, and he did not recover until he gave up his plan.

Thiele, II, p. 240.

THE FIRE AT STADARFELL

Iceland

In the winter of 1808 the farm at Stadarfell burnt to ashes. Just below the farm, on a cliff jutting out to sea, there was a large rock in which it was said that an elf-woman lived, but since the cliff was crumbling this rock half overhung the water; however, it was firm enough if no one interfered with it, and it might have stayed like that for a long time, because everyone was warned not to play the fool with this rock. But shortly before the fire, the farm workmen had sent the rock crashing into the sea, just for fun; and the next night old Benedikt Bogason dreamed of the elf-woman, and she told him he would be the worse off because his men had had their fun with her house. And shortly afterwards the farm burned down, and so the prophecy was fulfilled.

Árnason, I, p. 31.

GONA POOL

Iceland

Gona is the name of a pool between Refsstadir and Vestur River, upstream from Laxa River, which runs down that valley and is fed by a brook from that pool. Eyjolf, the district bailiff, who lived at Moberg in Langadal, had summer pastures and a dairy up in Laxadal. There was a young lad looking after the cattle there. One day this lad fished in the pool, though Eyjolf had forbidden him to do so. When he got back to the dairy, a cow which was due to calve soon was lying in the milking-pen with a broken leg. The boy decided that this would not stop him fishing in the pool, and next day he went fishing again. But when he got back to the dairy, the cow was dead. He had to admit it was his fault, and he stopped fishing. Since then, no one has fished in Gona Pool, though as a matter of fact there are no fish there nowadays.

Árnason, I, p. 483.

THE BIRCH TREE

Iceland

Near Horgsdal, in the Skaptafell district of eastern Iceland, stands a solitary birch tree, tall and beautiful, in the shelter of a ravine. No one was allowed to cut its branches or take anything away from it, whatever might be their need – and indeed, it is the only full-grown tree to be found in this part of the country.

One day, a woman was driving some cows near where this tree grew. The cows were being troublesome and were wanting to stray, and the girl had no dog with her, nor had she anything in her hand with which to control the beasts. As she passed the tree, it occurred to her that she could easily break off a branch to use as a stick, and so she does, and uses this branch to hit the most troublesome of the cows when next she wanders off the path. But at the very moment that the blow touches her, this cow crashes to the ground rump first, and breaks a leg. This was blamed on the fact that the girl had struck her with a branch from this tree, which nobody must ever take anything from, for any reason at all.

Árnason, I. p. 482.

THE TROLL IN THE CHIMNEY

Sweden

Jonte from Skorhult was a man who could see things that other people could not see. One day he was out haymaking on my grandfather's farm, but a thunderstorm came up, and so all the haymakers gathered for shelter in a crofter's cottage. All at once, a thunderbolt struck the chimney. A hole opened up just above the stove, and something big and black, just like a sack of coals, came rolling out. It looked as if there were legs kicking about inside the sack. Then it rolled out through the open door, and away it went down towards the lake – but then another thunderbolt struck it, and at that it simply disappeared.

But old Jonte, he said it was a troll, and that the thunder first knocked one of its legs off when it struck the chimney and then killed it down by the lake.

Klintberg, no. 137, pp. 141–2. Collected in 1932 from an informant born *c.* 1849.

CHRISTMAS EVE

Iceland

I have been told that it happened on a certain farm that whatever woman was made to stay at home on Christmas Eve had lost her wits when the others came home next morning; it was the custom then to hold a midnight service on Christmas Eve, and everyone would go to it, young and old alike, except one woman who would have to take care of everything at home. This went on for several Christmases at this farm, and there were not many left to stay at home, and yet the fact was that somebody would have to do it. Now there was a servant who had been taken on that spring, and it fell to her to stay at home on the first Christmas Eve that she was there. She knew what had happened to those who had done it before.

When the others had set out for church, she lit lamps and placed them here and there throughout the farm; then she sat down on her bed and began reading her prayerbook – she was a virtuous, pious girl. When she had sat there a little while, a crowd of people – men, women, and children – came into the farm. They started dancing all sorts of dances; they spoke to the girl, asking her to join the troop and dance with them, but she kept silent, sat still, and read her book. They begged her to come, and offered her this, that and the other if she would come. But she answered nothing, and sat still, as before. This went on all the time, but it was no use – she sat quite still, even though they offered her rich gifts. This went on all night, but when day broke they went away, and the people of the farm came back, thinking she would be bewitched like the others. But they saw at once that she was just the same as they had left her. They asked whether nothing had happened to her, so then she told them what had gone on that night; she said she had known that if she joined in their dancing she would have become like the others who had stayed at home before. After this, she was always the one to stay at home on Christmas Eve as long as she was there, and the same thing happened every time.

Árnason, I, pp. 119–20, from the writings of Ólafur Sveinsson of Purkey (1780–1845), who collected elf legends in the early nineteenth century to confirm his own strong belief in their existence. *Migratory Legends* 6015 'The Christmas Visitors'.

THE CAT ON THE DOVREFJELL

Norway

Once on a time there was a man up in Finnmark who had caught a great white bear, which he was going to take to the king of Denmark. Now it so fell out that he came to the Dovrefjell just about Christmas Eve, and there he turned into a cottage where a man lived, whose name was Halvor, and asked the man if he could get house-room there, for his bear and himself.

'Heaven never help me, if what I say isn't true,' said the man; 'but we can't give anyone house-room just now, for every Christmas Eve such a pack of trolls comes down on us that we are forced to flit, and haven't so much as a house over our own heads, to say nothing of lending one to anyone else.'

'Oh?' said the man. 'If that's all, you can very well lend me your house; my bear can lie under the stove yonder, and I can sleep in the side-room.'

Well, he begged so hard that at last he got leave to stay there. So the people of the house flitted out, and before they went, everything was got ready for the trolls; the tables were laid, and there was rice porridge, and fish boiled in lye, and sausages, and all else that was good, just as for any other grand feast.

So, when everything was ready, down came the trolls. Some were

187

great and some were small; some had long tails, and some had no tails at all; and they ate and drank, and tasted everything. Just then, one of the little trolls caught sight of the white bear, who lay under the stove; so he took a piece of sausage and stuck it on a fork, and went and poked it up against the bear's nose, screaming out: 'Pussy, will you have some sausage?'

Then the white bear rose up and growled, and hunted the whole pack of them out of doors, both great and small.

Next year Halvor was out in the wood, on the afternoon of Christmas Eve, cutting wood for the holidays, for he thought the trolls would come again; and just as he was hard at work, he heard a voice in the wood calling out: 'Halvor! Halvor!'

'Well,' said Halvor, 'here I am.'

'Have you got your big cat with you still?'

'Yes, that I have,' said Halvor; 'she's lying at home under the stove, and what's more, she has now got seven kittens, far bigger and fiercer than she is herself.'

'Oh, then we'll never come to see you again,' bawled out the troll away in the wood; and he kept his word, for since that time the trolls have never eaten their Christmas brose with Halvor on the Dovrefjell.

Webbe Dasent, pp. 62–3. *Types of Folktale* 1161 'The Bear and his Trainer'; *Migratory Legends* 6015. The Dovrefjell mountains in central Norway are traditionally noted for their trolls; cf. *Peer Gynt*.

ANNOUNCING A DEATH

Sweden

One day, a farmer from Ularp had been to the mill at Skeen. As he rode home, when he got to the bank at Marahult, someone shrieked: 'Go into the most southerly house in Värset and tell Stuva to go home, because Kisskusskolma is dead!' When the farmer reached Värset he went into the first house on the south side of the village and told the people there what the voice had shouted. At this, a sort of whirlwind swirled through the room, the doors flew open, and someone shrieked:

'Damn it, then I won't ever see my man again!' It was a she-troll who had got in there, meaning to steal the wort used in making beer. In her hurry she forgot to take her pail with her; long afterwards, the people at Värset still kept it.

Klintberg, no. 118, pp. 132–3. *Migratory Legends* 6070A 'Fairies Send a Message'. The troll's odd name may be a corruption of the Finnish words for 'one, two, three'.

'KASSERIKUS IS DEAD!'

Sweden

It was my granny on my father's side who told me this, so it's perfectly true. There was this stray cat which came to Ställberg, where my grandfather was living. The cat was sitting on the table one day when my grandfather came home, and grandfather just said to my granny: 'Fancy this,' said he, 'as I was going past Dromborgsberg a voice shouted from inside the mountain, "Tell Mäns to go home, Kasserikus is dead!"'

And as soon as grandfather said that, that cat shot out of the window and headed off into the forest, and they never set eyes on it again. And it was a troll-cat from Dromborgsberg, and it could understand what my grandfather said, and knew it was some sort of message to it.

Klintberg, no. 119, p. 133. Collected in 1932 from an informant born in 1876. *Migratory Legends* 6070B 'King of the Cats'.

The Troll from Brøndhøj

Denmark

Between the villages of Pedersborg and Lynge stands a mound called Brøndhøj, which is said to be inhabited by Troll Folk. Among these there was at one time a jealous old troll whom the others nicknamed Knurremurre ('Grumblegrowser') because it was so often his fault that there were quarrels and uproar inside that mound. One day this Knurremurre found some reason to suspect that his young wife was on rather too friendly terms with a younger troll, and the old fellow took this so badly that he even made threats against the young one's life.

So then this other troll thought the best thing for him to do would be to clear out, so he left the mound and took himself off, in the form of a ginger tomcat, to the village of Lynge, where he made his way into the home of a poor man named Plat. There he lived a long while, got milk and porridge every day, and lay all day long in an armchair beside the stove.

One evening Plat came home, and when he walked into the living room the cat was sitting exactly in his usual place, eating porridge from a pot and licking his paw.

'Well now, Mother,' said the man to his wife, 'I must tell you what happened to me on the way home! As I was passing Brøndhøj, out came a troll, who called out to me and said, "Listen here, Plat! You tell your cat that Knurremurre is dead!"'

At these very words the cat stood up on his hind legs, sent the pot flying, and dashed out through the doorway, crying 'What, is Knurremurre dead? Then I must hurry home!'

Thiele, II, pp. 187–8. *Migratory Legends* 6070B.

THE HUSBAND'S GARTER

Sweden

On a farm called Röckla, on the far side of Fremlingen, trolls once carried off a woman who had just given birth. And they carved a stump of alder-wood so well that everybody thought this thing was her, lying dead in her bed. And they prepared the funeral and were about to bury her, when the priest asked them whether they realized what sort of thing it was they were burying, and warned them that it was nothing but a stump of wood.

But later on her husband remarried, and at the wedding feast his first wife came back and appeared to him, and said:

> Give to me your stocking-band,
> And free me from the troll's harsh hand!

And he leapt right over the trestle table and wanted to run out to meet her, but the others held him back, because they feared the trolls would carry him off if he did go out to her.

After that, she appeared every Christmas Eve on a hillside called Käringabacken. And when she died, the same priest who had buried the wooden figure had an intuition of the fact, and he held a service of thanksgiving for her release. He was called Nilssen, that priest was, and he was parish priest of Virestad, where it all happened – Röckla Farm lies in Virestad parish.

Yes, it was a terrible business, that! And just think, some people actually overhead the trolls in the forest carving the wooden figure. There was one of them who shouted to another: 'Carve big paws – she has big ones, has Tora!'

Klintberg, no. 141, pp. 143–4. Collected in 1930, from an informant born in 1833. These events are alleged to have occurred in the 1670s, and a versified version of the story was written in 1840; the woman's rhymed appeal quoted by this informant comes from those verses.

THE CHANGELING AND THE COLT

Denmark

When a baby has come into the world, the lamp in the room where the birth took place must not be put out, otherwise the baby can easily be carried off by the Underground Folk. At one place in north Jutland, many years ago, it happened that a mother could not get to sleep in the room where she had just given birth so long as the lamp was alight. Then her husband agreed to hold the baby in his arms so as to take good care of it while the room was in darkness. But he fell asleep, without noticing on which arm he was holding the baby; and when he woke up, because something had jerked his arm, he saw a tall woman standing by the bed, and he realized that he was now holding two babies, one on each arm. The woman vanished at once, but he lay there with both the babies, not knowing which of them was his own.

Faced with this problem, he went to the priest, who advised him to try to get hold of an unbroken colt, which would be able to show him the truth of the matter. So then they fetched an unbroken male colt, which was so unruly that three men could barely lead him, and both babies were laid on the ground in their swaddling clothes, and the colt was brought in to smell them. And it was strange to see how, whenever the colt smelled one of them, he remained quite peaceful, and even tried to lick him; but whenever he smelled the other, he went wild, and tried to kick that baby. By this one could tell unmistakably which one was the changeling; but then, while they were all standing there, a tall woman suddenly ran towards them, snatched up the changeling, and disappeared with him.

Thiele, II, pp. 276–7.

THE CHANGELING IN THE OVEN

Sweden

A changeling – that's the kind of child where only its head grows. It's the Rå who makes the exchange, before there is time to baptize the baby.

There was one woman who had got a changeling, and someone advised her to throw it into the baking oven while it was good and hot. There would be no danger; the baby would come out again unburnt. The woman had her doubts, but in the end she obeyed and the baby did come out unburnt. But at that very moment in came the Rå and re-exchanged them, so that the woman got her real baby back. 'You scorch and burn, but I kiss and cuddle,' said the Rå.

Klintberg, no. 145, p. 147. Collected 1902.
A Rå is a forest spirit or water spirit – see
next chapter.

KEEPING THE CHANGELING

Sweden

There were these people living out towards Bogen who had their baby exchanged for a changeling. One evening they couldn't understand what had got into the child, he howled so constantly. Before that, he had never howled. What they had got now was a changeling.

Every Thursday evening they used to whip that baby till he howled. If a changeling is harshly treated, one should get one's own baby back. But they did it all for nothing. He was never really right not at any time in his life, and he grew up to be an idiot.

Klintberg, no. 147, pp. 147–8. Collected
in 1934 from an informant born in 1843.

THE CHANGELING SPEAKS ON THE WAY TO CHURCH

Sweden

There were these people who had a little boy who wasn't like a human being at all. He always had his tongue hanging out of his mouth, and he would tug at it, and dribble. He couldn't talk, and couldn't feed himself, and to cap it all he was hideously ugly. Clever folk said it must be a changeling, and they advised the parents to take him to church with them, and to choose their route in such a way that they would cross three river bridges.

So one Sunday they started off on this journey. And when they came to the third bridge across a river, the father heard a voice saying: 'And where are you off to now, chatterbox?'

The boy, who up to then had never once spoken, replied: 'I'm off to the Dingdongs to see what happenappens in there!'

The father knew that if he heard anything while crossing the river, it would be certain that the child really belonged to the Rå that lived in that river. So now he caught hold of the boy and threw him into the water. And what did he see then, if it wasn't his own little boy who came back up instead!

Klintberg, no. 152, p. 150. Collected in 1918 from an informant born in 1846. 'Dingdongs' means the church, in allusion to its bells, which trolls detest; the changeling's words are distorted and semi-nonsensical.

THE CHANGELING AND THE EGGSHELLS

Denmark

An old woman used to tell how her grandmother knew a woman whose baby had been exchanged by some of the Hill People. The woman did not notice it straight away, even though she did think it odd that the baby would not thrive at all. When it was three years old it still couldn't walk, let alone talk. But there was a cunning woman who advised her to take as many eggshells as she could get hold of and lay them under the cooking pot when she was brewing beer. Next she must lay the child in front of the hearth, so that he could see the many eggshells on the fire. And then she must go outside and keep quite quiet and listen whether the child would speak. If it did, it was sure to be a changeling.

The woman took this advice, and when she had brought the child in and had silently hidden herself, it began to speak: 'I've lived so long that I've three times seen Rold Forest planted and felled, but never, no never, have I seen anybody brewing beer in eggshells!'

The woman rushed in and shouted: 'So you're not my child, but a nasty old troll that I've been working myself to death for for three whole years!'

Then she grabbed the poker and started battering the troll. That put things right, for now her own child came tumbling down the chimney, though with a broken arm, while the nasty troll disappeared at once.

Bødker, pp. 172–3. *Migratory Legends* 5085 'The Changeling'.

INTRODUCTION

Fairy beings, as we saw in Part Six, were believed sometimes to invade human homes and to install one of their own race there as a changeling. They were even more commonly accused of luring humans into their own domain and keeping them imprisoned there, temporarily or permanently. As usual, certain real-life occurrences could be explained in terms of the belief, and thus would confirm it; children do wander away into the hills or woods, where they may later be found again, bewildered and with fantastic tales to excuse their wanderings; people suffering from amnesia or other illnesses may disappear for a while and then return, unable to account for their absence. Such experiences, interpreted as a *bergtagning* ('mountain abduction'), form a factual background for the more elaborated legends of children or adults stolen by fairies and/or rescued from fairyland.

Where, then, was the boundary between this world and the Otherworld believed to lie? On the whole, Scandinavian traditions do not envisage the Otherworld as a remote realm, but as lying so close alongside normal space that crossing from one into the other is only too easy. 'The Old Bride' and 'The Man Who Loved a Huldre' make this point clearly; in one, the Hidden Folk live inside a mound on the farm meadow, in the other they are in a peatbog just beside the road. But mounds and bogs, however close they are, are not as fully controlled and exploited by mankind as ploughed fields and pastures are; they are marginal areas, and hence are readily supposed to belong to supernatural creatures and to be subject to certain taboos (see 'Plomgårds Mound', p. 183 and 'The Fire at Stadarfell', p. 183). Humans who enter the Otherworld risk great dangers. They may vanish out of normal time and space for ever; if they do return, they may be permanently damaged, mentally or physically. In Icelandic tales, this damage is often symbolized by an indelible bluish-black mark which those who return from the Otherworld bear on their faces, and the intervention of a priest or a 'cunning man' is often necessary if they are to be brought back. Some tales, such as 'The Girl Whom the Elves Lured Away', teach that such returns are not in fact to be desired – those who have been too long in the Otherworld are no longer truly human.

It is also often implied that to enter the Otherworld deliberately is a sin. Scandinavian accounts of encounters between humans and fairy folk can be quite frank in their references to the sexual relationship involved, and there are in addition many instances where one may suspect that references to dancing with elves, or accepting food and gifts from them, are discreet ways of alluding obliquely to the same idea. It is probably no accident that the victims in some stories ('The Old Bride', 'The Man Who Loved a Huldre', 'The Bridal Crown') are young men or women who are about to be married; the tales seem to carry a half-hidden warning that chastity before marriage is essential, and that to give way under the strains and temptations of the betrothal period would entail supernatural danger. The Otherworld lover may come between the human being and his true sweetheart, as in 'The Man Who Loved a Huldre', or his Otherworld bastard child may return to shame him, as in 'The Elf-Woman Brings Her Baby for Baptism'; both motifs were used by Ibsen in *Peer Gynt*. On a more general level, tales about people carried off into the Otherworld often imply a warning against wandering out of doors after dark, and against going far from the beaten track; they could therefore be useful in restraining rash, unconventional behaviour, especially among the young.

Legends also tell of those who entered the Otherworld innocently, resisted its temptations, and returned unscathed – or almost unscathed. One widespread story concerns a midwife who, in the course of her professional duties, is summoned to help a fairy woman in labour; the visit itself does her no harm, though later she is blinded in one eye to punish her for disobedience and spying on the fairies. Yet so strong is the traditional dread of Otherworld visits that the midwife legend sometimes takes a more sinister turn: one version in Thiele's Danish collection says the woman was held captive a long time by the elves, and when her husband did rescue her she was so changed that 'he never had the least profit or pleasure from her. She sat at the kitchen table and wept continuously, and she was dumb, and remained so.'

A more cheerful popular legend, ending in triumph for the human hero, is Migratory Legend 6045, 'The Cup (or Drinking Horn) Stolen from the Fairies', represented here by 'The Chalice in Flakkebjerg Church', and also by an amusing Norwegian version, 'The Solunna Hag.' In many cases the story purports to explain the provenance of some unusually fine vessel belonging to a church or to some ancient family. The most famous instance is the Horn of Oldenburg, now displayed in the Royal Collection in Copenhagen, although in the sixteenth century it belonged to the German Counts of Oldenburg.

According to a German chronicle of 1599, Count Otto von Oldenburg acquired it in the year 990 by stealing it from a forest fairy who had offered him a drink; he tossed the liquor over his shoulder instead of swallowing it – fortunately for him, since it was so poisonous that it burnt the hair from his horse's back. The enraged fairy cursed him, saying his descendants would never know peace. This corresponds well with Scandinavian versions of the type, except that in these there is no curse; instead, the adventure generally ends in a frenzied chase in which the hero barely escapes from the owners of the stolen goblet.

In the mountain areas of Norway and Sweden, there is a close connection between one particular aspect of farming life and legends about meetings with supernatural beings. It was customary for women to leave the farms in the summer months and take the cattle up on to the mountain pastures. There they would live in the mountain dairies (*seter*), alone or in small groups, keeping watch on the cows and making large quantities of butter and cheese. It was believed that the Huldu Folk, the fairies who lived permanently in the mountains, also used the same pastures, and that their cattle might occasionally become visible. Various rituals were enjoined to avoid annoying them; in particular, it was thought necessary to leave one cow-stall unoccupied, in case a Huldre woman wished to put one of her cows there. The general rules of politeness, caution and generosity which were meant to govern human attitudes towards fairies applied on the *seter* with additional force, since there the humans were so near the fairies' own domains. If all went well, the Huldu Folk were good neighbours; but if not, the women and the cattle would suffer for it.

Seter life was no doubt pleasant in many ways, despite the hard work it entailed. But it generated anxieties too, both for the women and for their families in the valleys, since their freedom and isolation made them more vulnerable to seduction or even to violence and rape. The robber legend of 'The Twelve Robbers' in Part Two reflects this fear; so too, on the supernatural plane, does the widespread belief that a male Hulder might woo a girl at a *seter*, persuade her to marry him, and then keep her captive for ever. Two story-patterns evolved from this. In one, the girl herself is suspicious and reluctant, and tricks her fairy wooer into telling her which herbs have the power to drive him away. In the other, she succumbs, but the wedding is interrupted in the nick of time by her human sweetheart. Often it is said that some item of bridal finery given to her by the Hulder was kept as an heirloom by her family, or was given to the village church, in the same way as the stolen drinking vessels discussed above. Usually these two story-patterns stress the defeat of the supernatural lover and the fortunate escape of the girl; one example, 'Anne Rykhus' (p. 219), shows interesting modifications in that the standard ending has been altered to fit the personality of a real woman with a local reputation as a seer.

Some men also had work, as huntsmen, fur-trappers and charcoal burners, which took them to the mountains and forests and caused them to spend many weeks there alone. In Sweden, the supernatural beliefs associated with such work centre on the *skogsrå* ('Forest Ruler'), a female being with power over the forest and all the wild animals in it. She was thought to live alone, not in communities like trolls and Huldu Folk; she was said to be beautiful when seen from in front, but to have a hollow back like a half-rotted log, all covered in moss. Many accounts stress her wish to make love with human men, whom she rewards by magically helping their work. For charcoal-burners, she will keep up their fires while they sleep; for hunters, she ensures that their rifles never miss, and uses her power as mistress of wild beasts to send them plenty of game. Such fantasies are evidently wish-fulfilments, both erotically and as regards easy success in work. However, since sexual intercourse with Otherworld beings was thought sinful, there are also legends warning that a *skogsrå* works by trickery, for instance by deluding a man into thinking he is lying with his human sweetheart, when it is really her. Like all forest spirits, she is also held responsible when people lose their way there, wander in circles, are overcome with panic, or awake to find themselves in a ditch. Sometimes it is said she eventually drives her human lovers mad; she should therefore be driven off by any of the standard Scandinavian ways of exorcizing fairies – gunfire, throwing steel, carrying certain plants, uttering the name of Jesus, and so forth.

In Iceland, one high-risk occupation which took men to wild and solitary places was gathering gulls' eggs and trapping puffins and other birds on their nests, for which they had to be let down the cliff on ropes. When lives were lost through unexpected fraying of the rope, this might be blamed on the malevolence of cliff-dwelling giant trolls. Such trolls were also accused of drawing fishing boats on to the rocks and into caves. Legends on this theme emphasize the troll's huge, hairy grey hand.

Next comes a group of legends about the 'Wild Hunt', a theme well known in northern France and in Germany, and occurring sporadically in England too. It concerns a spectral or demonic huntsman who rides through the forests or across the sky, often in pursuit of woodland spirits. In parts of southern Sweden his quarry is the *skogsrå*, while in

Denmark it is the Elle-woman (female elf) or even sometimes a mermaid. This type of tale is exemplified here by two stories collected in this century, a Swedish one recorded in 1944 from a man of eighty-four, and a Norwegian one sent in response to the *Allers Family Journal* folktale survey in 1938. The former, brief and unadorned, is told with total conviction; the latter, evidently the work of a more skilled raconteur from the educated classes, is designed to make a good impression in a story-telling session, yet there is still an underlying implication that the story is at least semi-credible.

The tale of the supernatural huntsman and his fairy quarry has developed over the centuries from an earlier type, first attested as a sermon *exemplum* in the late twelfth century, in which the quarry is the ghost of an adulteress, doomed to be perpetually pursued and speared by her lover's ghost. A link with ghosts is also prominent in another type of Wild Hunt legend where it is not a single hunter but a whole host that sweeps through the air – a leading huntsman, his companions and their spectral horses and hounds. The leader is often said to be a king or nobleman condemned to hunt forever because in his lifetime love of sport led him into sin. Seen from this angle, Wild Hunt legends belong with those ghost stories which express the resentment of country folk against upper-class landowners; the enclosure of land for hunting reserves and damage to crops from reckless riders had long been abuses against which the peasantry had no redress. Swedish folk narrators say that the leader of the Wild Hunt, whom they call 'Oden', is a ghost of this type, a sharpshooter who went hunting on Sundays and is therefore doomed to pursue the *skogsrå* till the end of time. Many scholars (but not all) identify this figure with the Nordic god Odin, but even if the name is identical it would be rash to argue backwards from it that in heathen times Odin led a Wild Hunt, for medieval sources have nothing to say upon this point. In Norway there is less stress on the individual hunter; the Wild Hunt is envisaged as a horde of wicked spirits, the *oskorei*, who rush across the skies on winter nights, especially just before Christmas. Their name probably means the 'Terrible Host', and they may be thought of as ghosts, or demons, or a mixture of both. They are said to carry people off with them, or to invade houses at Christmas time as fairies do, but far more destructively. It is generally agreed that all these beliefs were strongly reinforced by misinterpretations of natural phenomena – winter gales, whirlwinds, the yelping cries of flocks of migrating birds.

Rivers, lakes and waterfalls were thought to be the homes of solitary supernatural beings, often dangerous to man. The commonest is the type called *näck* in Swedish, *nökk* in Norwegian, and *nykur* in Icelandic – a name derived from an ancient Germanic word for 'water monster'. Other names for him are *fossegrim*, 'Waterfall Goblin', and *strömkarl*, 'River Man'. Several interesting conceptions are embodied in the stories about him, and the moral ambiguity often attaching to supernatural beings is particularly striking in his case. His evil side shows itself in his responsibility for drownings, especially of children, as Faye describes (p. 230). There is a common anecdote, here given in a Danish version, telling how he turns himself into a horse to tempt children to mount him and then carries them into deep water to gobble them up. The tale of a voice crying 'the hour is come but not the man' (see Part Three, p. 71) can be presented as the story of an implacable *nökk* demanding human prey. All such legends are of course of great value to the community by training children and others to be wary of dangerous waters.

On the other hand, the *nökk* or *näck* is a fine musician, and many human fiddlers are said to owe their skill to his teaching – though at some risk, for he requires the offering of a black cat, or a meaty bone, or some drops of human blood, otherwise he will drown the would-be pupil. Moreover, the *näck*'s music can be sinister, like the Devil's; the tale of 'The Dancers Who Could Not Stop' (p. 231) is very like the Devil-legends at Hårga and Hruni (above, pp. 68–9, 74). So strong was the moral disapprobation of dancing, with its associations with drunkenness and sexual freedom, that any supernatural being connected with it would readily be presented as demonic in stories intended to frighten and to warn. In total contrast, another widespread tale about the musical water-spirit represents him as an innocent, cheerful being who longs for salvation and may well attain it (see p. 232).

Another ambiguous creature is the Mill Spirit, known as *kverngubbe*, 'Old Man of the Mill', or *kvernknurren*, 'Mill Growler'. Like the strong waters he symbolizes, he can work for good or ill; his strength turns the mill-wheel, but he can also drown people, and may capriciously cause the wheel to jam so that no corn can be ground. In so far as he is benevolently inclined, he is akin to the house-spirits, and like them must be propitiated with small offerings. On the other hand, when he shows himself visibly he is described as an ugly giant, and the commonest anecdote about him tells how he is put to flight by a lad who scalds him with hot tar.

Finally, a group of tales concerning sea-spirits in human form (the sea-serpents and dragons have been discussed in Part One). The commonest name for them in Icelandic, Norwegian and Danish is *marmen-*

nil, mermann, or the like. It would be pedantic to avoid the obviously related English words 'merman' and 'mermaid', but it must be stressed that the fish-tail so essentially implied by the English word is by no means central to the Scandinavian conception of sea-beings, which are far more commonly humanoid in appearance. Curiously, though the sea is dangerous, Scandinavian mermen are usually shown as benevolent; in some tales they prove their gratitude to humans by warning them of storms, while in others they give wise advice – though this may be double-edged or difficult to apply. Like most supernatural beings, they may abduct humans to be their lovers. 'The Forsaken Merman' is a Danish tale based on this theme, made famous in England by Matthew Arnold's poem; so too, of course, is Hans Andersen's literary variant, 'The Little Mermaid', which also draws on the belief that water-spirits may attain salvation.

In Sweden, water-spirits called *sjorå* are said to inhabit either lakes or the open sea. The males may be aggressive, and may try to capsize fishing boats; the females, like their forest counterpart the *skogsrå*, are helpful to men, bringing them good catches and warning them of storms. All the Scandinavian sea-spirits are imagined to have a world of their own on the sea-bed, with farms and pastures and cattle. Their fine cattle sometimes come up on land to graze, and any man who can capture one, or whose cows mate with a sea-bull, will greatly improve his livestock. This underwater world can also take the form of a magical island which occasionally rises to the surface for a brief while – a belief based upon experience of mirages and on the fact that floating mats of vegetation are sometimes found inexplicably drifting on the open sea.

The last story comes from Iceland. It is a version of a tale told wherever the large grey seal is found – not only in Norway, Iceland and the Faroes, but also in Ireland and Scotland – to the effect that seals are really enchanted human beings in animal skin, and that he who steals a female seal's skin can compel her to be his wife. Needless to say, like all fairy wives she eventually resumes her original form and escapes from her husband, though not without grief at losing her human children. Behind this shapely and pathetic tale lies a quite serious belief which once was widespread and backed with alleged proofs, such as the human-looking head and eyes and skeleton of seals, and the frequency of webbed fingers and toes as a deformity in human babies. Some said seals were descended from Pharaoh's soldiers, drowned in the Red Sea; in Sweden, the seal's barking cry was supposed to say 'Pharaoh! Pharaoh!' Certain families claimed to be descended from marriages of seals and humans, and to be good fishermen in consequence. As ever, the legend, as distinct from the fairytale, points the hearer back into the real world, and even its most seemingly fanciful inventions are interwoven with realities.

The Old Bride

Denmark

Once, when a wedding was being celebrated at North Broby, near Odense, the bride left the farmyard during the dancing and, without thinking what she was doing, went as far as a certain mound in the field there, where the Elle Folk too were having a merry dance on that very day. So, as she drew near the mound, she saw that it was standing open, raised up on red posts, and a man came and offered her a goblet of wine. She took it, drank it all, and allowed herself to be led into the dance. But as soon as that dance ended, she remembered her husband and went back to the farm.

Then it seemed to her that everything around the neighbourhood had quite changed, and when she came to the village she could not recognize the farmyards or the houses, and could hear no sounds of the wedding feast. Eventually she stood outside the farm where her husband lived, but when she went inside she recognized nobody, and nobody recognized her. There was just one old woman who, when she heard the bride's lamentations, exclaimed: 'So it was you who disappeared a hundred years ago, at my grandfather's brother's wedding!'

At these words, the old bride fell to the ground, and lay dead on the spot.

Thiele, II, pp. 219–20.

The Stolen Child

Iceland

At one time there was a couple living at Holar in Laxardal; they were well-to-do, and well liked by everyone. They had taken in a boy called Erlend as a foster-child; he was about three or four years old when this story happened. It was one evening when the whole household was out in the hayfield working there, or out gathering wood, except for one sturdy old woman who stayed at home to see that Erlend and the other children came to no harm. Some time in the course of the morning the old woman thought she saw the master of the house come to the door and lead the boy Erlend away, and she supposed he was going to the hayfield with him, and thought no more about it. Later, when they all came in for their midday meal, she asked about Erlend, but no one had seen him, and the master of the house absolutely denied having come to the door as the old woman thought he had. Everyone was full of foreboding at the boy's disappearance, and they looked for him far and wide, but in vain.

At that time, Arnthor was living at Sand in Athaldal. He was skilled in magic, and had often been able to help those who had been charmed away by the Huldu Folk or attacked by witchcraft. The couple from Holar decided to send word to Arnthor and invite him to visit them, to find out what had become of the boy and to get him back, if possible. Arnthor said that he did indeed know what had become of the boy. He was with the Hidden People who lived inside the stepping-stones upstream from Holar Farm, but it would not be too easy to get him back from there. Then he told the messenger to go back home, and said that he must come to him again if there was no news of Erlend within a week. And with that, the messenger went home.

Now, on the seventh day after Erlend's disappearance, everyone was sitting in the main room for their midday meal. And when they were least expecting it, the boy Erlend walked in at the door, and he looked just the same as he had always done, except that he had got a black spot on his left cheek.

Then the boy was asked where he had been, and what had happened to make him disappear and then return. He tells them that on the day he disappeared someone who seemed to be his foster-father, the farmer, had come to the door of the room and had led him away. He had gone off from the farm with him, and had crossed a small brook which was alongside the path. Now, when they had gone on a short way from the brook, they came to a small but beautiful house. Outside it, there is a woman dressed in dark blue, and she welcomes Erlend and is as kind as can be to him, but the boy does not like her at all. And when Erlend had been in the woman's house for some days, he burst out crying bitterly one day, and the woman tried all kinds of things to comfort him, but could not. She shows him gold and jewels and various treasures to divert him, and it is all no use. And so in the end the woman takes Erlend and brings him back across the same brook as was mentioned

208

before. There she leaves him, and as she is leaving she gives him a slap in the face, saying that's what he gets for all the trouble he's caused. And when the woman had left him, he saw the farm and found his way home. But the black mark he had on the cheek was due to her slap.

Erlend lived to be old, and was a wealthy farmer; many men are descended from him. But they say he had a black mark on his cheek as long as he lived.

Árnason, I, p. 49–50. The seer mentioned is a real person, Arnór or Arnthór Ólafsson, who lived in the seventeenth century.

THE GIRL WHOM THE ELVES LURED AWAY

Iceland

In the east of Iceland, it happened that a farmer's daughter disappeared from her home; they hunted for her far and wide but never found her, and her parents were very distressed. The farmer went to see a priest whom he knew to be more learned in many matters than most others were. The priest received him kindly, and the farmer begged him to find some good way of knowing whether his daughter was alive or dead. The priest then told him that she had been taken away by the elves, and that it would give him no joy to see her again. The farmer said that he could not believe that, and begged the priest to help him to get her back, and in the end, since the farmer pressed him so hard, the priest appointed a certain evening and told the farmer to come and see him then.

So now the farmer comes to the priest on the appointed evening, and when everyone was in bed the priest tells the farmer to come outside with him, and there he sees a horse, saddled and bridled. The priest mounts, and tells the farmer to mount and sit behind him, and so he does. Then they ride off, the priest and the farmer; the farmer cannot tell how long they ride till they come to the sea; there the priest rides into the water and so along the shore for a long way, till he comes to a high cliff or rock, and rides right up to the foot of it and halts at a certain spot on the cliff-face. All at once the cliff opens, as if there was a door in it; the farmer sees a light burning inside, and the whole place is bright with that light; he sees people going to and fro in there, both men and women. There he sees one woman go by; her face was quite black, except for a white cross on her brow. The priest asks the farmer how he likes this woman with the cross. 'Not at all,' says he. The priest says: 'This woman is your daughter, and I will get her out, if you want me to, but she has been bewitched into a troll through staying among these folk.' The farmer says that he does not want this at all, and begs the priest to come away as fast as he can, and says he has no wish to stay a moment longer. Then the priest turns his horse and they ride back by the same road and come home again, without anyone knowing of their journey. The farmer went back home very sad and troubled, and that is the end of his story.

People say this must have happened only a few years after this country became Christian.

Árnason, I, p. 56.

THE MAN WHO LOVED A HULDRE

Norway

A few hundred years ago there lived at Todneim a man who had a son called Lars. The father was rich, and the lad was betrothed to a girl at Raustein. One Saturday evening he went off to visit his sweetheart, and as he was passing near a peat-bog he heard some music coming from there. He was curious to see what it was, and who was celebrating Christmas in such a spot. He saw a light through the mist, and softly crept towards it. There were four men there, sitting round a table, wearing tall caps and drinking from silver beer-mugs. They had thick beards, but were no bigger than a five-year-old boy. The musician was sitting on a grass tussock, playing a marvellous tune which Lars had never heard before. There were four girls dancing, and Lars just stood and stared at them, for he had never seen such skilful dancing before, nor such pretty girls either. They wore bright green dresses, and they were prettier and more attractive than any he had ever seen, and more elegant than the finest ladies in Stavanger. As it happened, he did not see any of them from behind, and anyway he was not suspecting any evil. One of them came up and offered him a drink. Lars was a bit startled, but she looked so innocent, and he was thirsty too, so he drank, and it tasted good. Then a sort of door opened in a mound, and Lars went in with her – but he would never say a word about what happened to him in there. Next morning he came to his senses to find himself in a ditch in the peat-bog, feeling dead-tired and very unwell.

He never paid much attention to his sweetheart after that day; they did marry, but they had no children and were not happy. All this had happened around Christmas time, and the following Michaelmas people heard a baby crying down in the peat-bog, and during the long dark evenings Lars would sometimes leave the house and stay out late into the night. His wife knew very well that he had been somewhere he should not have been, yet she could not bring herself to complain to the priest, because she knew that if she did that Lars would be barred from taking Communion, and then there would be no hope left for him and he would go into the elf-mound for good and all.

Christiansen, pp. 102–3. Seen from behind, she-elves have tails or hollow backs which betray their true nature.

THE ELF-WOMAN BRINGS HER BABY FOR BAPTISM

Iceland

When Gisli, the ancestor of the Rev. Eyolf Gislason of Mula, was living at Hagi in Bartharstrond, it happened one Sunday during the service that a child's cradle was carried right into the church, though those who carried it were invisible. A woman was walking behind the cradle, and everybody saw her clearly. This woman goes straight to where Gisli was sitting and addresses him thus: 'I declare that you, Gisli, are truly the father of that baby lying in the cradle, as truly as I am his mother.' Gisli flatly denies being this baby's father. Then this woman looks very angry and says that he will pay for having denied that he was the baby's father, so that now it could not receive baptism. 'For ten generations after you,' she says, 'your descendants will suffer from constant exhaustion. However, I also decree that more good will come of them than seems likely.' Then she pulls off the coverlet that lay on the cradle and throws it into the chancel, and then she disappears, and the cradle too is snatched away. This coverlet was made into a chasuble, and it was given to the church at Brjanslæk, and it is called the elves' chasuble.

At the time when the Rev. Eyolf Gislason's parents were living at Brjanslæk, and Eyolf himself was four years old, he was in such great pain and sickness that it looked as if it would bring him to his grave, and they tried everything one could think of to soothe the pain, and yet nothing was any use. His mother knew a good deal about medicine, and her advice had often been helpful, and when she had tried everything she could think of, she sent someone to the church to fetch the so-called elves' chasuble. When it came, she wrapped it round the child at the place where the pain was; soon a change came, so that the pain was soothed and soon disappeared entirely.

This is true; but whether the chasuble had this power from the elves, or whether the appointed hour of healing had come from God, I do not know.

Árnason, I, p. 89; from the manuscripts of Ólaf Sveinsson of Purkey (1780–1845).

MIDWIFE TO A FAIRY

Denmark

One day, an Elle-woman was in labour, and she sent word to the midwife at Dunkaer to come and help her. When this woman had helped to bring the baby into the world, the Elle-woman gave her some salve which she was to smear on to his eyes, but in the process of doing so she got some of the salve on her fingers, and so it happened later that she rubbed her own eyes with it.

On the way home she realized that something strange had happened to her power of sight, for as she walked past a field of rye and looked at it, she became aware that it was swarming with little Elle-folk, who were running around snapping the ears off the rye-stalks.

'What do you think you're doing?' she exclaimed when she saw them stealing the grain from the field.

But the answer she got was: 'Oh ho! If you can see us, so much the worse for you!'

And with that they crowded round her and tore her eyes out.

Thiele, II, p. 202–3. *Migratory Legends* 5070 'Midwife to the Fairies'.

THE CHALICE IN FLAKKEBJERG CHURCH

Denmark

There was a farm-worker, once, who was riding from Skørpinge to Flakkebjerg. As he came up to a mound in which trolls lived, it was raised up on four posts, and he saw that inside it, in one corner, two trolls were fighting. He spoke to them and asked what they were fighting over, and one of them said that it was none of his business, but the other, who had only one leg, handed him a goblet and said that if he drank from it he would understand.

The man immediately tossed all the liquid in the goblet over his head and rode off with it. Both the trolls ran after him, and One-Leg came very close to catching him. Then the other troll, whose name was Two-Legs, shouted to him that he ought to leave the road and ride across the fields, which he did. At this One-Leg was so angry that he picked up a great rock and hurled it after the man, but it fell into a bog near Flakkebjerg; he had gripped it so tight that there are still finger-marks on it.

The man rode on, and by the time he drew near the wall of the churchyard, One-Leg had nearly caught up with him again, but the man jumped over the wall, and so now he was safe. At that very moment One-Leg caught his horse by the tail and flung the horse over the wall after him. It was dead by the time they found it. But the goblet can still be seen in Flakkebjerg Church, and one can still see that it was scraped against the wall, which has flattened it slightly.

As regards the rock, it is also sometimes said that there was a troll who lived over on Fyn who was angry with the priest at Flakkebjerg and took the rock and flung it at him, but that it fell in the bog, and that one can still see the marks of his fingers on it.

Bødker, pp. 37–8. *Migratory Legends* 6045 'The Drinking Vessel Stolen from the Fairies'. Some variants explain that riding *across* a ploughed field makes a pattern of crosses where the horse's tracks intersect a furrow, and that trolls fear crosses.

THE SOLUNNA HAG

Norway

My granny told me this story many times when I was little. I never grew tired of hearing it, and every time I went out to Byness on a visit she had to tell me again about the Solunna Hag. That's why I remember the story so well.

Solunna is the name of a very steep slope on the west side of Byness headland. Because of the way it faces, the sun never touches it, and that's probably how it got its name ('Sunless'). Inside that mountain, half-way up the slope, there once lived an old troll woman known as the Solunna Hag.

It happened one day long ago that the verger of Løveset Church had to ride over to the church very early one Christmas morning to get things ready for the service. As he rode past Solunna the wall of the mountain opened, making a cleft like a doorway, and out came the Solunna Hag herself. The verger was riding a dapple-brown horse, which took fright and leapt to one side, and the verger began crossing himself. But she was in a good mood, was the hag, and held out a big goblet and asked whether the man would like to taste her Christmas present. Now the verger was none too sure that everything was as it ought to be, and he thought that in any case he ought to be wary of drinking a troll's drink. So he took the goblet, but tossed what was in it over his shoulder, and set spurs to his horse. That drink certainly was strong stuff, for a few drops touched the horse's rump, and where they

214

touched it all the hair was singed off and the skin burnt. But the hag was not at all pleased that the verger scorned her gift, and shrieked at him: 'Wait, just you wait till I've put my Rolling Breeches on!'

She ran back into the mountain, pulled on her Rolling Breeches, and then down the path she came after the verger, as fast as a wheel. The verger soon realized that the only thing which might save him would be if he could reach the church before the hag caught him and if he could ring the church bell, and it was quite clear to him that his life depended on it. He forced his horse on as hard as he could, though the horse was half dead. Even before he was properly inside the church he grabbed the bell-rope and began ringing with all his might. The hag by then had just reached the crest of the slope facing the church, and as soon as she heard the church bells ringing she turned to stone, and there she remained, standing at the corner of the road.

The traces of all this can be seen on Byness to this day. There is the cleft in the rocks on Solunna which she came out by, and the big boulder beside the road is called 'The Solunna Hag' to this day.

Christiansen, pp. 91–2; sent in by Endre P. Ugelstad. *Migratory Legends* 6045, but with more stress on topography than on the goblet.

TROLLS AS BLACKSMITHS

Denmark

In the neighbourhood of Sundby on the island of Mors stands a mound inside which there lives a troll who is a blacksmith. At night one can hear him working. Also, some way inland from that mound, beside the village of Sœlberg, there is a sandbank in which this smith has a second workshop; one can hear the thud of heavy hammer blows coming from it. At midnight he often rides through the air from one of his work-places to the other on a headless horse, with his hammer in his hand and all his apprentices and workmen following him. It is not a good thing to meet him.

In the parish of Bur, by Nygårds Forest, there are three large mounds;

in one lives a Mountain Man who is a blacksmith and has his workshop there. Sometimes at night one can see fire coming up out of the top of the mound and, oddly enough, going in again through the side of it; this is how he heats his iron. If anyone wants to have some ironwork forged by him, all one has to do is to lay the iron on the mound with a shilling beside it to pay for the work, and also one must say aloud what kind of object it is that one needs. Next morning the shilling has been taken, and the work one has asked for is lying there, well made and properly finished off.

Thiele, II, p. 181–2. The first anecdote has points of similarity with Wild Hunt legends – see pp. 225–9 below.

GOOD NEIGHBOURS

Norway

There used to be many of the Hidden Folk around Tesse in the old days. At one mountain dairy called Brimiseter there was once a young dairymaid named Embjør. She had a lot of work to do all summer, and many cows to milk. As the summer wore on she developed such a bad sore on her finger that she was in great distress, for the finger gave her so much pain that she was at her wits' end what to do about it. It was the milking that was the worst.

Early one morning she was sitting at her milking and crying with pain, the finger was so bad. As she sat there trying her best, in came a girl of the Hidden Folk, with a milking pail over her arm and a little wooden pot in her hand. The girl spoke to Embjør, saying: 'You poor thing! Mother and I have seen how hard it is for you to do the milking with that sore finger of yours. I'd willingly do your milking for you, but you know how it is with such as me – if I were to milk your cows, they'd only give blood, for sure. But look here! I've brought something which you can put on your finger, so that you'll be all right again.' She handed the wooden pot to Embjør and said: 'Take the pot, and use what's in it for your finger. And keep the pot itself, as a gift from me, to remind you we've been neighbours this summer.'

Embjør smeared the ointment she had received from the Huldre girl on her finger and bandaged it well, and next morning the finger was perfectly all right. As for the pot, she took good care of it, and it still exists to this day.

Grimstad, p. 48.

BAD NEIGHBOURS

Norway

In our district there was a mountain dairy which was notorious because there were so many Hidden Folk up there. There was also a dairymaid who had spent many summers at that shieling. One day, during the last summer she spent there, she noticed an old woman sitting in the doorway of a house she had never seen before. The old woman was sitting there with her sewing, and it all looked so quiet and peaceful! The dairymaid walked towards her, hoping to have a chat, but then the old woman and all just vanished.

Now as bad luck would have it, it happened one evening not long after this that the dairymaid threw some boiling water out of the dairy door without saying anything first. She heard a child scream dreadfully. She was most upset, for she realized at once that she had forgotten to give any warning.

Well, on one of the very last days she was to spend up there at the shieling, along came an old woman she didn't know. This old woman said they had been neighbours during all the summers the dairymaid had been at the shieling – 'You've never done me any harm before, but now you've burnt my child very badly, and you'll have to pay for it.' Then she was gone. Next day, the dairymaid fell and broke her leg. As she needed to be nursed, they had to come and carry her down to the farm, and on the way down she said that as for the Hidden Folk, they could have the dairy all to themselves as far as she was concerned, and she wished them joy of it. At that, she heard shrill laughter from inside a mound a little way off.

The following winter, when men from the farm went up to spend a few nights at the shieling to fetch in hay and wood from the stores there, they found it impossible to keep the cart-horses quiet up there. They were restless all the time, and broke out of their stalls at night. On the last evening they were there, a man walked in, with his shirt-sleeves rolled up, and told them he had just slaughtered one of their horses. And with that, he was gone. Next day, as they were going home and had driven some way along the road, one cart-horse fell and broke a leg. There was nothing to be done but to slaughter it and leave the cart standing there until they could come back up the mountain with another horse to fetch the load home.

Grimstad, pp. 67–8.

THE BRIDAL CROWN

Norway

In Numedal there once lived a girl who was so lovely that even a Tusse fell in love with her, but although this Underground Man promised to give her a fine farm and much livestock – in fact, anything she could wish for – if she would let herself be betrothed to him, she still remained true to her former sweetheart. When the Tusse saw that he was gaining nothing by fair means, he seized the girl and carried her off by force. Accompanied by a whole crowd of Tusses, he was already on his way with his kidnapped bride to the church in the Underworld to marry her there, when her own sweetheart had the good luck to come upon the tracks of his vanished bride. He caught up with the bridal procession and shot steel over the girl's head, at which the whole enchantment disappeared, and he got back not only his betrothed but also a magnificent silver crown which the Tusses had set on her head.

This crown is still to be seen in the valley, and since it is believed to bring good luck to every bride who wears it, it is lent out for almost every important wedding.

Faye, p. 25. Migratory Legends 6005 'The
Interrupted Fairy Wedding'. It was custom-
ary for a bride to wear a crown in tradi-
tional Norwegian weddings.

ANNE RYKHUS

Norway

The Hidden People tried hard to draw Christians into their world. Sometimes they would lure away the young boys who herded the goats, and sometimes grown men, but the best of all was if they could contrive to marry a Christian girl.

At a mountain dairy called Jenså there was at one time a dairymaid named Anne Rykhus. She used to stay out late at pasture, because every evening an attractive young man used to come to her there, and he made himself so agreeable and spoke so persuasively, that in the end she agreed to marry him. There used to be dogs at the shielings in the old days, for guarding the herds, and Anne too had a dog with her. This dog knew quite well that it wasn't a real man that came there every evening, and in the end he ran off down to the village, where he acted so strangely that the farmer guessed at once that there was something going on up at the shieling which was not as it should be. He took his gun, as he generally did, and went up the mountains with the dog.

As soon as he reached the spot, he saw a crowd of people with horses saddled and bridled, looking as if it must be for a bridal procession. He could see Anne herself too: she was mounted on a glossy black mare, and was dressed up as a bride, with a gold crown and all sorts of other finery. A handsome young fellow stood at her side. They were just about to ride off, so the man had to do something quickly. 'In the name of Jesus!' said he, and fired a shot over the heads of the crowd. Everything vanished as if it had sunk into the ground. Only Anne was left, and she just sat and stared straight ahead of her. 'How are things with you?' asked the man. 'I want to go home to the village,' said she, and began to weep.

He took her home, but from that day she was never like other folk. She used to say that when the farmer fired that shot up there at the dairy, the man she had been about to marry shouted to her: 'You'll see much, but understand little.' And so it was. She could see all sorts of beings which were invisible to others. Sometimes she would see the path so full of them that she would take a stick and drive them away. She could also see things which would come true later. She once declared she could see wagons on wheels going up the valley of their own accord, and fifty years later the railway came through Fron, just outside the house where she had lived. What's more, she declared she could see things like huge birds high in the sky, and some years later aircraft passed over the village. After some years had gone by, Anne Rykhus was no longer considered to be odd, but wise.

Grimstad, pp. 41–2. Migratory Legends 6005.

SHOOTING A DOG AND A CAT

Sweden

This happened somewhere in an upland parish. Two old fellows were out hunting one autumn. One evening they came to a mountain hut where they meant to spend the night; but when they went in, they saw that there were two women inside there, and that one of them was just about to give birth to a baby.

Since the women didn't seem to have anything to wrap the baby in, one of the men took off his neckerchief and gave it to them, and the other gave them some other garment. The women were very pleased and began chatting with these old fellows. Then the women left, and the one who had borne the baby said: 'Tomorrow one of you will shoot my dog, and the other my cat.'

Next day, they shot a wolf, and a lynx. After that, they believed that these women were Skogsrå. Johan Ersson of Flata is descended from one of these forest huntsmen.

Klintberg, no. 24, p. 89. Collected in
1908 from an informant born in 1824.

A Reward for Making Love

Sweden

There was an old fellow in this village who was called Jan Nilssen. He and his maidservant were away fom home, mowing hay up on the mountain. They slept in the barn. During the night the girl saw a woman come into the barn and lie down beside the old fellow. This stranger was beautiful to look at, but from behind she looked like a fir tree all covered in rough bark.

Next morning the girl asked her master what kind of a woman had come visiting him during the night.

'You just keep quiet about that,' says he, 'for today I'm going to get myself a fine big buck.'

An hour or so later, along came a huge great bear which lay down on a rock right in front of the barn, so that the man could shoot him with no trouble at all.

'So now you see,' says he, 'that I've been very well paid for taking her into my bed.'

It was of course the Skogsrå he had been lying with, or so the old folks have always said. But it all happened a long while ago.

Klintberg, no. 25, p. 89. Collected 1912 from an informant born in 1843.

The Widows

Sweden

There was a man called Olle Skytt. He lived in Hästhagen by the river, near Haugsjön, and he was the best huntsman there ever was. He only needed to blow on his gun-barrel for a little while and the whole place would be full of wild animals, which came and clustered round his cottage. Birds would sit and sing on his chimney, and elks and hares would come and wander around outside his windows.

Now when he was dead his widow sat on the edge of the bed and wept, for she was thinking of herself and the three children; what would become of them? Then in came ever such a fine-looking woman, with her skirt trailing behind her like a long green train. And she sat herself down beside the widow, and she said to her: 'Now then, don't you cry! It's far worse for me. I had seven children by him, I did,' said she.

Klintberg, no. 28, pp. 90–1. Collected in 1912 from an informant born in 1829. This story assumes the hearer will recognize the Skogsrå by her green clothes and the train which conceals her tail.

THE BISHOP AND THE CLIFF-TROLLS

Iceland

The island of Drangey lies roughly in the middle of Skagafjord, rather nearer to the west shore than the east. It is like a sheer stack of rock, about a hundred fathoms high at its highest point, and is uninhabited. But yet it has its value, and is full of people in the spring, for many men go out there to hunt sea-birds which nest in hordes on the cliffs all round the island, and also to fish. The island belonged to the See of Holar in the Middle Ages, so the Bishops of Holar controlled the island and had most of the profit of its birds and fish.

But catching the birds was no easy task in those days, for Drangey rises up from the sea in sheer cliffs on every side. In those days, people in our land were brave, strong, and full of spirit, so they would fearlessly let themselves down the cliff-face on ropes, but this sometimes led to great loss of life; men would slip from the ropes, be killed by falling rocks, or smash against the cliffs and break all their bones. And people soon noticed that of those who died on the rocks, there were just as many who had stout ropes as had inferior cords, which did not seem reasonable. And when their ropes were drawn to the clifftops, they were seen to be cut clean across, as if they had been hacked with an axe or cut with a blade, and some even wondered whether they had not heard the stroke of some weapon on the rocks, just before the men slipped from their ropes or the ropes themselves snapped. So the word

222

went round that there were those living in the rocks who did not want men from the mainland to take their wealth away, and who regarded the creatures of the island as their own. And because of the losses they had suffered, people became frightened to go to the island at all.

This went on till Gudmund Árason the Good became Bishop of Holar. Gudmund, as is well known from the saga about him, was very good at chanting prayers and giving blessings, and went round the country curing various ills and driving away evil spirits. He was generous to the poor, and would not only take them into his own home when he was there, but would also have others in his company as he travelled the country, and so food would sometimes run short, and they would have to find more where they could. So he sent his men to Drangey in the spring to get wild birds and fish, but very soon the beings who lived on the island started attacking the Bishop's men as they had the others, and there were many deaths. Then the Bishop was told how his men were losing their lives on the island, and he resolved to go there himself with his clergy, and with holy water.

On a beach on the island is a raised slab of rock which looks as if it has been set up purposely, and it is known as Gudmund's Altar. They say that when he disembarked he said Mass there, with that rock as his altar, though others say he merely prayed there; and to this day it is the custom that no one lands on Drangey, or leaves it, without saying his prayers at that rock. Having done this, he went to bless the island, starting just north of Hæringshlaup and working his way round the island clockwise, from the top of the cliffs to the bottom and out to sea too; and when he could not go along the beaches he would go down the cliffs on a rope, so that he covered the whole island with his readings, chantings and holy water, and his clerks went with him.

It is not said that he came across any harmful creatures till he got back to Uppgaunguvik at the north tip of the island. There he went over the cliff on a rope, as he had already done elsewhere, and when he had gone as far down as he thought fit, he began his blessings and readings, as he had done elsewhere. After a little while, out of the cliff there came a huge paw, grey and hairy, and a red sleeve on it, and it was holding a big dagger with a very sharp edge to it, and this was drawn across the rope which the bishop was hanging on to, and it cut through two strands of the rope at once. What saved the Bishop's life was that the dagger did not bite on the third strand, which had been most intricately blessed. At the same time, the bishop heard a voice saying, from inside the cliff: 'Don't bless any more now, Bishop Gudmund; the wicked do have to have somewhere to live.' Then the

Bishop called for the rope to be hauled up, and himself too, and said he would not bless the remaining part of the cliff between there and Bergisvik. He said he was sure that all the parts that had been blessed would do no more harm to his men or to anybody else, which has indeed proved true. The section which he left unblessed is still unblessed to this day, and so it is called 'Heathen Cliff'; it is said that more birds nest there than anywhere else on Drangey, but the belief still holds, and men hardly ever go over the face of 'Heathen Cliff'.

Árnason, I, pp. 144–6 (slightly abridged). Bishop Gudmund the Good died in 1237. A variant of this story, in which a rope blessed by the bishop saves a fowler's life from a cliff-troll, occurs in a fourteenth-century collection of his alleged miracles.

THE TROLL'S FINGERS

Iceland

Thorvard, the son of Björn Skafin, lived at Njardvik after his father's time. He kept his household in great style, and everything he owned was of good quality. He had a sturdily built boat for sea-fishing. It is said that one day he rowed out to the fishing bank called Deep Kettle, and when he had been there for a while there came up so thick a fog that one could not see further than the boat itself, and a heavy swell at the same time, so that they could not keep their station on the fishing-grounds. Thorvard told the crew to row against the swell, but it was no use, however hard they tried – the boat was swept along, as if in a strong river current. This went on a long while, till they sighted land and saw that the boat was heading for a cove just north of Njardvik which is called Kogur's Cove. There is a large cave in the rocks surrounding this cove, and it is known as Kogur-Grim's Cave. The boat ran into the cove as if it were in a rushing torrent.

As soon as Thorvard saw where the boat was heading, he told the crew to stand ready with some gaffs and barge-poles they had on board to try to pole it out of the cove if they got a chance. But he himself seized a big axe they had in the boat and went to the bows. The boat swept into the mouth of the cave, and just as its keel touched bottom, an enormous hand clutched its gunwales. But Thorvard chopped the fingers off, so that they fell into the boat. The crew were ready with the poles, and so they got the boat back to the mouth of the cove. Then, catching them unawares, a great rock came hurtling from inside the cave and fell just short of the boat, setting up huge waves. But Thorvard and his men got away around the headland called Skalanes, where they stayed for a while; then they rowed back to the fishing banks and had a good catch. Thorvard kept the fingers to show people and everyone thought they were amazingly huge.

Árnason, I, p. 165.

HUNTERS' TALES

Norway

One autumn evening in 1898 we were sitting by the fire at Elgesrud. My brother and I had bought this little estate that summer. We were planning to go hunting hares next morning, and had invited a few neighbours to stay the night. Elgesrud is a pretty little place, rather isolated, due south of Elge Pond, on the boundary between the parishes of Aker and Ski. There was bright moonlight that evening and a peaceful, romantic atmosphere out of doors, while indoors the fireside talk turned to fairy-tales and old beliefs.

'No, I've never heard of anything like that round here,' said Gustav Holstad. 'The only thing I know of is that in the old days a man once had to climb a tree near here on account of a bear, but that's not supernatural. And out in the middle of Lake Sværs there's a rock called Bride's Rock. A whole wedding procession is supposed to have been drawn inside it, but I don't know any more about it.'

'Well now,' said Per Myrer, 'I've heard tell about something that happened to two fellows who once spent a night camping out of doors by a bonfire, over by the river Langås on the far side of that pond there. It was two woodcutters who were camping there, and in the course of the night they heard two gruff bitches give tongue as they began hunting in Asurdal, over by the Gråben Caves. The cry went up by Teien and then came northwards along Langås River. The sound was strange and eerie, and they asked themselves what kind of bitches would be out hunting at such an hour, on a pitch-black night. They crept nearer to the fire and remained lying there, listening to the strange gruff cry of the bitches, which was coming nearer and nearer. Then came a bare-foot girl running for her life, her hair streaming loose, right past their fire; and away she went southwards, towards the marshes south of the river. She was wearing a white smock and a short green petticoat. Before they could even draw breath, there came two big black hounds in full cry following her trail, and their baying could be heard going southwards to Kloppa, then up along the Oskrud track, and on to Del, where a shot rang out, after which everything was silent.

'They were frightened, and sought comfort round the fire once more, and wondered what kind of a hunt this had been. But then twigs snapped in the woods somewhere, and shortly afterwards along came a huge man with a big black beard, who went striding past. They could see him well by the glow of the firelight. He had the two bitches on a leash and was carrying a big blunderbuss over his shoulder, and the girl was hanging down his back, with her legs tied together and passed over the barrel of the gun, just like any hare one has shot. The woodcutters said nothing, and the man said nothing, and off he went into the dark night; but they felt sure the girl had been one of the Hidden Folk.'

Christiansen, pp. 95–6; contributed by C. Norenberg of Ljan. *Migratory Legends* 5060 'The Fairy Hunter'.

HUNTSMEN SEE ODEN'S HUNT

Sweden

My father and my grandfather were out hunting in Solerud Forest one day. That evening they heard a strange barking; there was one hound barking very shrilly, and there were also two with a deeper cry. They stood still and waited. All at once, a woman came running by with her hair streaming out behind her. Next came the hound that barked so shrill, and then the two others. Shortly after, along came a man with red hair and beard. He had a gun with him. He just went straight past. Father said this was Oden's hunt.

Klintberg, no. 9, p. 82. Collected in 1944 from an informant born in 1860. *Migratory Legends* 5060.

ODEN WAS A SUNDAY HUNTER

Sweden

If you are out of doors at night on great festivals, you can hear Oden's hunt. It goes by high up in the air, moving along over the forest. It moves faster than a bird can fly. It is really three dogs barking; two have a gruff cry, and the third a shrill voice.

There was once a man called Oden. He was a fine marksman, and went hunting on Sundays. As a punishment for this, he must hunt the Skogsrå until the end of the world. Many of the old folk round here have heard the hunt on Kroppefjäll Mountain; I can remember one old man who declared that he had heard it once on New Year's Eve when he was going to a dance.

Klintberg, no. 8, p. 82. Collected in 1947 from an informant born in 1861.

THE FLYING HUNTSMAN

Denmark

All over Denmark there can occur a terrible form of haunting, which everyone who has seen or heard it speaks of with horror. What happens is that at certain seasons one hears whistling and roaring up in the sky, howling and clamour, cracking and clattering, just like when a hunting party is careering along through the woods and fields, with horns blowing, hounds baying and huntsmen galloping wildly. This, say the peasants, is 'the Flying Huntsman', and they fling themselves face down on the ground or hide behind a tree till the monstrous company has passed by.

It is also called 'King Volmer's Hunt'. For King Valdemar is now condemned to go hunting every night, all the way from Burre to Gurre, as a punishment because when he was alive on this earth he used to say that Our Lord could keep his Kingdom of Heaven for himself if only he, Valdemar, could still go hunting in Gurre. He generally comes riding through the air with his hunting party. As he draws near, one first hears howling, clamour and the cracking of whips, and straight afterwards comes the hunt itself; at the head are coal-black hounds that run rapidly to and fro, snuffing the ground, with long glowing tongues lolling from their jaws. Next comes 'Volmer' astride his white horse; sometimes he carries his head under his left arm. If he meets anybody, especially any old people, he orders them to hold a couple of his hounds, and then either leaves them standing there with the hounds for hours, or else fires a shot soon after, at which the hounds snap all leashes or chains and race off, following the hunt.

When King Volmer goes hunting, one hears him smashing gates down, and if ever he wants to pass through a farm, the bolts all fly open before him when he comes. It is said there are certain farms through which he regularly takes his course, in at one gate and out at the other, and that people leave the gates open at times when he is likely to come. There is one farm at Bistrup, behind Roskilde, about which (among others) this tale is told. At some other places his regular course passes *over* the buildings; there is supposed to have been one roof at Herlufsholm which had sunk right down in the middle because he rode over it so frequently.

Thiele, II, pp. 113–14. Valdemar IV (Valdemar Atterdag) reigned 1340–75; 'Volmer' is a colloquial abbreviation of his name.

The Green Giant

Denmark

On the west coast of the island of Møn there is a forest called Grønveld in which the Green Giant goes hunting every night on horseback, with his head under his left arm and a spear in his hand, and many hounds around him. At harvest time farmers put out a sheaf of oats for his horse, so that it should not trample their grain down during the night.

One night the Green Giant was hunting in the Borre Forest. He stopped his horse outside Henryk Fyenbo's door, knocked, and ordered him to hold the hounds. Then off rode the hunter, and Henryk meanwhile just stood in the doorway for two whole hours, holding the hounds. In the end, the Green Giant did come back, and there was a mermaid which he had shot lying across his horse, and he said to the farmer: 'I've been hunting her for seven years, but now I got her at last, over near Falster.'

Then he demanded something to drink, and when he had had it he handed Henryk Fyenbo a gold coin – which simply burnt a hole through his hand and disappeared into the ground. Then the huntsman burst out laughing and said: 'You've got a fine story to tell now, how the Green Giant shook hands with you! But so that you can't say I drank in your house without paying, you can keep the leash with which you held my hounds.'

The huntsman rode away, and Henryk Fyenbo took the leash and kept it for a long time under lock and key, and during this time he grew constantly richer. In the end, however, he despised the leash and threw it away as useless rubbish, so then he became poorer than he had been in the old days, and died quite destitute.

Thiele, II, pp. 119–20. There are several Neolithic chambered tombs on Møn; a very fine one on the west coast is called Grønjægers Høj, 'Green Huntsman's Mound'.

THE NÖKK

Norway

This type of water-troll usually lives in rivers and lakes, but sometimes in the fiords as well. Every year he claims a human being as a sacrifice, which is why one sometimes hears it said of this or that river or lake that at least one man is lost in it every year. When someone is fated to die soon, the Nökk is often heard calling out, in hollow tones, 'Cross over!' This ominous cry can also be a wailing, moaning voice, like that of a man on the point of death. The Nökk can change his appearance to look like all sorts of things – sometimes like half a boat on the water, or half a horse on the land, and sometimes like gold and valuables. If you row out towards them, the Nökk gets you in his power at once. He is particularly greedy for little children. Moreover, he is especially dangerous after sunset. When one comes near a stretch of water at that time, it is no bad thing to say: 'Nyk, Nyk, nail in the water! Our Lady Mary throws steel in the water! You sink, I float!' . . .

It was a Nökk, or some other water-troll of that sort, which shouted from the water late one evening outside the priest's house by Lake Hvidesø: 'The hour has come, but not the man!' As soon as the priest heard this, he ordered the people to keep watch for the first man who might come along and want to cross the lake, and prevent him going any further. Very soon there came a man riding at full gallop, who demanded a ferry-boat as fast as possible. The priest urged him to abandon his journey, but when neither pleas nor threats were of any use, the priest told his men to use force on him. The stranger then collapsed unconscious, and he remained lying there until the priest got someone to fetch water – from the very lake from which the shout had come – and gave him this water to drink. No sooner had he drunk the water than he gave up the ghost.

Faye, pp. 49, 51. Second anecdote: *Migratory Legends* 4050 'The Hour has Come, but Not the Man'; compare the Swedish version given in Part Three, p. 71.

THE NÄCK'S FIDDLE

Sweden

If a musician wants to have his fiddle really finely tuned, all he need do is to leave it beside a river and the Näck will tune it. When a Näck tunes a fiddle, he brings another fiddle along with him, and tunes that one too. So the musician must make a mark of some sort on his own fiddle, for if he took the Näck's fiddle instead, it would play so powerfully that the very tables and chairs would skip about.

Klintberg, no. 53, p. 101.

THE DANCERS WHO COULD NOT STOP

Sweden

There was a fiddler who had been taught to play by a Näck. Well, he was at a party, and someone there asked him to play for them. Then he played the Näck's Reel (which is a tune the Näck will teach a fiddler who lets him suck blood from his finger), and they were forced to start dancing, every one of them, and even the furniture danced too. They had nearly danced themselves to death, all of them, only there happened to be one girl who had been outside giving the animals their fodder for the night, and she had pinned a four-leaf clover to her clothes, and so when she came back into the room she could see the Näck sitting just behind the fiddler. So she stepped forward and cut all the strings on the fiddle, for that was the only way to get them to stop. If not, they would surely have gone on dancing until they all dropped dead.

Klintberg, no. 55, p. 102. Collected in 1935.

THE NÄCK LONGS FOR SALVATION

Sweden

There was a boy from Gylltorp who was going home one evening after doing a day's work on the manor farm. When he came to the river, he saw the Näck sitting on a rock in the middle of the stream, and he was playing his fiddle and singing:

> On Judgement Day, on Judgement Day,
>   God's mercy will be mine.
> On Judgement Day, on Judgement Day,
>   God's mercy will be mine.

The boy yelled at him: 'You'll never get God's mercy, you're far too ugly for that!'

When the Näck heard this, he was so bitterly upset that he began to shriek so loud that one could hear it a long way off. So when the boy got home, his father was standing out in the yard, and he asked him what all the hullabaloo down by the river was about. When the boy told him what it was, his father said: 'Now, you just go back to the river, and you say to the Näck, "My father has read a lot more than I have, and he says that you *will* obtain God's mercy."'

The boy ran back and said those exact words. The shrieking stopped at once, and the Näck started playing his fiddle most beautifully and sank down in the waters of the river.

Klintberg, no. 50, p. 100. Collected in 1922. *Migratory Legends* 5050 'The Fairies' Prospect of Salvation'.

THE WATERFALL GRIM AND THE
MILL GROWLER

Norway

Akin to the Nökk is the Grim or Fossegrim, a musical being which lives near waterfalls amd mills. He generally plays on quiet, dark afternoons to lure people to him; also, he will teach a man to play the fiddle or other stringed instrument, provided he offers him a white kid on a Thursday evening, throwing it into a waterfall flowing northwards. If it is a thin beast, the pupil will learn no more than how to tune his fiddle, but if it is fat, the Fossegrim will grip the player's right hand and guide it to and fro for such a long while that blood spurts from every fingertip. Now the pupil has been taught all there is to know, and he can play so incomparably well that trees dance and waterfalls hang motionless in their fall.

The Grim appears in all kinds of shapes. Once, when a man was in the mill in Nissedal, the door suddenly burst open and in stepped a goat which was so tall that its horns touched the roof. But it went out again quickly, and the frightened man did not dare follow it, though he did watch where it went – it vanished all at once into a big rock near the mill. The man was glad to be rid of the Fossegrim so soon, for that was who it was.

Just as he has various shapes, so he has various names. In some places he is called Fossekallen ('Old Man of the Falls'), in others Kvernknurren ('Mill Growler'). In Gjerrestad in the old days people used to put out a bowl of ale or some such thing beside the millstones, so that the Mill Growler would multiply the grain in the sacks. At one time, long ago, he used to live in Sandaker Falls. There was a man who owned a mill there, and whenever he wanted to grind corn the millstones would jam and stop. Knowing it was the Growler playing tricks on him, one afternoon when he wanted to grind he took a pot of pitch along with him and lit a fire under it. No sooner had he set the mill going than it jammed, as usual. He jabbed a pole down into the water to drive the Growler away, but in vain. Finally he opened the door to have a look, and there in the doorway stood the Mill Growler with his mouth gaping wide – so wide that the bottom lip rested on the threshold and the upper lip was above the lintel. He said to the man: 'Have you ever seen such a wide gape?' But the other snatched up the boiling pitch at once and flung it into the gaping mouth, saying: 'And you, have you ever tasted such hot porridge?' The Mill Growler disappeared, howling, and nobody has ever seen him there since.

Faye, pp. 53–5.

THE RIVER HORSE AND THE LITTLE GIRLS

Denmark

One evening, a group of little girls came to the brook called Bækgren, between Borup and Blaus, and wanted to cross over. The stream was swollen with rain so that the foot-bridge was well under water, and they couldn't think how to get across. One of the girls exclaimed: 'If only we had some old nag or other, we could ride across.'

At that very moment, along came a grey horse, and stopped right beside them. One of the girls mounted at once, and it was clear that there was room enough for one more. So a second girl mounted too, and still there was just as much room as before. Now several more girls mounted, and all the time this horse was growing longer and longer, so that eventually all the girls found room to sit on his back.

When they were all mounted, the horse waded out into the river carrying them. Up till then the girls had not uttered one word, from sheer astonishment, but when they were in mid-stream one of them exclaimed:

What a long horse,
By Jesus' Cross!

But at that word the horse disappeared from under them, and all the girls were left floundering in the middle of the water. Most people think it was some kind of a troll that they were riding, and that it had to retreat when the Cross was mentioned.

Bødker, pp. 158–9. In some Swedish variants the creature vanishes because he thinks he hears his name, Näck; the smallest child tries to say *jäg räcker inte*, 'I can't reach', but mispronounces it as *jäg näcker inte*. Similarly in Icelandic tales he flees at words which sound like his names Nykur and Nennir.

234

The Merwoman and Her Cattle

Denmark

Off the northern coast of Zealand, according to what people say at Tisvilde, there lives a merwoman who used at one time to drive her cattle ashore at Strandbredden and let them graze all day on the meadows at Tibirke. The farmers in this district, being pretty tight-fisted, as they have been from time immemorial, did not care for this at all, and plotted to round up her cattle. So one evening they posted lookout men, and contrived to drive the sea-woman and all her cattle into a pound near the village, and refused to set her free unless she paid them for having grazed on their land. She told them she had no money to give, so then they insisted that she should give them the belt she wore at her waist, which looked very costly and glittered like precious stones. She was forced to agree, and bought her freedom by giving them the belt. But later on, as she was driving her cattle down to the sea, she said to her big bull: 'Now dig!', and he at once began to furrow the ground with his horns and stirred up the sand all along past Strandbredden. And so, when next the wind blew from the northwest, the sand swept inland over the fields towards Tibirke village, so deep that it nearly buried the church. And as for the costly belt, the farmers got little joy from it, because once they got it home and had a proper look at it, it was simply woven out of rushes.

Thiele, II, p. 257. The area round Tibirke was liable to damage from shifting sands till forests were planted in the eighteenth century.

THE WISE MERMAN

Iceland

On Sudurnes is a small isolated farm called Vogar, but its real name is
Cows' Vogar, and it is so named in the medieval *Book of Settlements*. In
the old times there was a farmer living there who went fishing a great
deal – even nowadays one can make excellent catches off Sudurnes.
One day this farmer rowed out as usual, and there was nothing particularly remarkable about the fish he caught on this occasion, but the
story goes that he did make one very heavy haul and that when he
pulled the net to the boat he saw something human-looking in it and
took it on board. Then the farmer found that this man was alive, and
when he asked him how things were with him, he replied that he was a
merman from the bottom of the sea. The farmer asked him what he
had been doing when he got tangled in the net.

The merman answered: 'I was busy adjusting the cowl on my
mother's kitchen chimney. Now throw me back into the water.'

The farmer said he would do no such thing, '. . . and you will have
to remain with me'.

They said nothing more to each other, and indeed the merman
refused to utter another word. When the farmer thought fit, he rowed
back to land, taking the merman with him. There is nothing worth
mentioning about this until after the farmer had beached his boat, when
his dog came running to meet him and leapt up at him, at which the
man grew angry and struck the dog. At this the merman laughed for the
first time. Then the farmer went striding across his meadow and tripped
over a tussock, and cursed it; then the merman laughed a second time.
The farmer reached his house; his wife ran to meet him and welcomed
him warmly, and he showed pleasure at her warmth. Then the merman
laughed for the third time.

Then the farmer said to the merman: 'You've laughed three times
now, and I'm curious to know what you're laughing about.'

'I won't tell you on any account,' said the merman, 'unless you
swear to take me back to the same fishing-bank where you caught me.'

The farmer promised, and then the merman said: 'The first time I
laughed was when you struck your dog, who fawned on you because
he is devoted to you. And I laughed a second time when you tripped
over that tussock and cursed it, because that particular tussock has
treasure buried under it and is full of gold. And I laughed once more,

for the third time, when you were so pleased at your wife's flattery, for she is deceiving you and is unfaithful to you. Now keep your word, and take me back to where you first caught me.'

The farmer said: 'For two of the things you have told me, my dog's devotion and my wife's fidelity, I have no way of proving the truth; but I can find out whether you spoke truly about there being treasure buried in that tussock, and if it proves true, then it's likely that the two other matters are true too, and then I'll certainly keep my promise.'

The farmer then went and dug up the tussock and found a lot of money there, just as the merman had said. As soon as he had done that, he put to sea again and took the merman back to the same fishing-bank where he had first caught him. Before the farmer threw him overboard, the merman said: 'You have done well to send me home to my mother, farmer, and I'll certainly reward you for it, if you have the wits to profit by what I send. Goodbye and good luck, farmer!' Then the farmer put him down into the water, and now the merman is out of this story.

Not long after this, it happened that the farmer was told that seven cows, all as grey as the sea, had come into his meadows near the beach. The farmer rushed out at once and hurried to where the cows were, but they were running wild and seemed very nervous. Meanwhile, he noticed that they each had a bladder on the muzzle, and he felt pretty sure that he would lose the cows unless he could manage to burst these bladders. He struck one of the cows on the front of her muzzle with a stick he had in his hand, after which he was able to catch her. But he lost the rest, and they plunged back into the sea. He felt sure that the merman had sent these cows in gratitude for being released.

This cow was the most valuable heirloom that ever came to Iceland; a whole race of cattle is descended from her, and they are spread all over the country now, and all are grey in colour, so they are called 'sea-cow breed'. As for the farmer, he was a prosperous man all the rest of his life. He also added to the name of his farm, which had been called simply Vogar, and called it Cows' Vogar, after the cows which appeared on his land.

Árnason, I, pp. 133–4. *Migratory Legends* 4060 'The Mermaid's Message'. Árnason also gives a grimmer version, dating from 1644, in which the merman's third laugh is at hearing the farmer grumble at the quality of some new boots, when in fact he is fated to die three days later. In that version there are no sea-cows and the treasure under the tussock is never found.

THE MERMAN'S SOCK

Denmark

One cold winter's day a fisherman had put out to sea to fish. A strong wind began to blow and he decided to return, but he was finding it difficult to make headway. All at once he saw an old man with a long grey beard come riding on a wave, straight towards his boat. The fisherman realized it was a merman that he had in front of his eyes, and he knew too that to see one means a storm is brewing.

'Ugh, how cold it is!' said the merman, who was shivering with cold, for he had lost one of his socks. The fisherman took off one of his own socks and threw it to him. The merman disappeared with it, and the fisherman came safely to land.

Some while after this, the fisherman was at sea again, and a long way from land. Suddenly the merman popped his head up over the gunwale and sang into the boat:

> Listen, man who gave the sock!
> Turn your ship and sail straight back,
> There's thunder over Norway!

The fisherman hurried back to land as fast as he could, and soon there came such a storm as nobody had ever seen the likes of, and many men were lost at sea. This warning was his reward for his sock.

Bødker, p. 155. *Migratory Legends* 4055, 'A Grateful Sea-Spirit Gives a Storm Warning'. In most versions the gift is a glove, and the merman or *sjörå* later addresses the fisherman as 'Glove-Friend'.

THE FORSAKEN MERMAN

Denmark

At Frisenborg there once lived a poor couple who had only one daughter, called Grethe. One day when they had sent her down to the shore to fetch some sand, a merman came up out of the water while she was standing there collecting the sand in her apron. His beard was greener than the sea itself, but he had a handsome face and he spoke many kind words to the girl, saying: 'Come with me, Grethe! If you do, I'll give you as much silver as your heart could wish!'

'That would be no bad thing,' she answered. 'We've got little enough of that at home!'

So she let herself be persuaded, and he took her by the hand and led her down to the bottom of the sea, and there she became, in due course, the mother of five children.

But after many years had passed, and she had almost forgotten all her Christian beliefs, she was sitting one morning, on a holy day, rocking her baby in her lap. Then she heard church bells ringing far above, and there came over her a great longing to go to church. And as she sat there weeping and sighing over her child, the merman noticed her grief and asked what her trouble was. Then she begged him, from the bottom of her heart and with many loving words, for a chance to go to church again, just once. The merman could not resist her sorrow and led her back up on land, but urged her most earnestly to hurry back soon to her children.

Half-way through the sermon, the merman came to the outside of the church, calling 'Grethe! Grethe!' She heard it well enough, but she still thought she would hear the sermon to the end. When the sermon was over, the merman came to the church a second time and called: 'Grethe! Grethe! Are you coming soon?' Yet she did not obey. Then at length he came a third time and called: 'Grethe! Grethe! Are you coming soon? Your children long for you!' And when she still did not come, he wept bitterly, and plunged back down to the bottom of the sea.

But Grethe remained with her parents from then on, and left the merman to look after the wretched little children himself. And one can often hear him weeping and lamenting in the depths.

Thiele, II, pp. 259–61. This story is also found as a traditional Danish ballad, 'Agnete og Havmanden'.

The Merman at Nissum

Denmark

Once, a corpse was washed ashore at Nissum and was buried in the churchyard. But no sooner had this been done than sand from the beaches began to be blown inland. This went on for three days, and it was getting worse and worse all the time. People began to think there was something uncanny going on, and so they turned to a 'cunning man' for help. When he heard that the sandstorm had blown up immediately after a corpse from the sea had been buried in the churchyard, he said that it must undoubtedly have been a merman, and that the sand-drift had begun because of him being laid in hallowed ground. They must now dig him up again immediately, and see whether he had sucked his forefinger into his mouth far enough to cover the second joint. If he had, there was nothing to be done; but if not, they must re-bury him in the sand dunes, and the sand-drift would stop.

So they dug the merman up again, and he was lying with his finger in his mouth right enough, but he had only sucked it in just up to the second joint, not over it So they buried him down on the dunes, and the sand-drifting ceased. But from that time onwards, all corpses washed up on shore have been buried in the sand dunes.

Bødker, pp. 157–8.

The Magic Islands

Norway

In the middle of Åfjord there lies an island called Løvøya, of which it is said that it was at one time an elvish land. It was then only occasionally visible to human beings, when it rose up out of the sea with its green fields and hills. At first it would show itself simply as a small strip of land just above the crest of the waves, then little by little it would rise up out of the sea, like a mirage. Many people tried to reach this island, but as soon as they got anywhere near it it would sink down into the sea and disappear. They tried using holy words and prayers, but nothing was any good – there was no way of landing there.

On the mainland, further up the fiord from this island, lies a farm called Olden. The people there had a sow with seven piglets, and one day when the island was visible she swam across to it and went ashore. These pigs roamed about on it all day, but swam back to the mainland in the evening, and then the island disappeared again. So it went on, for many days on end. As soon as the island showed itself, the pigs would swim out and go ashore on it. So one morning, the man who owned the pigs hung a steel knife round the sow's neck before he let them out of the pen. When the island became visible again, the sow swam out to it with her seven piglets and went ashore, as usual. But from that day on, the spell was broken; the island never disappeared again, and nowadays there are large, well-stocked farms on it.

Christiansen, pp. 88–9.

'BETTER THE SKIN THAN THE CHILD'

Iceland

It is said that there was a man, either a widower or unmarried, who had occasion to go down to the sea-shore on Midsummer Eve, and there he saw many people lying on the sand stark naked, and each had a sealskin at his or her side. The man thought this strange, and as he wanted to find out what it all meant, he ran among them and snatched one of the sealskins. Then all the people lying there jumped to their feet, and each slipped into a sealskin, and they all slid into the water, except for one woman who could not find her skin. She was most unhappy because she could not get her skin back, and she pleaded with the man as earnestly as she could to give it to her. But instead, the man invited her to come to his house, and she agreed.

There he gave her some clothes and kept her with him, and after some while she seemed content with this too, and gradually they grew closer to one another, and in the end they married. They got on well together, and had children. The woman took good care of the house, and she kept the keys to all the rooms and storehouses, and looked after everything very efficiently. But there was one key which her husband never entrusted to her, and which he kept with him all the time. This key belonged to an old chest outside in the smithy. The woman often asked the farmer what was in this chest; he said there was nothing in it but old scrap-metal and his blacksmith's tools.

Now some years had gone by, when the farmer had to leave home one day for a short while. Then the woman began looking for the key of the chest, as she often had done before, but could not find it anywhere. So she went out to the smithy, where she met her eldest son, and asked him whether he had ever happened to look into this old chest. The boy said he had not. 'Don't you know either where the key to it can be?' said she. 'No,' says the boy; 'Father always keeps it on him when he's at home, and when he leaves home he hides it somewhere in a hole in the wall.'

'Do please look for the key for me,' says the woman, and the boy does, and in the end he finds the key and gives it to his mother.

She lost no time in opening the chest, and what does she see in it but her own fine sealskin, and then she says: 'Better the skin than the child. The skin never speaks, but a child may talk.' Then she took the bag and went down to the shore. There she paused, thought a little, and then said:

> Woe is me, woe is me!
> I have seven bairns on land,
> And seven in the sea!

When the boy saw that his mother had gone to the shore and wanted to slip the skin on, he begged her and pleaded with her not to do it. But it was no use; she put the skin on and flung herself into the sea.

Árnason, I, pp. 10–11. Told in 1871 by a woman informant born in 1844. *Migratory Legends* 4080 'The Seal Woman'.

FOR THE BEST IN PAPERBACKS, LOOK FOR THE

In every corner of the world, on every subject under the sun, Penguin represents quality and variety – the very best in publishing today.

For complete information about books available from Penguin – including Pelicans, Puffins, Peregrines and Penguin Classics – and how to order them, write to us at the appropriate address below. Please note that for copyright reasons the selection of books varies from country to country.

In the United Kingdom: For a complete list of books available from Penguin in the U.K., please write to *Dept E.P., Penguin Books Ltd, Harmondsworth, Middlesex, UB7 0DA*

In the United States: For a complete list of books available from Penguin in the U.S., please write to *Dept BA, Penguin, 299 Murray Hill Parkway, East Rutherford, New Jersey 07073*

In Canada: For a complete list of books available from Penguin in Canada, please write to *Penguin Books Canada Ltd, 2801 John Street, Markham, Ontario L3R 1B4*

In Australia: For a complete list of books available from Penguin in Australia, please write to the *Marketing Department, Penguin Books Australia Ltd, P.O. Box 257, Ringwood, Victoria 3134*

In New Zealand: For a complete list of books available from Penguin in New Zealand, please write to the *Marketing Department, Penguin Books (NZ) Ltd, Private Bag, Takapuna, Auckland 9*

In India: For a complete list of books available from Penguin, please write to *Penguin Overseas Ltd, 706 Eros Apartments, 56 Nehru Place, New Delhi, 110019*

In Holland: For a complete list of books available from Penguin in Holland, please write to *Penguin Books Nederland B.V., Postbus 195, NL–1380AD Weesp, Netherlands*

In Germany: For a complete list of books available from Penguin, please write to *Penguin Books Ltd, Friedrichstrasse 10 – 12, D–6000 Frankfurt Main 1, Federal Republic of Germany*

In Spain: For a complete list of books available from Penguin in Spain, please write to *Longman Penguin España, Calle San Nicolas 15, E–28013 Madrid, Spain*